The Moody Man

John Milne

The Moody Man

NO EXIT PRESS

This edition published in 1999 by No Exit Press
18 Coleswood Road, Harpenden, Herts, AL5 1EQ

http://www.noexit.co.uk

A CIP catalogue record for this book is available from the British Library.

ISBN 1-874061-89-0   The Moody Man

2 4 6 8 10 9 7 5 3 1

Printed by Caledonian International Book Manafacturing Ltd, Glasgow

For my family

Part One
The Girl of My Dreams

Chapter One

I was in a mews in Kensington. The houses had pink or white or lemon-yellow walls, all freshly painted. Doorsteps were varnished mahogany. Fake Georgian doors boasted fake, highly polished Georgian brassware. Hanging baskets seemed to be outside every mews cottage, and were filled with winter-hardy plants. The plants bent and drooped in the steady, heavy rain. New gutters gleamed under the re-roofed roofs and carried the rain away from the paintwork. In the street, new cars were bumper to bumper along the carefully conserved and repaired cobblestones.

The rich have to spend their money on something.

Floodlights which would have held their own on a film-set lit the mews. I moved forward, a single actor on an echoing, empty sound-stage. Each footfall rang along a tunnel of brightness. The floodlights kept the October night at bay, and the rain fell steadily on the cobbled street even through the glaring brilliance.

I shivered and squeezed up my eyes so I could peer at the door numbers further along the mews. I was looking for the house of a friend. An old friend. Peter Moody. I hadn't seen Peter since... well I don't know since when. Since a few years. I had been surprised to find he lived somewhere so rich. The mews must have been too expensive to keep cars or horses in for a long time, *I* knew. Not many people could pay their way to live here . . . not me, for example. That's a rotten example.

I leaned on a Jaguar car and the beads of rainwater on its roof soaked through my sleeve. Rain was soaking through my mackintosh – both across my shoulders and under my collar, too, so that my shirt was clammy.

I moved slowly down the mews, still looking out for Peter Moody's door number. I wasn't happy. He had dragged me out in the rain so I blamed him for making me leave my umbrella on the tube train. I didn't particularly want to see him . . . meetings between estranged friends are usually embarrassing. The rain kept falling and I was getting more and more soaked. I was *resentful*. What the hell did he want me for?

A door opened about a hundred yards down the mews and loud classical music burst out. A tall dark figure ran from the door. He was going the opposite way from me, so I only saw his back. He staggered through a big stone archway at the far end of the mews. He disappeared into the night beyond the arch. I thought it might have been Peter. The figure looked like Peter from the back.

I yelled, 'Hey! Hey Peter! Hold on!' But he didn't hesitate and I couldn't run after him. He just ran into the night and I thought maybe he was running to his car. It's easy to get things out of proportion when you have strange messages left on your answering machine by long lost friends . . . the imagination goes into overdrive. I told my imagination not to go into overdrive. I didn't *know* the figure was Peter, anyway. The light plays tricks on you sometimes. I only yelled the once, then I felt foolish.

I moved on down the mews. After a few more yards it became clear Peter's house was going to be the one with the open door. I pushed the door back on its hinges. All the lights in the downstairs rooms seemed to be on. Beethoven's *Ode to Joy* was belting out of a music machine in the drawing room. The sound was on the edge of pain.

4

'Peter! Peter!... Anyone home?' I yelled as loudly as I could.

No reply.

The inside of the house was like the outside; newly painted, everything done without concern for the cost, lots of expensive furniture, lots of polish... everything immaculate. Everything immaculate excepting the big smear of blood on the wall at the bottom of the stairs. Everything immaculate excepting a trail of blood splashed into the plain, grey wool carpet that led up the stairs. I went into the drawing room and pulled the plug on a compact disc player. The relief at getting rid of the sound was physical. Then I went back to the entrance hall and followed the trail of blood up the stairway. I'm a mug for mysteries. Sometimes I wish I wasn't.

There were more blood smears all the way up the stairs. I should have turned back then. I could make out palm and finger prints in the smears; small prints too, made by a woman. I followed the trail on the carpet up to the landing. I turned the landing light on. The trail led into a woman's bedroom. A woman was in it, I could make out her figure in a chair. She was leaning forward over a dressing-table. She didn't move or turn when I came on to the landing and she was sitting absolutely still in the darkness. I didn't think she was going to turn out much of a conversationalist, somehow.

I went into the dark room. There was light from the hallway and two gas fires, one in the hearth, one in the corner of the room that gave out a red glow. The room was *so* hot. I loosened my collar. I felt as if I were in a steam bath. I approached the woman.

She was young – not over twenty-five – naked and dead. She was sitting on a veloured dressing-table stool. Her head was on the dressing-table. It was a woman's dressing-table and the contents of a make-up kit were flung all over the tabletop... as if the woman's arm had swung across it at some stage. Her face lay against the polished, veneered top of the dressing-table and the mirror in front of her had an 'R' written across it in blood. The last leg of the 'R', the downstroke, was dragged across the mirror and into the table-top. The trail of blood thickened and deepened as it approached the woman. It was hers. She'd bled to death.

I didn't tread in the blood, but I went close to her, close enough to touch, close enough to smell and feel death. I grabbed a handful of hair and lifted her face off the table.

Her classic Middle Eastern features were warmed in the fire-glow light. As I lifted her head her whole body fell back into my arms, and I had to drop the coarse, thick hair quickly and grab her shoulders. I could see her face very clearly now in the light falling from the hallway. She had sallow skin, an almond-shaped face and thick black hair, no dyeing.

And she was cold. Very cold. I was surprised, considering the fires. Considering the fact that I was sweating. I couldn't work it out at first. The girl's head fell back into the crook of my arm. I saw she might once have been beautiful. I also saw the first stab wound in her neck, a wild and angry plunge of a big knife, then I saw two more stab marks, neat, clean-looking ones this time, but done with the same big knife; one in the flesh stretched over her clavicle, one in her breast between the upper ribs. None of the wounds had bled. That was strange. Then my grip slipped a little on her skin and she really fell back. Her legs buckled under the stool and she slipped from my grasp, folding neatly into her own blood at my feet. I saw her cold, white hands had been clutched around a cut in her abdomen. The hands fell away from the cut easily as she went down. The cut was ten inches long and ran from her solar plexus to below her waistline. That wound might have stopped the others bleeding if it had happened first. But it was an incision, a surgical-type cut. How had she been the victim of a surgical-type cut? How had she been kept still while it was inflicted on her?

The girl's eyes were open. I knelt with some difficulty,

6

but I closed the eyes. I stood back. The fact that she was so cold still worried me. I took a good long look at her face. I wouldn't forget it. Her flesh was as cold as ice and I was sweating. I kept thinking about the fires in the room; a conventional gas fire fitting in the hearth and a second gas fire in the corner of the room. Both were full on. The second was one of those fires powered by a propane gas cylinder. You can move them from room to room. They're used in boarding houses or hostels. They're used by poor people, people who can't pay their electricity bills, or people who can't pay to put heating in. The propane fire was all wrong for that kind of house. You just don't find them in posh joints in Kensington . . . Peter's place had central heating anyway. I crossed the room and felt a radiator. It was full on. The metal surface burned to my touch.

I went back to the door and snapped on the electric light. I looked at the girl. I turned her over on the floor. There were dark, bruised marks on her back and backside. I looked around the room. I took my time. I had to think. Then I took out my handkerchief and wiped all round the room, all the places I could remember touching. I wet the handkerchief a little under the bathroom tap and I wiped the 'R' off her dressing-table mirror. I went downstairs to the open front door. No crowds of neighbours were there, no flashing blue lights. I peeked around the door for a while, till I was as sure as I could be that no one was spying and no one had been spying. I didn't think anyone should be. I slipped out into the floodlit yard. I didn't lock the door, which was going to be a bit unfair on Peter's postman or milkman in the morning, but I couldn't help that. I couldn't afford the time to find the key and the door had two Ingersoll mortice locks with their bolts shot back. There was no night latch. That puzzled me, too. It's very unusual not to have a rimlock of any description, even in Kensington.

In ten minutes I was in Gloucester Road tube station and felt I'd signed up as a human being again. In forty minutes I was alive and well and drinking a large scotch in the front room of my flat in Stoke Newington. I'd put my handkerchief in a plastic bag and the plastic bag in a big envelope ready to post. I'd addressed it to a private pathology lab with a request that they identify the type of blood on the handkerchief. They get stranger requests and anyway they knew me. I threw the envelope on my sideboard and drank some more scotch. So far only *I* knew that I hadn't spent the evening watching game shows on TV and reading thriller novels. Only the big brown envelope addressed to the path lab said I hadn't. I took a seat where I couldn't see the envelope. By the third gulp of scotch I wasn't sure I'd been in Kensington. By the third glass I was sure I hadn't.

At some horrible hour in the a.m. my friend Peter phoned me.

'I'm sorry I missed you,' he said.

'What the hell do you want?'

'I have a problem.'

'You're telling me, Peter,' I said. 'This is "goodnight", old buddy.'

He tried to argue but I put the phone down. He rang again and I said 'You have reached a wrong number,' and put the phone down again. It was the most I felt like doing for him. Even that was taking loyalty to its outer limits. What I really felt like doing was ringing Kensington Police and telling them there was a stiff in Peter's house and it looked to me like my old buddy had done it. I didn't believe that was true for a moment . . . but a sensible man would cover himself. I'm not a very sensible man. When Peter rang for the third time I simply went over and unplugged the phone. I didn't call the police. I should have done.

By five a.m. I was dreaming of butchers' shops and weekends in Tenerife. There lies an uneasy conscience. Kensington Police could do their own detective work. By six a.m. I was certain my pal Peter would be in France at least. If he had real sense he'd be on a plane to Brazil or Paraguay or somewhere. It's so much easier to argue your corner with the cops when you can have a lawyer of your choice and you're not in custody. As an ex-policeman himself, I was sure Peter would know enough to hit the channel ports before anyone found out what a state his house was in . . . or what was in it. As an old friend who'd become unwittingly involved, I reckoned the best thing I could do was not know anything about it. I didn't believe Peter could have murdered that girl . . . but if I had been the Metropolitan Police detective given the case I'd reckon on putting Peter and me in separate police stations and talking us into the ground until our stories checked out. How the hell the stories *would* check out is beyond me. The way I saw it the only thing going for us was lack of evidence. The police wouldn't be able to prove a case against me, at least, but I didn't fancy a week or two in the slammer while the cops made up their minds whether I was innocent or not. I'd done all I was ever going to do for Peter by taking that 'R' off the dressing-table mirror. Whatever corner Peter was in, he'd have to get himself out of. I'd carried enough of his baggage already.

Chapter Two

The next day I stood by the window in my dirty little office in Canning Town. I had my hands flat on the windowsill. An orange, autumn-evening sun smudged its way through the greasy glass. A spider crawled along the sill, stopped, suspicious of my presence, then went on towards my hand.

'You made the wrong decision,' I said very softly.

'What?' said a woman's voice behind me.

'Nothing.'

Her voice began, explaining. I leaned forward and let the cool glass touch my forehead. Outside I could hear engines and shouts and cars sounding their horns. I pulled the sash up and let it all in. I could see the automatic streetlamps flickering redly under the flyover. I could smell the oily, blowsy aroma of broken-down leads and cast-off carbons. There was a screech and some yelling. I leaned under the sash bar to see the street better. A Mercedes owner was arguing with Sammy, a stunted decrepit who sells copies of the *Standard* to drivers by dodging between the traffic on the flyover sliproad. Sometimes Sammy doesn't dodge quickly enough and then his papers and his bag end up spilled all over the road. One day Sammy will end up spilled all over the road, too, and then people will come round with a hat so's we can all contribute to buying him a decent second-hand suit and some secondhand dentures to get buried in. Sammy waved at me from among the cars and I waved back.

Living as a tramp is one thing, but no one would like to think of themselves being buried as one. I leaned back in and pulled the window down.

'Well, Jimmy?' said the woman behind me.

The spider crawled up on to my hand. I held it out of the window and blew it into the street. A spider that doesn't know when to keep still won't last long.

'No,' I said. I shook my head without looking round at her.

'I'm going to offer five, Jimmy,' she said. 'It's a lot of money for two days' work only. A lot of men would be glad of it.'

'Let those men do it, then,' I said. She didn't pick up that one. 'I just don't want to help him again. It's not just the money. It's not just that. I've just had enough. It's a crazy scheme, anyway. I don't want to do it.'

The woman came and stood close to me. At first I didn't look at her, but I could feel her presence next to me. I caught a whiff of lemon soap and French perfume. I didn't need to look at her to know how this woman looked. Once I had loved her. Even that's not true... once I had been totally infatuated with her. I had been infatuated the way a schoolboy would be, only at that time I was no schoolboy. At that time I was in my early twenties. Now, more than ten years later, that smell of lemon soap was enough to bring a pang – nostalgia? Lost innocence? Something.

I turned and looked at her. Her face was close to mine. She stepped back, looking steadily into my eyes. Clare was about five-eleven in her high heels and she was slim, wearing a tie-at-the-front autumn weight coat. When she'd come to my office she'd worn a silk scarf on her head. As she had come in she'd pulled off her scarf and shook her head so that her hair fell on to her shoulders. As she did that I was lost. I haven't seen Clare for years, but even now she can turn my stomach over. She has thick, dark hair that flows down on to her shoulders, a high brow above big brown eyes and the kind of mouth men stare at and wonder; full and rich and wide and easily pursed and easily smiled with. As soon as a man sees Clare he's going to want to kiss that mouth.

I turned back to my window. Clare came close again.

'He was your friend,' she said quietly into my ear.

'That's right . . . *was*. He's not now,' I said. 'I don't know what he's mixed up in but he's not playing that "friend" card any more. You were my friend, too. You're not playing it either.'

'Six then,' she said. 'Six thousand pounds is a great deal of money. It's money you could do with, I know. *Everyone* knows. . . .'

'Nothing. Everyone knows nothing,' I cut in quickly.

'Everyone knows you're short of money, Jimmy Jenner.'

Well, I don't have investment brokers breaking down the door, it's true. But this isn't the kind of thing I like having bandied about. I lied.

'Everyone knows wrong,' I said. 'As usual.'

I turned and looked into her eyes. She smiled. Orange light from the sun washed her face.

'It's not the money, Clare,' I said. 'It's really not the money. It's him. I don't know what Peter's doing to himself. Something funny. But one thing's sure . . . he is not involving me.'

She ignored my answer. She stared through my open window at a car down the street. The bonnet was up and a man in workman's overalls was leaning over the engine. A lorry roared past, blocking him from view, and Clare looked closely into my face again.

'Talk to Moody,' she said. 'Just talk about it.'

I shook my head.

'Talk to him,' she said. 'What harm can it do you?'

I shook my head again. I turned and looked out of the window, then pulled the sash down. The man playing in the street with his car had let the bonnet down and was inspecting his wheels. Given another five minutes he'd be changing the exhaust. I pointed at him.

'He's shaved his beard off. That's a bloody good disguise. Fool anyone, that would.'

A car hooted at Sammy the newsvendor again and he sold two evening papers.

'Grow up, Jimmy. What's he supposed to do?'

When I didn't answer she said irritably, 'Why's the room full of cardboard boxes?'

'Daz.'

'Daz? You mean the washing powder? Your office is full of washing powder?'

I nodded.

'*All* these boxes are Daz?' she said.

'Oh no. Some are Omo and some Ariel. The four big ones in the corner are fabric conditioner and all those ones down the wall are Murphy's Crisps.'

'Six thousand five hundred,' Clare said. 'You can buy a lot of wholesale groceries for that.'

'They're not my groceries . . . *how* much did you say?'

'Seven. Seven thousand English pounds. I have it here.'

She dipped into her small, black, designer handbag and pulled out a wad of notes. The money nearly filled the bag. I closed my eyes and leaned back against the windowsill.

'No,' I said. 'Take it away. I don't know what he's been up to and I don't know what you've been up to. I don't know what was at the bottom of last night and I don't want to know. Peter Moody will have to come to terms with the coppers on his own. I did him one very big favour last night and I'm not doing any more. I'm not going on any day trips to France or even to Southend with your boy. I wouldn't take seventy thousand pounds to spend a day with him, leave alone seven. You can tell Peter Moody I consider our friendship terminated and all debts on both sides are now paid up. Even if I did feel I wanted to do something for him that something wouldn't include spending a few years in chokey as an aider and abettor of murder. You might also tell him that standing outside a fellow's office and mending a car for a couple of hours is a rotten disguise and I would have expected better of him. Nearly as pathetic as shaving your beard off. He'll be dyeing his hair yellow next. He must be getting old.'

I said all this with my eyes closed. She waited a while and then I heard her reply, 'We're all getting older, Jimmy. The only difference is you'll be old and poor.'

I kept my eyes closed until I heard my office door slam, then the clip-clop of her high-heeled shoes on my stairs. Those shoes were probably worth more than all the money I possessed in the world at that moment. I didn't need the expensive high heels, but I could have used the money.

I kept my eyes closed until I heard the outer door slam, too. When I opened them I saw she'd left the bundle of money on the desk. I turned and looked down the street again. Cars had their lights on, even though it wasn't quite dark. I saw the tail lights of the broken-down car swing out into the traffic and then it was gone.

I leaned for a long time against the windowsill thinking about the past and about my friend Peter Moody. I stayed there for an hour at least. When I decided to move the room was dark. Headlamps from the flyover panned across the ceiling of my little room. I could hear my landlord, Chardray, talking to himself and rattling the shutters to his shop as he closed them. Chardray talked to himself every time he rattled those shutters either up or down, and since he runs an Asian 'sell-everything' shop open three-hundred-and-sixty-five days a year, that's an awful lot of rattling and chattering to get through in a lifetime. I edged slowly past Chardray's soap packets. I have a disability, a false right leg, so I didn't 'edge' too well. I can't run very well, either, which is why I hadn't been able to catch Peter Moody when he ran out of his house the night before. I fell over some boxes, heard Chardray shouting 'Okay Jenner? Okay?' up the stairs and decided to ignore him. I pulled the filing cabinet open, took out the scotch and put in Peter Moody's money. Then I locked the cabinet. I poured two fingers of scotch and indulged myself in a little momentary guilt for not putting my neck on the chopping block to help poor old Peter. Neither the guilt nor the whisky lasted long. Streams of light poured over the concrete bridge outside my window. The light crossed the room, crossed me. I poured another whisky. I heard a woman's shoes on the stairs again.

'This shop's shut for business tonight!' I yelled. 'All emergency calls must be directed to our answering service, Whitehall one-two-one-two. Our usual hours are nine to five. Bye now!'

The footsteps kept coming.

'How's your hearing, girl? I said this shop's shut. All enquiries to be forwarded to New Scotland Yard.'

She said nothing. She didn't even come into the room. She stood at the top of the stairs and waited.

'Come on, I've had a tough day. Give a fellow a bit of peace, eh?"

Nothing.

'Well?' I said.

Clare took half a pace into the room. She leaned against the jamb for a long time, then pushed herself off and took a step forward.

'Turn the light on, Jimmy,' she said.

'Clare, I said no. Please. . . .'

'He's gone now. And I'm sorry. I'm ashamed to have asked you. Let's just talk.'

'No. No talking. Leave it, eh? Take your money. It's in the filing cabinet. Here's the key.' I held up the key. 'Take your money back and leave me alone. Please.'

She leaned over my desk and turned the anglepoise lamp on. She ignored the offered key. 'Let's just you and me have dinner tonight.'

'No, I have a date.'

Even I wasn't convinced by my voice.

Clare poured some more whisky into my glass, picked the glass up and drank. She laughed.

'Maybe you have. Come and have dinner with me. Cancel

your date. I promise no more Peter Moody talk. He imposed on me just as I imposed on you. I'm sorry to have imposed on you. I said I'm sorry and I meant it. Let's just have dinner and talk. My treat.'

I didn't answer.

'It's a long time since we've talked, Jimmy. Don't let's worry about Peter now. I came and asked you, just as he asked me to. You said no. I've told him that. That sets us both free of any obligation to Peter, doesn't it?'

I took my whisky glass back.

'What do you want to talk about... sport? Politics? The Middle Eastern situation? My nearly ex-wife's feelings towards me? How about crime and punishment? The sentencing of serious criminals and those who assist them? Or the Metropolitan Police's clear-up rate for murders?'

'It wasn't what you thought. Forget it, anyway. Talk about you and me.'

'You and me.'

'And dinner,' Clare said. She leaned right over me. I could smell the lemon soap again.

She was hamming and she knew it and I knew it. The whole point of flirtation and flattery, though, is that you can see it for what it is and still like it. And still want it. I was hungry, anyway. I hadn't eaten. I kissed her once, briefly, on the lips, then turned my typist's chair halfway round and stood.

'Give me my stick there, will you?'

I took a look round the washing powder cartons. They looked as impassive as the stones must have done on the side of the road to Damascus. What's it to them what men do?

I opened my filing cabinet again.

'Here's Peter's money.'

'It's no good to me. I don't expect to see him.'

'Well I don't have a safe, Clare. It's a lot of money to leave lying around in an office.'

'I don't have a safe either. Hold on to it. I'm sure he'll contact you when he wants it. In any case he won't miss it.

16

There's plenty more where it came from.'

'I thought the seven was all you had.'

'Would more money have made a difference?' She smiled that all-knowing, superior smile again. I put Peter's money back in the filing cabinet, then I put the whisky in, nestling up against Peter Moody's seven grand. I locked the cabinet good and proper on them both. Some security. A good sneeze or a wallop with a Cumberland sausage would be all you'd need to break into that.

I locked my office door and followed Clare down the stairs.

In the street I bought a newspaper from Sammy. He asked how my leg was.

'It's gone dead,' I said. Sammy laughed. Sammy must think that crack hysterically funny. Every time I buy a newspaper from him he asks how the leg is, and every time he asks I say the same thing. He always laughs, too. We walked down the street to Clare's car. I opened my paper. Halfway down the third page was the caption DEAD GIRL POLICE SEEK MAN. The type was none too big. The journalist gave a description of a man, but it was neither Moody nor me. Maybe the police knew something I didn't. No maybe, of course they did. They always do.

I showed Clare the paper. She smiled and handed it back.

'I thought we'd eat at Cyril's in Dean Street,' she said.

'Take me to your Cyril.'

Chapter Three

Some years ago I was a policeman. During that time I had a friend called Peter Moody.

People used to say Peter Moody and me looked like each other. I don't know. It's so long since we met and so much has changed in between for both of us it would be hard to make a judgment now about how we were in the old days . . . even about how we looked. If the people who said we looked like each other were right Peter would be just over six feet and weigh fifteen stone. He'd be middling- to dark-brown-haired, with very dark eyes. He has a square jaw so I guess I must have one too. That's a good description of me and it's a good description of Peter in our twenties. It says nothing, though, about his way of smiling, especially at women, and I certainly never had his lazy way of leaning on everything as if all of life were slightly too much bother. Peter gave everyone, even his bosses, the impression that if you weren't on top form, witty and intelligent while you were with him, you would quickly lose his attention. It made the bosses dislike him and Peter had the confidence not to care.

I wasn't like that. I wasn't that cool. I never had his wry smile because I never had the confidence to find everything amusing the way he did. I was never a big hit with women like him because I never believed I would be. Peter never believed he wouldn't. I never had his taste for expensive clothes, either.

No, if ever I looked like Peter Moody it was when we were about twenty-two and twenty-seven, me and him respectively, and the resemblance was entirely superficial. It was because we were both tall and dark and well-built and roughly of an age. Maybe it was because we both wore that blue uniform people thought Peter and I looked like each other. Nowadays his weight has gone up by two stones and mine has gone down by one, so we don't look alike. There are other differences . . . he's grown a beard and I've lost a leg. How different can two men be?

I remember when I first met Peter.

I was at that stage in a young copper's life when the desk sergeant thinks you might not be a complete disaster turned loose on Joe Public. It was a Saturday night. I took a call over my personal radio for the Trocadero Danse Palace. It was the usual thing. Fifteen pints of lager and everybody wants to break each other's skull. A dance hall fight should represent no problem for me, the beat copper. I wasn't expected to go along and make like Flash Gordon and Tarzan all rolled into one. I just had to stroll down there in my big hat and direct traffic, that sort of thing, until a Transit van full of heroes would turn up. Then we'd *all* go in. The received lore of this type of policing, not the sort of thing they spend a lot of time on in training schools, is that it is unwise to go wandering around furious dance halls, pubs or cinemas (even houses) without all the lights on, without everyone knowing you're a copper, and – most importantly of all – without having arranged some sort of back-up. Your black belt in judo or origami or whatever will do you no good at all when some small but vicious guy comes up behind you in the dark and breaks a bottle over your head.

I forgot all those rules. When I arrived in front of the Trocadero Danse Palace there was a distinct absence of flashing blue lights and friendly, familiar faces. I couldn't even hear a siren in the distance.

The monkey on the door didn't want me anywhere near the place. He was a squat, muscly man with grey skin, a thick, purple lower lip and a forehead all of one inch high. The face was topped with the worst toupee in the world.

'No trouble here, officer. You was misin... misin... someone told you wrong. There was a rumble but the boys involved had it away on their toes.'

It was possible. I looked around.

'Why are you on your own?' I asked.

His eyes narrowed. I could almost hear his brain ticking.

'I ain't,' he announced suddenly and looked happy. Newton must have looked like that when his apple fell. We two stood alone in the foyer. Neon lamps flickered greenly about us. The silence was broken only by the tapping of the monkey's patent leather shoe. Then listening hard I could hear the faint hum of music two floors above. I looked around again. The monkey followed my gaze anxiously.

'What's that on the floor?' I said.

We both stared down at the white marble. He lifted his head slowly and his brow furrowed again.

'Blood,' he announced. 'It's blood. One of the other bouncers caught a noseful off some fruity-pie during the rumble.'

'Well,' I said. We both stared at the patch a little longer. It was a foot long and six inches wide, allowing for all the scuffing that had gone on since it had been left there. 'Is it fresh?' I said.

He nodded.

'Oh yes. The others have taken him to hospital. Should have got there by now I would think, if you wanted to talk to him. . . .' His voice drifted off and he looked towards the street, clearly hoping I'd go back on to it. I looked at the patch again.

'Your colleague must have a very big nose,' I said.

'A whopper. It's down the hospital. I think someone got him in it with a knife.'

'A knife?'

Just then a muffled scream came along the corridor behind him. I tried to ignore it. I wanted to ignore it. I'm not big on muffled screams and generally avoid them wherever I can. Then it came again.

I pushed past the monkey. He said, unbelievably, 'Have you got a warrant?' People watch too much TV. I took no notice of him. I drew my stick and leaned on a set of emergency doors behind the ticket stall. They gave on to a blue-lighted atrium with another set of emergency doors on the far wall. The screams were coming from behind the second set of doors. I could hear the wet slap of a steak being slammed on a slab, then another slap, then another, then another. There were no screams now, just throaty coughs to follow the first two slaps and a strangled, gargling sound following the third. The steel bars to the emergency doors were down and the doors were about an inch ajar. I pushed the doors an inch wider so I could see better. There was a small dark yard about twenty feet square. It was full of big dustbins, tall as a man and four or five feet across. The only light in the yard came from a narrow alleyway that led back to the street. I drew back into the blue light and safety of the atrium. I lifted my radio mike to my mouth and called softly. It didn't work. Often the older ones didn't work indoors. I tucked the radio back into my tunic, held my stick up and went forward. My hand was sweaty on the grip.

Slap!

Slap!

The sounds came again. I leaned out the doors and could see shadows moving between the bins. Some big men were there, using another man as a punchbag.

Slap!

The man they were hitting didn't have it in him to groan even, by now. I stepped out.

"That'll do,' I said firmly. 'Let's just break this little party up, boys.'

You've got to say something. The couple of big men turned out to be three, and for some reason they didn't just surrender there and then. I heard the man they'd been thumping fall down and wondered how long it would be before I joined him. Two of the men jumped me, but instead of fighting they just wanted to batter me to the ground and get away. Very reasonable, from their point of view. They went through the emergency doors. I came out of it with sore knuckles, a face even more sore and my pride on the floor. I got up but my pride didn't. I had a piece of cloth in my hand. I'd lost my truncheon and my helmet in the dark somewhere.

I looked up.

I could see the silhouette of the third man in the alley. He seemed to be laughing at me, I couldn't be sure. I heard his victim groan between the bins. I decided I'd hold *one* of them no matter what. My pride wanted him. I stuffed the cloth I was holding into my pocket and started forward.

'Don't make me laugh,' the silhouette said. It had quite a soft voice, not harsh at all.

I threw myself at him. He punched me in the face and I stopped short, staggering back. I remember the feel of the brick under my hands as I slammed back against the wall. I remember the iron taste of my own blood in my mouth. My mind was operating in a dull, ringing world; as if someone had dropped a length of steel nearby. Steel in my head, iron in my mouth, steel in my face again as he hit me a second time. Did I hear someone move behind him? I didn't think so.

He began to move back down the alleyway quickly. I threw myself at his back. He shrugged me off. I threw myself at him again. I felt a sharp pain in my left forearm and he punched me hard to the side of the head. I fell back again. I still hadn't seen his face but I'd felt his fist. The silhouette was a lot better at fisticuffs than me. I was on the ground. I began to raise myself once more. Then I saw the knife in his hand and knew what the pain in my forearm had been. Light glinted on the blade and the silhouette advanced. I was half-standing, half-kneeling, fixed to the spot, waiting for the blade. Then I caught a movement behind the silhouette and he went down like so much coal tipped into a cellar. A handlamp snapped on and an outraged voice said, 'I've broken my bloody stick!'

I staggered down the alley to the street. A policeman followed me.

'He's got a knife,' I said.

'I've cuffed him.'

'And there's a bloke all mashed up behind those refuse bins.'

I leaned on the corner of the alley. My tunic was filthy and blood was dripping from the fingertips of my left hand. I was trembling all over. I looked up and was surprised to find myself surrounded by a small crowd. Young boys and girls, dressed in their Saturday night gladrags, stood arm's length away, staring. Waiting for me to speak or move. A sergeant and a constable pushed past me, flashing the alley with handlamps. I had a glimpse of the dirt I might have died in, then the lights moved on.

The copper who'd followed me from the alley was leaning against a shining white rover, picking unhappily at a split truncheon. He looked up.

'What a bonce, eh? He broke my stick.'

The crowd's eyes swivelled from me to the broken stick. No one outside of us two spoke.

'Thanks,' I said, then, 'Why no siren?' angrily.

The policeman pushed his stick into his pocket and held his hand out.

'Peter Moody,' he said. 'It was my idea, I'm afraid. I didn't want any fights breaking up before I had a chance to join in.' He grinned and I saw he meant it. I took his hand.

'James Jenner. Jimmy. You could have got me killed,' I said. I meant it, too.

Moody shook his head and held the car door open for me.

'No, I'd been in the alley there for ages. I just didn't think you'd appreciate me joining in before you'd had a chance at him on your own. You did all right, considering.'

'Considering what?' I groaned, and eased myself into the Rover's passenger seat. The crowd still stared. Everything ached suddenly. I saw the blue lights of an ambulance turning the corner. Peter Moody said, 'Considering that matey was a very nasty piece of work. You did well.'

I let my head fall back and closed my eyes.

'Cheers, mate. Here.' I pulled the piece of cloth from my pocket and held it up to him. 'Somewhere in that club is a bouncer with no bow-tie. He shouldn't be too difficult to find, unless they've all taken their bow-ties off.'

Chapter Four

Peter Moody was new to our station, which is why I'd never met him before. When I met him he was twenty-seven and had been a policeman for four years. Such was his personality that there were plenty of rumours about what he'd been doing before, but one night while we were patrolling together he told me he'd been a soldier for three years, and had been a career soldier but had got cheesed off with it. Later I met a traffic cop from Catford who'd been to Hendon with Peter. He said he was sure Peter had been in the army okay, but as an officer in the infantry. It sounded unlikely to me.

I always considered Peter saved my life that night behind the Trocadero Danse Palace, and I'm usually able to forget that it was partly his fault I'd been at risk in the first place.

Peter and I became good friends and he saved my bacon more than once. He had a knack of getting us into terrible trouble and then getting us out again. I became his sidekick, his catechumen in the ways of life. I wasn't that much of a beginner when I met him, but Peter always made me feel like one. He was forever explaining things to me that I already knew. I didn't mind... he explained lots of things I didn't know, too. It was a good time in many ways, and the good time lasted a little under two years.

We even shared a house for a while. It was a big posh one in Chigwell and it belonged to a girl I met one day when her car had been stolen. I took the stolen vehicle report, chatted her up, all that nonsense. She was in the import/export business and her car had been full of imitation fur ready to go to East Germany. It was the gear she was worrying about more than the car, because losing it meant losing a customer.

I said all the right things to her, tried to get her to relax a bit. What's a few yards of imitation fur? It was nothing beside her. She was a cracker. Thirty, tall, flowing dark hair, big brown eyes and the kind of figure that would keep you awake at nights wondering what it would be like to lean against. I leaned against her once or twice over the next couple of months. It was okay.

This girl came into our nick one day wearing a dripping wet gaberdine trenchcoat and carrying a big leather briefcase. Her hair was soaked and she pouted across the Formica counter-top, complaining about her lost car. She was so lovely I wanted to give her mine. Instead I told her to park herself in a boozer down the street till I finished duty, then I'd run her home. Two hours later I was sitting in the drawing room of a big, airy, red-brick house in Chigwell with a scotch in one hand and the girl in the other. It was her house and she was only there about six months a year because of business, she said, so she was at present looking for a couple of trustworthy people to share it with her. Real *regular* people, she wanted. She slipped down the sofa a little towards me, dipped her chin and said, 'It can get very lonely here. I get very insecure sometimes.'

I lifted her chin and kissed her lips.

'You mustn't be frightened. What kind of people are you looking for?'

'Trustworthy, like I said.' She smiled and kissed back.

'Policemen, that sort of thing?' I ventured.

'Policemen would be perfect.'

Well, I can take a hint. I volunteered myself as lodger and boyfriend. I got both jobs. I volunteered Peter Moody as the second lodger. I suppose some thought like 'he needs a decent roof over his head' or 'we could share the journey to work' must have been in my mind. I must've been mad. I should have gone and found the dirtiest, ugliest slob I could find in our nick. That's what I should have done... but I didn't. Within a month I was lodger still but only second string boyfriend. Peter had looked at my lovely new acquaintance, or smiled, or said hullo or something. I know that one night they were going out to supper and it was obvious I wasn't welcome. Peter got the woman, the lodgings and the use of the Alfa Romeo (it had been recovered, minus the immo fur) while she was away on her business trips around Europe. *I* got the elbow. I moved into a section house – a posh barracks for coppers – in Wanstead. I was a bit fed-up with him, but there was no point in getting angry ... I don't think Peter even knew he was doing it.

Oh yes. The girl was called Clare. Clare Fisher. She called herself Austrian, but that was only because her father was from a German-speaking part of Italy. She'd been brought up in Paris and held a British passport. I don't know how many languages she spoke... I think it was seven. I only speak three... cockney, English and rubbish.

Although we worked together still, things weren't the same between Peter and me after the business with Miss Fisher. It was natural. A couple of months later he moved into the section house, too, but by that time I was on my way again, transferred to Romford. We lost touch for nearly a year, and I didn't mind losing touch. I'd found another girl... one he wasn't getting his hands on.

I heard of Peter next from a guy who'd transferred out to Romford too. Dave something. I don't remember. I can't even put a face to him. He knew my friend Peter Moody, okay. He said everyone knew him. Peter was famous. He'd been caught nicking peppered smoked mackerel from Tesco's, Dave said. Maybe he'd cracked up. I don't know. I mean, *peppered smoked mackerel*... it's such a humiliating thing to get thrown out of the job for. I tried to find him. I went round to all the people who knew Peter. No joy. I went to Clare Fisher's house but a tough-looking guy there said she was in Poland and he didn't know when she'd be back. He didn't expect her for months.

'No address there?' I asked politely. 'No phone number I could have?'

'No,' he snarled. 'She's travelling around.' And he slammed the door on me. At the time I put it down to a jealous boyfriend.

I tried our old nick. No joy there. I even tried Staff Records, which was in Tintagel House, Vauxhall, in those days. I made out to be a pay clerk after a National Insurance number.

'There's a flag on the file,' the girl said. 'Refer to Head of Section. What's your office, Mister Proust? I'll have him ring you back.'

I told her I was in the Permanent Record Enquiry Office (whatever that is) and gave her the number of a minicab firm in Bermondsey.

I tried CRO, too. If someone had been convicted of a crime like theft *and* they'd been a policeman they *must* be on CRO, I reasoned. They must be there on two counts . . . once for being a policeman and once for being a thief. I got a detective constable friend to fill in a CRO enquiry form for me. It came back a week later marked 'Nothing Known.' This was in the days before they had computers, of course. It seemed the Metropolitan Police was determined to convince itself that Peter Moody had never existed. Maybe that's what happens to black sheep. Maybe we're proud in some way of coppers who go spectacularly bent, but those who are caught nicking peppered smoked mackerel are a source of shame to us all, and are given the 'non-existent' treatment. It's so *petty*.

All that happened in mid-November. In January I had a phone call from Clare.

'I've bought a new house.'

'That's nice for you, Clare. I'm pleased.'

28

'Why don't you come over and see it, Jimmy?'

'I couldn't do that, Clare. I'm involved with someone, you know? I don't think it would be fair for me to come over and see you.'

'Come and see it,' she said. A shiver ran up my spine. Who's interested in houses when you're talking to Clare? The shiver ran down again.

'How's Peter?' I said. 'Do you ever see Peter nowadays?' It was the best subject change I could do.

'No. I haven't seen him for more than a year. I went to your old station once to see him, but no one there had heard of him. I'm afraid we rather lost touch. Do you see him?'

'No,' I said. 'Have you seen him since the fish?'

'What fish?'

'The business with the fish, Clare. Have you seen him since then?'

'I don't know about any fish, Jimmy. Have you been drinking?'

So she didn't know about the fish and she hadn't seen him. I didn't explain it to her . . . I'd let Peter make his own explanations if and when he saw her next, I thought. Clare said she'd got this house on the marshes past Corringham, in Essex. A big, old, seventeenth-century job, she said, with herringbone bricks and black timbers and all that caper. If she'd said mackerelbone bricks I'd have worried.

'When's your day off next week, Jimmy?' she asked.

'Wednesday.'

'Get the six-ten from Fenchurch Street. I'll pick you up at Stanford-le-Hope Station and we'll have supper together. I've some nice Polish ham a client gave me. We'll have that.'

'We won't,' I said, but she'd rung off. She hadn't left me either the new address or the telephone number. I rang the telephone directory and asked after her number, but they didn't have any Clare Fishers in Corringham or Stanford-le-Hope. None they were doling out numbers for, anyway. I just had to go and have dinner with the lady, it seemed.

Chapter Five

The winter of 1975 was cold. I wore underclothes, over-
clothes, woolly mittens, fingerless gloves under the mittens,
a scarf around my neck and a bobble hat on my head which
I had to turn inside-out because it said 'WEST HAM
RULES' all round the outside. When I arrived in Fenchurch
Street I was the only one there in a claret-and-blue hat with
ƨƎＬUЯ MAH TƨƎW round it. I was *freezing*. So was the
rest of London. The City was suffering from the 'down'
everyone gets after Christmas. There were still decorations in
shop windows, but now they looked tawdry, not gay. Everyone's face had that puffy, unhappy appearance, a combination
of too much plum duff and alcohol and the prospect of months
of freezing gloom before they could dash off to Majorca.
You'd think a nation that gets as much winter as the English do
would grow to like it. But we don't.

That January evening I stumbled down Fenchurch Street
with thousands of my fellow countrymen and women, all of
us refusing to look at one another, each of us intent on
hunching our shoulders against the wind and the cold, each
of us simply getting where we had to go as fast as possible. I
was early for the train so I pushed into the crowds in the East
India Arms and had a glass of beer called 'Winter Warmer'.
Two of those and it would have been 'Winter Fall Over'.
The beer was thick and dark and salty-sweet and seemed to
stick to the sides of my throat. People pushed and shoved

each other, called for two more over here; there was no-where to sit but the main thing was we were *warm*. Every intake of breath didn't hurt my teeth. Some feeling had re-turned in my toes. My cheeks and forehead had become a little less numb.

I decided to take a chance on another glass of Winter Warmer. I suppose I thought it might make the journey into frozen Essex a little more bearable. I would pass the train ride in a pleasant, alcohol-induced haze.

'I'll have another of these!' I called to the barman. I was leaning across some fellow's back.

'Get out!' yelled the barman, a slim, blue-eyed young man with an anxious face. 'You're not to come in here! You're not to be served!'

It seemed a bit drastic but when I followed his eye to the door I could see what he was so upset about. The pub's more or less exclusively used by City types wearing smart suits and their girlfriends in formal blouses and navy-blue skirts. The character the barman had shouted at looked like a walking rubbish tip. He had a shock of dirty black hair and a dusty beard. I could smell him from ten feet away. He'd been for a good long soak in booze and urine. People drew back from the man. He was really ugly. His face was flushed red from the drink and the winter wind. His eyes were deep-set and mad-looking. He wore a thin, dirty jacket and he had a collarless cotton shirt on, undone halfway to his waist. He wore no hat, no overcoat, no sweater even.

'Out!' called the barman again. The drunk's face screwed into anger, then his eyes met mine. We stared across the room at each other for a few seconds, then he was gone.

'Thank God,' the barman muttered. The burble of conver-sation filled the room again. A young man laughed a ner-vous, high-pitched cackle of a laugh. He wanted to impress someone, he was laughing at some joke. Other men laughed more quietly.

'Yes, sir?' the barman called to me. I still had my arm outstretched, holding my glass towards him. I dropped my glass into his hand and pushed my way outside.

After the fug in the bar room the freezing winter's evening was like a slap in the face. I drew in my breath and pulled my hat on. The air was so cold my lungs hurt. The sky and the side streets were inky black. Only the yellow streetlights and the brilliant shop neons kept the darkness from Fenchurch Street. I breathed onto my mittens. Rime formed on the woollen surface. Tiny, dusty flakes of snow were whipping past me on the wind. Over the street I could see the drunk, whirling through the crowd, a bottle of cider or sherry in one hand, the other holding his thin jacket across his body. He crossed the street again, running into Railway Place. There's a tatty piazza in front of the station, dropped there a few years before in an attempt to smarten the joint up. In the centre of the piazza is a raised flower-bed, just the right height for everyone to drop litter into, and down the side of the flower-bed are some benches. The drunk reeled across Railway Place. A black cab just missed him. The driver leaned on his horn and yelled. The drunk made his way towards the benches. A couple of his own kind were already there. I walked into the station booking-hall and leaned against one of the big dusty grey doors there. I wanted to watch what happened next. I could hardly believe what I was seeing. The drunk I'd followed was Peter Moody. I could have no doubt . . . he'd recognised me, too, I thought. There was Peter, sitting across the way from me with a school of down-and-out drunks, tipping his bottle back and offering it to the next man along the line.

I crossed over to them. Thin snow eddied about my feet. I stood before the drunks, slapping my mittened hands together, stamping my feet like a guard on some foreign border post.

'Peter,' I said. He ignored me. I stood over him and shouted, 'Peter!' He still ignored me. I pulled his arm. When he looked up his eyes were glazed and dozy. He blinked slowly and said, 'Hullo, James, I thought it was you.' He gave a stupid smile and stood. I could see his unwashed, pale body, blue-white grimy flesh inside the half-open shirt.

'Peter,' I repeated, softly, uselessly. I didn't know what to say. He was rolling drunk on a bench full of rolling drunks, all of them eagerly waiting their turn at the cooking sherry. I just didn't know what to say. How much can a man change? Nine months ago he'd been a policeman. For almost two years I'd been his close colleague. I'd never in all that time seen him with anything stronger than a glass of lager. He was the one who always drove home.

A policeman forced me to act.

'Any problem?' It was a City of London copper, crept up behind me.

'No problem,' I said. I won't repeat what he said about Peter and his pals, but it wasn't very kind of him to talk like that in front of men's faces. Any men's. I suppose if I'd been standing there in the Gilbert-and-Sullivan outfit my attitude might have been similar. I pulled out my warrant card. The City copper took it from me.

'Mets, eh? You keep some funny company, PC Jenner.'

I couldn't argue.

'The one in the middle's an old friend.' The policeman stared at me. 'Of the family,' I added. 'Falls off the rails every now and then. You'd be doing me a really big favour if you could get one of those cabs to carry us.'

'I know I would.'

He did it, though, which is more than I ever expect of City of London coppers because they're a haughty bunch of big lumps. The cab driver we chose didn't like the deal one bit, but the presence of the City copper and me flashing fivers did the trick. I didn't *give* him any fivers, of course. I just showed them. Fifty pence would be quite enough tip for a cab journey from Fenchurch Street to Stoke Newington (where I'd recently bought a flat) even today. The cab driver was a miserable sort and made a fuss about the money . . . but then they always do.

Chapter Six

He came round at five in the morning. If I'd been asleep he'd have woken me with all his crashing around in the bathroom and stumbling against my furniture. As it happened, I was lying in bed wondering about life, the future, the past and all the other junk that fills people's minds when they're awake at five in the a.m., so Peter's noise didn't matter. I went into the kitchen and made coffee. Peter came in too, wearing only his stinking trousers. I fetched him a shirt and jeans and took his gear to the rubbish chute. It was good for nothing else. When I came back he was in the living room.

'What happened?' I said.

'Nothing.'

'*Nothing?*'

'Nothing to speak of.'

He sat on my sofa with a beaker of coffee cupped in his hands. The beaker was shaking and so was he. His eyes were red-rimmed. I'd stuck him under the shower as soon as I'd got him home the night before so his beard and his hair simply looked scruffy and wild, not dirty like he'd looked at Fenchurch Street. He looked like one of those poets, an Irish one perhaps, who is totally preoccupied and doesn't notice he looks wild and handsome. He had raw cheeks and a surly look on his lips. Peter was about twenty-nine at this time

. . . a good age for poets and drunks both. Twenty-nine going on fifty.

I stood before him drinking coffee too. I said to him, 'A few months ago you were my friend. Then I don't hear from you, as if you'd dropped off the world. Then a fellow turns up in my nick saying you'd been slung out of the job for pinching mackerel. This seems very strange to me. Then I find you drunk and incapable with a load of down-and-outs. This seems even stranger.' He was nodding as I spoke; once every few words he'd nod his head, as if he were assenting. I went on, 'And after all that you tell me nothing happened.'

He kept nodding.

'And what about this mackerel business, is that true?'

'Yes.' He was still shaking. His beaker of coffee was still shaking. 'I think so. I don't remember the incident very clearly.'

I pulled the curtains open. Outside was still dark. My figure reflected in the glass, Peter's behind me on the sofa. Even with the wild hair and beard he looked like me. I could see his reflection shaking with the drinker's ague.

'I've got a couple of cans in the fridge if you want one,' I said. He didn't answer. '*Why* didn't you come to me, Peter? Or to Clare . . . or anyone? How long have you been like this?'

He gulped the coffee, winced and said, 'Since my late teens, on and off. It's what got me thrown out of the army, though my CO managed to keep it off the record.'

'When did you start again?'

I heard my own voice clearly, suddenly. I sounded like a probation officer. I can't stand that sort of sickly, *now-tell-me-all-about-it* do-gooding, yet the tone was in me, I knew.

'When I split with Clare. It wasn't her . . . it was never that serious. I was just ripe to fall off the wagon and sure enough . . .' His voice trailed off. He began to sip the coffee, more as a way to avoid conversation, I felt, than any real desire for the coffee. By this stage I didn't mind him not wanting to talk. The way I'd spoken to him had made me feel pretty embarrassed. We sat in silence for a long time, staring at the carpet and sipping cold coffee.

'Could you sleep now?' I said eventually.

He shook his head.

'No. No chance.'

'Let's go for a walk, then.'

We walked the streets of Stoke Newington wearing, between us, virtually every item of winter clothing I owned. Peter looked so much like a malnourished and unshaven version of me it was uncanny; like walking beside yourself. The night was as cold as the day before had promised. We talked – or rather, I talked – rubbish. I nattered about any subject I could come up with. We walked and I talked for hours. I phoned in work and reported sick. Peter leaned on the outside of the phone box blowing dragon's breaths of condensation into the cold night air. I said I had toothache. The nightshift skipper didn't seem convinced, but since he had no responsibility for me he didn't question me too closely. I hung up and Peter and I walked round and round some more. Milk carts passed us, then early red buses. Commercial vans clunked gears. We must have looked fierce, because several times I noticed people cross the road rather than pass us by on the same side of the street.

'Where do you live?' I said.

Peter shook his head.

'Nowhere. I was in what's called a "hotel" in King's Cross, a glorified flop, really, but I've been out of there for...'

'For how long?'

We were outside Clissold Park. The shrubbery looked strange and foreign, dark leaves glinting in the artificial light. Frost was all over the surfaces of the leaves, like sugar coating. Peter leaned on the railings and looked as if he would break down. His throat was choked when he said, 'I don't know. I really don't know how long. A few days. A

36

week, maybe a week-and-a-half. No more than that on the street, I don't think. Something like that. I never had room rent.'

I fought down the urge to say 'Why didn't you *ask*?' again in that wounded tone I'd used earlier.

'You can crash out at my place for a few days while we work out what to do with you. Have you any plans?'

He smiled for the first time then.

'No. I don't have any plans.'

A man came to unlock the park gates. He was a small, intense-looking black man and he'd put on even more clothes to ward off the cold than me. People were passing by. Suddenly the street seemed busy.

'What's the time?' I said to the small black man. He looked at his watch.

'Eight-thirty-two. Any complaints?'

We walked away. There's no point in upsetting a man at the beginning of his working day. Maybe he thought we were checking up on him.

'I thought I might go to Canada,' Peter said suddenly. 'I've got a sister there.'

I shook my head. 'You can't just go to places nowadays. You have to have permits and things.'

'I don't. My mother was Canadian. I was educated there.'

We were making our way back to my flat. The pavements were covered in white hoarfrost. The passage of feet had made skid marks on the frost. The kerbstones, for some reason, weren't frosty. Steam rose from a sewer cover. I looked at our feet, at his shabby shoes. I looked at him wearing my clothes. They fitted him all right, but it was still a queer feeling to see him in my clothes.

'You should shave and get a haircut,' I said. He stroked his beard suddenly, as if he'd just become aware of it. His hand was very shaky still and his face was deathly white.

'Yes. I could lose this.'

I pointed to the lights of a supermarket down the road.

'Do you need anything there? There's no booze in the

house apart from the lagers in the fridge.'

'No . . . a razor. I could use a razor.'

'I've got that. Come back and I'll make some breakfast and we'll see if we can't fix you up a bit.'

I didn't hear from Clare about our missed dinner date for nearly a week. Then she called and gave me a hard time. I told her about Peter but she didn't seem interested in it. I told her I hadn't been able to phone her but she ignored that.

'I'm in the book, Jimmy.'

'You're not.'

'Of course I am. Anyway, I thought policemen were meant to be resourceful. A girl guide could've done better than you.'

'Thanks. What do you know about Peter and this drinking business?'

'Nothing. Don't bother asking for any more dinner dates, either, Jenner.'

She hung up. I said something very rude into an empty British Telecom line (or Post Office line, as it was then). I lay back on the sofa and drank some of the Canadian Club I'd bought in case Peter fell off his self-imposed wagon again. He'd left the night before, air ticket in one hand, my best winter clothes in a suitcase in the other. The few days we'd spent together hadn't been too bad. Peter drank gallons of tea and coffee but no booze at all. He phoned his sister in Toronto who said 'Come on home all is forgiven' or words to that effect. I had enough money in the bank to buy him an air ticket and make sure he didn't turn up in Toronto completely potless. He seemed very emotional all the time and could hardly speak to me sometimes. I put it down to him coming off the juice.

He wouldn't let me drive him to Heathrow. He gave me a pawn ticket for his Nikon and spare lens and said if I got it out of hock it was mine, then he shook hands and tramped down the stairs from my flat without looking back. I remember sincerely hoping, praying even (though I don't know who'd listen to me), that he made out in Canada. I suppose he did make out in his way.

Chapter Seven

Looking back on it, I might have done quite a few things differently. I might, for example, have asked my old pal Peter why he didn't seem to be listed by the Criminal Record Office, despite qualifying both as a copper and as a criminal. I might have asked why only supervisors could read his file at Staff Branch. It was queer . . . but since I didn't really expect anyone to read his file to me over the phone I just dismissed it. Looking back on it I might have asked for a clear account of the mystery of the missing mackerel . . . in which branch of Tesco's did the incident take place, for example, and was there a subsequent court case? Most of all I might have asked exactly *what* had caused him to fall off the wagon.

I might have asked and I might have insisted on an answer, but I didn't. I would ask if the same thing happened today, but it's always easy to be wise with the advantage of hindsight. I had been pretty shocked to discover Peter almost literally in an underworld. Cleaning him up and giving him a start was a chance for me to play the Samaritan . . . for less than two hundred quid. Given the mentality of the twenty-three-year-old Jimmy Jenner, it was cheap at the price. Helping Peter made me feel good, and I wasn't much inclined to question how this opportunity to help him had come about. If I had been, things would have worked out differently. But I was a naïve and sentimental young copper.

I'd been given the chance to be the good guy. It's a chance which doesn't come your way often, and it's a pretty cheap route to personal sainthood and general smugness. I took it without question.

I was surprised to hear from Peter within a week. It was in the form of a letter posted in Toronto.

Dear Jimmy, he had written, *sorry to have imposed on you recently. Encl. is a cheque which should make us about square financially. It's not my money, of course, it's from my sister. She doesn't think we should owe money outside the family. I guess she's right, too. I hope the Nikon's working okay. Take some pictures of yourself and the boys and send them to me if you ever get a chance. I'll always owe you one.* (signed) *Peter*

P.S. The money isn't a gift from her to me ... it's an advance on wages. I'm working in her husband's business.

The letter contained a counter clerk's cheque from the Royal Bank of Northern Ontario to the sum of four hundred pounds, made out in sterling. I sat down to read the letter again. Peter had never mentioned the existence of a sister until a week befor . . . now she'd insisted I should have four hundred pounds of her money. Where was *she* when he was down and out in Fenchurch Street? I looked the letter over again. Peter must have sent it the day after he landed in Toronto. There was no return address, just the postmark 'Yonge Street, Toronto' and the date. I'd heard of Yonge Street before. It's famous . . . for being eighty miles long. You could hardly walk up and down knocking on doors: 'Anyone here know a bloke called Peter?' There's old Peter, being elusive again. And what was the 'pictures of yourself and the boys' phrase in there for? Peter was one of the 'boys' like I'm a member of the Society of Jesus. I ain't and he wasn't.

Peter's behaviour looked very irrational, and I began to wonder seriously if the booze hadn't pickled his brain good and proper. I wondered if I shouldn't follow him up, make sure there actually was a sister and that things were okay for him over there. I tucked the cheque into the breast pocket of my tunic, hanging behind my bedroom door. I lay on the bed and read the letter over and over. No matter how many times I read it, there was something enigmatic about that letter.

Peter went to Canada in 1975, which was about the time I clearly formulated two policy decisions about my life. The first was the admission that I was very involved with my girlfriend of the time (a policewoman called Judy Williams), the second was that I should go for detective. I had always wanted to be a detective, but that time – my fourth year of being a police constable – was when it appeared in my mind as being really urgent. If I didn't get going soon I wasn't going to have a brilliant career in the Criminal Investigation Department. If I didn't get going I wasn't going to have a career at all. I decided to concentrate my energies on the twin goals of becoming a detective and excluding the dozen or so other keen males from Judy Williams's life. Perhaps I would even make her Judy Jenner. I was *so* pretentious.

I didn't give up on Peter, though. I thought I might try to find him through his sister. At some time in her life she must have been Moody-not-married. I went to Camden Library and checked the international phone book for the name Moody in Toronto. There were hundreds. Then I tried the London phone book. There were thousands. I rang a couple of fellows who'd known Peter when he was a copper. They both said that if I didn't know about his family then nobody would, because nobody was closer to him than me. I tried Clare. I rang directories to see if she wasn't listed yet. She wasn't. I even got the name of a fellow in the Post Office Special Investigation Branch from a detective sergeant in my own nick. The SIB bloke owed my bloke a favour for something. I rang him to see if I could get Clare's number but he drew a blank, too. There had been no phones connected to anyone called Fisher in Corringham recently, he told me over the phone.

'How far back does "recently" go?' I asked.

'Six months.'

'And you're including ex-directory entries?'

'I certainly am, PC Jenner.' He leaned on that 'PC' like it was a garden gate. He didn't like my detective sergeant friend doling out his number to mere PCs. He told me so and he asked me to let my detective sergeant friend know. I did just that, and the sergeant's reply had to do with pride, the Post Office SIB and the fellow's anatomy. I won't repeat it here.

I even rang a couple of removal companies in Chigwell to ask whether they'd moved any spectacularly good-looking young women from Chigwell to Corringham. Nobody had. I did the same in Corringham. Nobody had there, either. I didn't try too many . . . I mean, it's hard to know where to call a halt. My brief foray into the investigation business had been a non-starter. I couldn't find Peter and I couldn't find Clare. They'd both disappeared leaving tracks all over the place and I couldn't find them. So much for my chances of getting on the detective strength.

The next two weeks I was on nights, then for two weeks after that I was on a driving refresher course at Hendon (compulsory . . . I'd bumped a wall with a panda car). The mystery of the disappearing Peter didn't get my attention again for four full weeks. By that time we were in the middle of a wet February and looking forward to a wet March. I was in my flat on a Monday afternoon feeling resentful about the rain. I hate the winter, and we certainly didn't have spring yet. I took Peter's cheque from a drawer and spread it on the dining room table. I held it down with the forefinger and thumb of each hand. I stared at the paper, wondering why Peter had to make everything such a mystery. He had even been mysterious about his time in the army . . . *of course*. The army. That traffic cop had told me Peter had been an officer. And the identities of army officers are a matter of public record. I went to the public library and asked a woman with enormous breasts and an even more enormous blue chunky-knit sweater, did they have a copy of the Army List?

'No,' she said. 'There's no call for it. There's an old one in reference but it's from 1970 . . . or 1969.' She held a novel by D. H. Lawrence close to her enormous breasts and looked dreamily past me. I never knew the Army List could have that effect on people. Maybe she'd been involved with a soldier once. I went to the reference section and pulled the book. It's big and brown, a sort of soldier's *Wisden*, full of the names of serving army officers. Sure enough he was there: 'Moody, P.R. 2nd Lt. The Mendip Regiment.' So I had proof he'd existed. In 1969 Peter Moody had been a Lieutenant in the Mendip Regiment of the British Army. Sherlock Holmes, eat your heart out.

I rang the regimental headquarters, which was rather unsurprisingly in Somerset. I explained to the clerk that I was trying to get in touch with an old friend who'd been an officer in that regiment, a Lieutenant Moody.

'Is he still in the army, sir?'

'No,' I said, 'he's not. I think he's in Canada somewhere. I want his parental address, so I could get in touch with him that way.'

'I don't think I could help you there, sir. I should think the very best we would be able to do would be to pass something on . . . leave it with me and I'll see if we can do that. Can I have your number?'

I gave him the number but he didn't ring back, not for three days. By that time it didn't matter.

Chapter Eight

'Jimmy! How are you?'

The voice was metallic and distant but it was clearly Peter Moody's. There was a pinging sound in the silence that followed his greeting. It made me think of birds landing on an overhead telephone line, then taking off again.

'Where are you Peter?'

'Toronto, mate. I've got myself fixed up with a room in the YMCA and I'm working out of town for my sister's husband.'

I turned my bedside clock around so I could see it.

'Good, Peter. I'm pleased. It's two a.m., you know? Why call me at two a.m.?'

There was a silence, then he said, 'I'm sorry. I just forgot about the time thing . . . you know how it is.'

'Of course,' I lied. Maybe the grape had got him again. How can you forget a five-hour time difference? 'What's the job you're doing for your brother-in-law? You'd better tell me now you've woken me.'

'Are you on earlies?'

' 'Fraid so.'

'Oh, I'm sorry. I'll go.'

'What's the job?' I insisted. 'I'm already awake.'

'Well . . . he's a market gardener in a little place southwest of here, towards Niagara. It's a huge outfit he's got and he has fellows going into gardening stores, hardware stores, that sort of thing, selling bulbs. It's very seasonal work and I've come during the season.'

'I thought people planted bulbs during the autumn?' I said.

The pinging sound came on the line again. They can land a man on the moon but they can't stop transatlantic telephone lines pinging.

'Maybe, I don't know. You can't order them one day and have them on the shelves ready to sell the next, you know. It's a big business. It needs planning. They have to grow. Like babies... that's what bulbs are, baby plants. So I go around with a catalogue taking orders and my brother-in-law's company produces the bulbs. When they do it is their business, not mine.'

I groaned and sat up. I could hear rain beating against the bedroom window. Peter was still talking about bulbs, black earth and Windsor, Ontario. I don't know how Windsor got into it but it did. I pulled the eiderdown about myself and said, 'What the hell's all that money you sent for? Are you trying to buy off some guilt trip or something?'

'No. I took the clothes and I used your place. You paid my fare. I just reckoned up what I owed you plus the inconvenience and I paid you that. I just wanted to pay you back properly.'

'Why no return address? I've been ringing all over England trying to find you. I even tried to get you through your old regiment.'

He laughed – nervously, I thought.

'What did *they* say?'

'Nothing. What did you expect them to say? I got some regimental clerk on the phone who offered SFA... that's what. I was beginning to wonder if you weren't a figment of my imagination... which reminds me...'

'What?' he yelled. 'I can't hear you very well.'

'I said, "which reminds me".'

46

'Jimmy! Jimmy! Are you still there, Jimmy?'

'I'm still here. Can't you hear me?'

'Hello? Hello?'

There was a click and the line went dead.

I didn't swear. I didn't even get angry. I got up and dressed and made coffee. I opened the living room curtains so I could see the rain beating against the glass. The night was black, pierced by streetlights. Each droplet of water that clung to the glass carried its own beam of light. I was reflected in the glass too. I sat at the table and looked at the window and drank my coffee and thought about Peter, and about his reflection being behind mine in that glass. It seemed a lifetime ago. Then I wrote him a letter. I can't say exactly what I wrote in the letter... it's nearly ten years since I wrote it. I know I tried to be friendly and supportive. I said that if he ever wanted to fall off the beam again the place to do it was among friends. I said I considered myself his friend and he could crash down in my place just any time he felt like. I wrote words to that effect, anyway, and I put in a cheque for the amount I reckoned he'd overpaid me, two hundred quid. I still reckoned then that somehow the juice had ruined his brain... we were, after all, a very short time from Peter running round the streets like a wild man and drinking rough cider from the same greasy bottle as a load of other down-and-outs. I wondered who the other down-and-outs belonged to. I reckoned I shouldn't be too hard on Peter. There was a hole in his life... called alcohol. That was enough. When I finished my letter to him I phoned the night international telephone operator and got the address of the Toronto YMCA off him. He insisted on giving me the telephone number too. I didn't argue. It seemed to make the operator happy.

When I left for work it was still dark and raining. I didn't have an 'airmail' envelope so I put my letter to Peter in an ordinary one and wrote 'airmail' around each side of it and 'c/o YMCA' above YMCA and the address all in red ink. By the time I'd reached the letter-box some of the ink had run in the rain and I was worried the letter wouldn't get there. That's the kind of detail that sticks in your mind over the years, as if it has a life independent from your memory. I can see the rainmarks clearly in that red ink even now.

Chapter Nine

I wrote two letters that morning before I started early shift. The first, and what seemed at the time the most important, was to Peter. The second was a request to transfer to a central London division, preferably the West End. I'd decided that the quiet life of the last couple of years working in good old Romford *had* to change. I was always looking in to London, I realised. I had an ambition – to be a detective – which could best be realised by working in the centre of the city. I had a rather beautiful WPC (as she was then) girlfriend who was working at New Scotland Yard – central London again. Even my flat was closer to central London than to Romford. Romford was an orbit, the West End was the sun. I put in my transfer request, duly signed. I didn't let it get wet in the rain, either.

I didn't hear again from Peter for nearly eighteen months, a little longer even. I didn't hear back from the Commissioner-of-Police-for-the-Metropolis for nearly as long, which was just as much of a surprise in its way. In the meantime my affair with the ever lovely WPC Williams developed into the all-singing-and-dancing-this-is-the-real-thing thing. She was promoted to sergeant in the Criminal Intelligence Section of New Scotland Yard. She learned to be brilliant about computers and all sorts of stuff that I would never understand. I was never going to be that sort of material. I wandered merrily round Romford and its environs doling out parking tickets, reporting nineteen-year-olds for having no tax on their Mark 1 Ford Cortinas and threatening – idly, usually – to arrest middle-aged couples who got pissed on Saturday nights and broke the crockery over each other's heads while they resolved thirty-year-old passions about squeezing the toothpaste tube from the middle. The only consolation was having Judy round to my place once a week so I could give her supper and show her my etchings. Boy, did those etchings ever take a hammering. Sometimes she'd have me round to her place and we'd get a take-away so we could get down to the serious business of studying flow-charts. I discovered algorithm is near algolagnia in more than just the dictionary sense. Judy was in her early twenties then. Good skin, blue eyes, lovely figure, ridiculously young to be a sergeant already, destined for the top. I don't know what she thought she was doing hooked up with me . . . but I was pleased that she was hooked up and I wanted to hold on to her. I believed that putting myself in central London and making myself a good candidate for the detective branch should just about keep me believable as her man.

So it was that I felt I had my chance before me when the Commissioner wrote and asked PC James Jenner to present himself at Tottenham Court Road Police Station at eight a.m. on 1st September 1976.

I took my chance. It nearly killed me.

The career in the West End didn't last long. Days rather than weeks. I had two days in the nick, familiarising myself with the place and their procedures, three days on the beat being shown round by a senior constable, and that was my lot. On the third day a couple of Arabs went in for a spot of self-immolation while we were questioning them. Questioning's an exaggeration. They spotted us, one ran while the other closed the wires on a car bomb he was sitting in. The two coppers I was with got issued with a harp and a cloud each. Same for the Arabs, or whatever is the appropriate Mohammedan equivalent. I was the lucky one . . . at least I think I was. I ended up with my right foot missing and only one ear working. If there's an afterlife those Arabs are in it and so's my foot . . . stalking them. One day the swine'll get a big kick up the arse from a disembodied English foot and wonder why.

So ended my brief career in central London. I'm not bitter. It doesn't make me wish I'd stayed safe in my suburb cracking gangs of garden gnome thieves. But I do hope my foot finds the Arab who closed the wire on that commercial explosive. And I hope it's still wearing my steel toe-capped boot when it finds him.

I never woke up properly for two weeks after being blown up. I had a tube up my nose, one in my arm and a stubby little Irish girl came along and stuffed a needle in me every time I woke up. For all I know she stuck the needle in me every time I went to sleep. I don't know. I lost track of what was waking and what was dreaming. I knew what had happened but I could still feel my missing foot. One of the nurses, either the dream stubby Irish nurse or the real one, was injecting me with morphine. Often Judy came to see me but she often said things she wouldn't say or talked in voices that weren't natural to her, so I thought that probably was dreaming. A couple of senior coppers came in and leaned over me, crushing their scrambled-egg uniform caps to their breasts as they leaned and murmured things I couldn't understand. They looked like nothing so much as a couple of undertakers sizing me up for a coffin. I thought that at that time I was probably conscious but was suffering from a sort of near-death fantasy. Once Peter Moody came and stood at the base of the bed looking long-faced and unhappy. He'd put on a lot of weight and grown a beard like old King George's; a naval beard with a point. He hung around my sickroom for a long time looking gloomy, peering out through the venetian blinds, then turning quickly to stare at me. At one point he came close and stared into the glass vessel which was slowly decanting fluid into my arm. Rubbing his forefinger gently against the glass as if he were clearing a patch of condensation from a window, a schoolboy peering out of a classroom. We never spoke and Peter left as suddenly as he came. I closed my eyes for a moment and he wasn't there. He hadn't spoken while he visited and I knew he was a figment of my imagination and I'd been dreaming. Then when I was properly awake there was a brown envelope on my bedside table which I got a nurse to open and read for me.

Jim, on a flying visit. Keep well. So sad to hear. I'll be in touch. Peter.

'What was the man who delivered it like?' I asked the nurse. 'When did he come to visit? Did he have a pointy beard?'

'I never saw him. I'll find out.'

Next time she came the nurse said, 'Staff says he came the day before yesterday and saw you but you were asleep. He asked if he could leave a note because he didn't live in England. She said she presumed he was one of your relatives.'

There was a cage over my legs, supporting the blankets. The nurse touched the blankets over it with her hand, straightening some imagined rumple.

'Why was that?'

The nurse lifted a finger to her lips like a schoolgirl asked some sudden, embarrassing question.

'I saw him myself. I remember him now,' she said. 'He was a big fellow standing in the corridor outside here . . . and he *did* have a beard.'

'I don't understand,' I said. It was true. I didn't feel then as if I could understand anything except the simplest ideas expressed in the simplest sentences. Complexities about the staff nurse's meanings and this nurse's imagination were beyond me.

'What did she *say?*' I asked impatiently.

The nurse smiled and leaned over me.

'She said even though he has a beard and you don't he

looked exactly like you. She presumed he was your brother. Wasn't he?'

'In a way,' I said. I closed my eyes and the nurse pulled the cord to snap down the venetian blinds before she left the room. Outside, food trolleys squeaked on the linoleum flooring and in a distant corridor a doctor's personal bleeper sounded insistently. Then the heavy door clicked shut and I slept.

Chapter Ten

My career in the Metropolitan Police ended effectively then.
I don't mean they weren't generous. They certainly offered
me jobs. But after all, I wanted to be a *detective*. Who's ever
heard of a one-footed police detective? I didn't want a job
pushing paper in NSY, so in my mind I left from the first day
what had happened sunk in on me. It was a full two years
before the physical leaving came about. In between, the
mystery of the disappearing Peter seemed solved.

The first time I saw him after the hospital visit was in
April 1977. I was lolling around in a convalescent home
near Hastings, reading piles of junk novels and staring
through huge windows originally intended for tubercular
cases. The place had been built in the 1930s when there had
been a boom, if not in the building trade at least in the TB
market. The windows had rotting iron frames, all covered
with thick, crusty white paint. Every now and then a sheet of
glass would carry the orange stain where rust had scarred the
iron surround. I was staring blankly through one of these
stains when Peter's face appeared.

'Jimmy.' He held his hand out. It was strong and brown
and sinewy. 'You look better than the last time I saw you.'

'So do you.'

We laughed a lot and talked a lot of rubbish. I was in a
wheelchair. Peter was pushing me across one of the huge
clipped lawns of the TB hospital. We were going towards the

sea. A light shower of rain was falling and a nurse was calling us back.

'Ignore her,' I said.

The path led through a shrubbery. Rhododendrons as big as trees closed over us. At one point there was a great magnolia stretching above us like an arch. The air was full of the smell of the sea and wet earth.

'How long are you in this for?' Peter asked.

'Not long. I don't have to use it now. I've got crutches.'

We came out of the shrubbery on to another lawn, only this one was uncut. I could see the sea, but there were houses between us and it.

'Far enough?'

'Far enough. Are you still in the horticulture business?'

He laughed.

'Yes. It's going along nicely. What have you been doing?'

Since I'd spent the last few months in the newspapers we both had a good laugh at that.

The light rain kept falling. Peter stood before me with his arms folded and rain in his hair and on his beard.

'You should go on a diet,' I said. We both laughed out loud. I ran my hand along the cool metal tubing of the wheelchair. 'I'm going to get a false leg fitted, get good at walking on it and then make myself a detective. A private detective.'

'Do they have them in London, Jimmy?'

'They will have when I get going.'

We both laughed again, though it wasn't a joke. I meant it.

We spent an hour there, getting wet and talking. He asked at one point if people had come enquiring after him when he went to Canada.

'Like debt collectors?' I joked. He laughed too. It was a strange question to ask, though. I told him that a very well-spoken bloke had come round after him at our nick, ages after he'd left.

'And?'

'Got a flea in his ear and told to sling his hook, I should think.'

'Can you describe him, Jimmy?'

Peter was staring out to sea.

'I never met him. Do you know who it was?'

He shook his head and suddenly laughed again, turning to face me. 'No, Jimmy, I don't. Maybe it *was* a debt collector.'

We talked on. Peter told me he was completely off the booze and had been for a long time. He was doing well and had bought a place in London. He gave me the address. It was a posh one in Kensington. I put the piece of paper into my shirt pocket and carefully buttoned the flap. I treated the piece of paper like a diamond.

Back in the hospital we both got bawled out by a nurse, then when she'd gone we promised each other we would never lose touch again. We were too good friends to allow ourselves to lose touch again. We promised each other with firm handshakes and tears in our eyes . . . what a couple of romantics. We were both absolutely sincere in saying it, too. I was.

All that happened eight years ago. I didn't hear from him again during all that long time. It wasn't only his fault. I suppose we both had a lot on our minds. I got married and lived in Spain at one stage. I've no idea what became of the precious piece of paper with his address. I expect it went into the hospital laundry the same evening he visited.

I finally heard from Peter again this autumn, and when I did hear from him it was a telephone message passed by a third party over my telephone answering-machine. The third party passed on this invitation to come to Peter's house. 'I'm calling on behalf of . . .,' in a dark brown, muffled voice, all that nonsense. Essentially, someone was asking me to come and find a corpse in Peter's Kensington home. If that person was really calling on behalf of Peter it wasn't very friendly of him. If they weren't . . . then my old pal Peter Moody was in the chocolate.

And maybe I was too.

Part Two

Autumn Leaves

Chapter Eleven

Cyril's, the place Clare took me to work on me about Peter, is a supper-only restaurant. I don't know if they're supper-only because they can't be bothered to cook lunches or if it's because their particular clientele doesn't get up in time to eat lunches. Maybe both reasons are true.

I've been there before. It's in Dean Street. The restaurant is made up of three enormous rooms over a strip joint. On the floor above Cyril's is a film-editing outfit full of young guys who'd have you believe they were Cecil B. De Mille, all the Kordas, Stephen Spielberg and Mae West rolled into one. Those boys in the film-editing place are *full* of themselves. What they don't know or haven't done would fit on the back of a postage stamp, and they'll tell you all about everything they know whether you're interested or not. They don't care if you're sitting at the next table or walking downstairs in the street; they're talking and you're listening. The film-editing boys all come down to supper in Cyril's and talk big through the early evening. I could hear them now, puffing their egos and their French cigarettes.

I munched a game chip and looked about myself. At one time, in the early nineteenth century, the building would have been the home of quite a grand family. Nowadays the place is just a supper restaurant, clean and with good food, but nothing *too* special – no specially imported French chef, for example.

I tried to imagine the grand early nineteenth-century family who'd owned the house . . . maybe had it specially built for themselves. I wondered what they'd think of us filling our faces in their first-floor drawing rooms. I wondered what the nineteenth-century family would think of the strippers of all nationalities (leave alone shapes and sizes, if the comings and goings in the street were anything to go by) bumping and grinding in what had been the cellar and the kitchen of their grand house. I wondered how the master would feel about the whisky-swilling movie-trade chancers setting up shop in his bedroom.

I sat there thinking that if Cyril (whoever he is) didn't keep his restaurant a bit fuller than this it would end up being an ex-supper restaurant. I was by one of the tall windows at the front of the house. I leaned forward and tapped my fingers on the glass for no other reason than the need to touch the fabric of the building. I looked down on Dean Street and watched the Soho neon lights and bustling pavements. I could hear taxi horns and then some girl yelling down the street after a fellow. A uniformed copper was talking to two black kids under some scaffolding across the road. They weren't discussing football or girls and they weren't swapping racing tips. The black boys were edgy, just wanting to get away, but the copper kept them there, talking, talking, talking to them. They didn't seem to answer much.

Clare sat opposite me spearing pieces of langoustine with her knife, looking lovely and not saying much either. Every now and then she'd break the silence with some word about how poor old Peter had been hard-done-by having a stiff found in his house. She made no mention of how the stiff might feel . . . or rather how the person who was now the stiff might have felt. Clare hadn't seen the stiff, of course, and so she didn't know. I had seen the stiff and didn't want to discuss it. I wasn't really listening. I reckoned it was none of my business. I wanted to talk about us, as promised. I wanted to talk over old times and flirt some more. I didn't want to hear a damn thing about old Peter. That's the story I told myself, anyway. Looking back from now, I can be objective. I can say that I must have known before we came that Peter was going to be on the menu just as much as soup of the day was going to be. I'd never have let myself be talked into coming if I hadn't wanted to talk about him.

I tuned in when she suddenly looked up and said, 'Can't you?'

'Can't you what?'

'Can't you *help*, Jimmy?'

I shook my head.

'I don't see how. I'm a private detective. He needs Harry Houdini.' I paused to let her carry on, but she just twirled a piece of dead crustacean around on the end of her fork and smiled at me. I went on, 'If he was framed he should go to the coppers and say so. If he *really* felt he was being framed and he *really* believed nobody could help him he should have run out as soon as he knew.'

I nearly said, 'He should have kept running that night.' I nearly said, 'If the coppers can't help him I don't know why he should think I could.' Instead I said, 'Why should anyone frame him anyway? What the hell is there to frame about a wholesale garden supplies merchant?' I asked the question and really didn't want to hear the answer. Sometimes the mouth beats the brain to the draw.

'Somebody killed that girl and framed Peter,' Clare insisted.

At this point I should have paid the bill and called a taxi. I should have asked Clare to go on somewhere with me and do something that didn't involve talking. 'My place' would be an example of the somewhere. The non-verbal activity doesn't need illustrating with examples. I didn't do that, though. If I'd had any sense I should have choked on my supper and got myself a nice long stretch in hospital with a strained throat that couldn't do any talking or helping. At the very least I should have thrown a fainting fit and refused to recover for an hour or two. I should have done anything except ask another question about Peter Moody.

'But *why* would someone frame Peter? What's he got for God's sake?' Mouth beat brain again.

'I don't know why!' She was raising her voice. If there'd been anyone other than the film-types in the restaurant they'd have noticed.

'The dead girl in his house, was she his girl?'

'He's not saying.'

'He's not saying,' I repeated after her. I found the idea of him being coy at this point hard to take. 'Well, did he manage to say why she was killed?' My voice came out more sarcastic-sounding than I meant it to.

'No. Not to me.'

'Well, dammit, Clare, who *else* is he talking to?'

'No one. I don't know,' she said loudly again.

I waved my hand to quieten her.

'And why are you helping him? What's in it for you?'

'Someone has to help. He asked me to.'

'What makes you think someone was trying to frame Peter?'

'He said so. And he knows who and he's got something on them.'

'Got something on them? He's not on the juice again, is he? He's not back on the wibbly-wobbly way? I mean, people do some funny things when they've a skinful. Peter does.' I didn't dare mention smoked mackerel in the presence of so much dead shellfish. She said nothing. I pushed my food around my plate for a while, then said, 'What's he been doing that makes him worth framing, Clare?'

'Guns.' She put her knife and fork down and looked me straight in the eye. When she looks like that it's usually impossible to believe she could lie. Clare knows it, too, and she does it on purpose. 'Selling guns,' she said.

She might as well have said 'selling tickets for the space-shuttle' or 'selling autographed copies of *War and Peace*'.

'Not bulbs? Not flowers?'

'No.'

64

'Not green twine to hold up clematis plants?'

'No.'

'Never?'

'No. He's been selling guns since you sent him to Canada. His brother-in-law was dealing in surplus military equipment from Vietnam. Peter's very well known in his own world. He's known all over the continent.'

'For selling guns?'

'For selling guns.' Clare poured us both some more wine. So that was it. Guns. I felt bitter. The wine felt as if it had stuck in my throat, like a lump of unchewed bread. I kept feeling, 'I must have been some mug all that while'; after all, it was me who lent him money to go to Canada and it was me that was so pleased to see him get going in the gardening business.

'So why can't his gun-selling pals get him out of the country?... No, no.' I held my hand up. 'Don't tell me. They killed the girl, right? *They're* stitching him up, right?'

'So he said to me.' She seemed to mean it.

I let my fork drop with a clatter.

'If that's true the police really are the only ones who can help him. He's not Lord Lucan.'

'Phone, sir.' A waiter was standing next to me. I don't know how long he'd been there. No one knew I was going to the restaurant except Clare. I guessed that meant Peter must know, too; and it would be Peter on the phone. I went out to the stairway. The phone was a wall-box. Not only was I going to give it to him straight about the law of the land and the coppers being entitled to see him if they reasonably wanted to, I was going to give him a piece of my mind about lying to me, too. I picked up the handset from where the waiter had left it on top of the coin-box. I just got a dialling tone. I went upstairs to check Peter wasn't playing games, but I met a locked door. Coming down again there was nothing to see but a battered plush-red carpet. I went out to the street and walked twenty yards in either direction. No Peter. Back in the restaurant I couldn't find our waiter. He'd gone. So had Clare. A new waiter was clearing our table. He was a nervous, spotty kid, and he looked like he was flinching as I walked past; waiting for a blow. I didn't even bother to question him. I went to the kitchen but couldn't see the waiter who'd given me the message. I couldn't see Clare, either. The cooks said nothing. I pushed open the back door and turned back to look at them. The kitchen people still said nothing. I went out and climbed down some steel emergency stairs into an alleyway. It was a dark and dirty alleyway. It smelled high. Restaurant rubbish. The alleyway turned a corner and I could see light at the corner reflected back off of Dean Street. I went towards the corner and the light.

'Jimmy,' a voice said. I turned. The voice had come from behind me but I wasn't sure where. I could only see the metallic reflections of the steps and handrails of the stairway from Cyril's kitchen. Beyond the foot of the stairway was inky darkness. A little light fell from the frosted windows of the kitchen.

'Go to the police,' I said. 'You're a bloody mug. I don't know what you're into this time and I don't want to know but just *go to the police*.'

'I can't. They can't protect me. I'm dead mutton, Jim, if I don't get out of the country.'

A cat moved on the wall. Its silhouette shape passed against the night sky, then I heard it leap and saw it on the steel stairs, sniffing around.

'I thought your friends were framing you,' I said. 'I thought that was your story? What's to be scared of if they're framing you? No one would take the trouble to do that *and* try to kill you too. If it's a frame go to the police and tell them. I don't see what the problem is.'

There was a long silence. Then Peter said, 'No. The girl was a warning. They were warning me. I'm next. If they get hold of me.'

'I was there that night. You know what I'm getting at? I was *there*. What warning? I saw that situation.'

66

He didn't answer. I felt the anger rise in me.

'You've got a cheek, cock, asking me for help. Why did you tell me you were in the bulb business, for God's sake? Why not tell me the truth?'

I heard the voice in the darkness sigh.

'It's too long, Jimmy. It's a long story.'

The cat came down the stairs and disappeared into the darkness at my feet. I said, 'I'm waiting. I've got time.'

I stepped towards the voice. I still couldn't see him. I was very unsure of my footing in the alley, but I wanted to get close to him.

'Please.' He seemed to have withdrawn a little further into the darkness.

I stood still and said nothing for a while. Then I said, 'Go to my flat in two hours. My car's in the yard in front. It's an old green Hillman Hunter automatic. My passport will be in the glove box. I'll leave the insurance and ownership document there too. The boot'll be open and the key will be under the spare tyre. If you get stopped you nicked them both, right? You knew where I kept my spare flat key and you nicked them both. Make sure you're not being followed, too.'

'Okay. I'll go there. I'm not being followed.'

'Just make sure. Meet me in Boulogne mid-day two days from now. Saturday mid-day. Have you a gun?'

'Yes.'

'Well, dump it. Don't go riding round in my motor with no guns, right? Do you know Boulogne?'

'No.'

'Nor do I. Make it the railway station bar. I hope to heaven there's only one. Better say the railway by the ferry terminal.'

'Okay.'

I turned and walked away without saying any more. Even now I wouldn't be able to say why I agreed to help him. And there were good reasons why I shouldn't have. Very good reasons.

67

Chapter Twelve

I've been to France plenty of times – and I don't like it. I've only been to Boulogne twice in my entire life, but it seems much like the rest of France. The first time I went there was on a school trip. I was about nine or ten, and we spent all our time staring over the lock gates into the inner harbour because either a dead dog or a dead very hairy pig was there. It was bloated and bobbed about in the water. Then a harbour policeman saw us and asked would we mind leaving the location. Loudly and in French. That's what I remember of Boulogne . . . that and some frog lifting half my week's pocket money for one tatty ice-cream. I don't think France is a lot of cop and I don't rate Boulogne even more than I don't rate France, which is saying something.

My second visit to Boulogne was in order to meet Peter Moody. I got up at four on the Saturday morning and took the first train from Charing Cross. I took three hundred smackeroos out of Peter's seven grand that Clare had left with me. I thought it was only fair that he should pay the expenses. By seven-fifteen I was buying a day-trip ticket at Dover ferry terminal and telling criminal lies about the whereabouts of my passport, just so I could get myself issued with an excursion identity card. It worked, no one ever queries it.

I went on the bus down to the immigration hall. Only in England are the police as paranoid about who goes out as they are about who goes in . . . other countries are only too pleased to see the back of you. The immigration hall was a big grey room and every movement echoed sounds about the place. I was holding my breath, then breathing slow and low, consciously calming myself. Before me was a lectern with just one bored clerk propping it up. Steel crush barriers guided us passengers towards the lectern. The clerk was staring idly at some photostatted papers on the lectern, interrupting himself every now and then to wave someone through. He didn't seem interested. I thought maybe it was too early in the day to be interested in mere comings and goings, even if it were your job. The clerk looked very intent on his reading. Suddenly he pulled a passport and looked up. A beautiful, proud-faced African woman stared him straight in the eye.

'Got a return visa?' said the clerk.

'Visa?'

I was next. I had to stand there and look cool. I hadn't even brought my stick. I didn't want to stand out from the crowd. I stood stock still behind the black woman with my leg hurting, trying to look as if I were only bored by the whole business. I shivered, the hall was cold. A couple of grey characters with grey gaberdine macs came into the immigration hall while I was waiting for the immigration man to finish with the woman. The grey man stared at the passengers; first the African woman, then at the rest of us mugs. Special Branch. I don't know why they don't wear uniforms . . . they might as well.

I was worried for a minute. They would be looking for me, of course.

That's my ego playing me up again. They weren't looking for me. Why should they be? My imagination responds badly to dead bodies and conversations in dark alleys. It makes me twitchy. I needn't have worried. No messages went between the detectives and the immigration clerk. The clerk politely pointed out to the African woman that she shouldn't leave the country without sorting out her visa situation. It was easier to do that from inside Britain than outside, he said. The clerk was being helpful. The two Special Branch men just gave everyone their regular 'I'm a tough guy' stare and tried to look busy. I sweated buckets inside my own version of the grey gabby mac, but everyone ignored me. Why shouldn't they? I'm just a mug in a gabby mac going to raid the hypermarket in Boulogne.

I crossed the water with a load of schoolkids – albeit schoolkids out of uniform. Their teachers drank English beer, spoke bad French to each other and yelled to the kids all the time as if they (the kids) were deaf. Maybe they were. Some old ladies were on the boat, too, trailing trolley shopping-bags and comparing past trips with each other. Right behind the old ladies was a family that found owning a Volvo a stressful situation. That was all the ferry carried except for some unhappy, greasy-looking lorry drivers. If you had to be past Lille before you could have your lunch maybe you'd be unhappy too.

Boulogne hadn't changed much in the twenty years since I'd been there. Of course, the station had been redecorated but then some vandals had obligingly turned it into the same mess it had been before redecoration. We foot passengers were made to clump up the same steel ramp as the cars and lorries. We left the Volvo family still on the ship's car deck, opening suitcases on the shiny steel decking. A frontier policeman gave my identity card a cursory glance, then waved me on to France proper. Lucky me.

The ferry terminal's on two tiers. It's like arriving on the ground floor of a multi-storey car park. There were engines revving above me somewhere, and the wind whipped the noise and dirt and diesel fumes past me. There was a mesh fence between me and the railway station bar. The only gate was firmly locked. I followed the fence for what seemed like miles until it led into one of those echoing tunnels they use in airports to guide you to your plane. It's surely a journey into or out of a corrugated steel and plastic womb. The tunnel turned sharply several times. On the last turn a howling

70

wind buffeted me. I turned and entered Boulogne in the breech position.

When I came down the steps and out of the tunnel I turned again and found myself on Boulogne sea front facing the information bureau (which was shut). The railway station was in the distance behind me with an entire harbour in between us. The tunnel I had come from was empty and silent, save for the wind and its sound. Another empty and silent tunnel stood next to it. I couldn't see Peter. I couldn't see my Hillman. I had a plastic bag with duty-free cigarettes in it – I don't smoke – an apple and a half-eaten Toblerone. Boulogne was empty and windswept around me.

I went up the steps of the other steel and plastic tunnel and took the long walk back. This time I ended up on the station and found my way into the waiting room and bar. I went up to the counter and ordered a coffee. I put a fifty franc note on the counter . . . my usual technique. That's how I manage in France, since my pronunciation of French is none too hot. I just give out big notes all the time and collect the change. I'm never sure, otherwise, how much they're asking me for. By the time I get home I have a wheelbarrowful of French small value coins.

The waitress gave me the forty-five-and-a-half francs change and a scowl, then busied herself slamming microscopically thin slices of pink ham into split and halved French loaves and wrapping them in cellophane as if to indicate they were totally hygienic and untouched by human hand.

The clock above her said eleven o'clock. I sat and stared at it. No matter what time I leave England I seem to get to France at eleven o'clock. When I lived in Spain I used to go through Cherbourg a lot. No matter which ferry we got from Portsmouth we seemed to arrive in Cherbourg at eleven.

I stayed in the railway bar from eleven till twelve drinking the coffee I'd bought and several of its close relatives. Then I took my life in my hands and had one of the rolls. Then I had a beer and another and another. At one-thirty two coachloads of English came in, scoffed all the rolls plus a lot of beer and were on their way in the twinkling of an eye. No one else came into the railway bar. No one apart from a porter and a policeman even went past it. I asked the waitress if she'd seen *un grand homme anglais, comme moi*. It exhausted my French and her patience. She shrugged and turned away. I went back out to the steel and plastic tunnel and started the long walk back into town. Then I saw a little boy before me in the tunnel, about fifty yards away.

He was about eight or nine, dressed in the windcheater, jeans and sneakers uniform of kids of that age throughout Europe and America. He was leaning against the wall of the tunnel and being pretty cool, as eight-year-olds are wont to be.

He called up to me, 'Shenner! Shenner! You are Shenner?'

I looked around to check there was no one else in the tunnel. There wasn't. I was the Shenner he wanted, okay.

'Shut up!' I yelled. 'Do you have to shout it from the rooftops?'

The kid shrugged and held out a buff envelope. I grabbed it off him. He ran away while I was opening it. Inside was a note in Peter's handwriting. It said . . . *You are being followed. Meet me in the café Deux Magots, blvd St. Germain, tonight, nine-thirty. Make sure you lose them and burn this letter.*

By the time I'd read the note a couple of times even the kid's footsteps were gone. I was all alone in the tunnel. I could have been all alone in the world. If anyone was following me they must've been disguised as a handrail. Nine-thirty p.m. Almost another eight hours in Boulogne. Could I stand it? I'd have to. I went to a bar in the town and bought an English newspaper and a box of matches. I burned the note, just like Peter asked. Then I asked the guy behind the bar where Deux Magots, boulevard Saint Germain, was. He didn't understand. I asked all round the bar and no one understood. An old woman took me to the door and pointed up

the hill. She gave me a shove and set me on my way. I came
to some old city walls and climbed them and asked several
people there. No one understood. Eventually a man led me
by the arm into a butcher's shop. The woman there, the
butcher's wife, was from Manchester.

'A friend of mine left word for me to meet him at Deux
Magots, boulevard Saint Germain,' I said to her. 'But I can't
find it.'

'Spell it, love, will you?'

I spelt it. The woman frowned and said was it supposed to
be in Boulogne?

'Why?' I asked.

She gave me a friendly Mancunian smile and said she'd
asked because the only boulevard Saint Germain with a café
called Deux Magots she'd heard of was famous and in Paris.
Did my friend expect me to meet him in Paris?

I didn't take it very well. I had to have a walk round the
block and calm down. So Peter wanted me to go to Paris.
When I came back I asked the woman was she sure the
boulevard Saint Germain in Paris was the only one?

'It's not the only one. But that bar on that street... *that's*
in Paris. It's famous, duck,' she said. Duck indeed. I
couldn't leave Peter to wander around France getting up to
all kinds of mischief with my passport in his pocket. I would
have to go to Paris if I was ever going to set eyes on my
passport and my Hillman again. And that would mean
spending the night in France. I asked the Manchester woman
where in Boulogne a man could buy a walking stick. She
gave me a very funny look but told me. Then I went and
bought the stick and headed back for the station. Even then
there was no train leaving from that station and I had to take
a cab out to the hover terminal.

The train I took from Boulogne didn't leave till after four. It
seemed to stop at every cattle-halt in northern France. We
arrived in Paris North at seven p.m. I went round and round
on the metro system, changing train lines and directions so

many times I got thoroughly confused myself. I can't believe anyone was following me. Then I took a cab over to Saint Germain, the area where Peter's chosen café was. The cab driver got shirty because I wanted to sit in the front with him. I only got the tone, not the words. I think it was just as well. When the cabbie dropped me off I still had an hour to spare. I decided to wander around a while. I watched two bad guitar players wailing a Bob Dylan song into the wind and plucking their strings with frozen fingers. In boulevard Montparnasse someone tried to sell me religion, in Vaugirard someone else thought I was their cousin. Oh yes, I got to learn all the Paris street names. Eventually I ended up at a table in the corner of the Two Maggots by the window where the terrace was closed off for the winter. I was drinking what felt like my hundredth cup of coffee of the day and trying to look as if I wasn't furious. Peter didn't show at nine-thirty. What a surprise!

At a quarter to ten Clare Fisher came into the café and sat down before acknowledging she knew me.

'Hi. Thanks,' she said. She dropped the car keys on to the table-top, then fished a car-park ticket out of her bag.

'Where's Peter?' I said. 'Where's my passport?'

'In the dash, where you left it. Do you know where this car park is?' She waggled the car-park ticket. 'The address is on there.'

'I'll find it. I'll get a cab if I have to. I just want my car and my passport, pronto pronto.' I paused to let her speak. She didn't offer, though. Eventually I said, 'Where's Peter? Why are you here?'

'He couldn't come. He's driven mad by the idea that he's being followed.'

'I thought it was *me* he thought was being followed. He sent me a note to that effect in Boulogne.'

She smiled sourly for an answer.

I looked into her face for a long time. I wanted to see what was there. All I could see was a good-looking woman in her mid-to-late-thirties. After all these years I didn't even know exactly how old she was. All I could see, all I could know about this beautiful woman of indeterminate age and shady background was that she was beautiful, of indeterminate age and shady. I couldn't even plumb the depth of her relationship with Peter. I wanted to know more and I didn't want to play games. I rubbed my eyes with my hands. I was tired.

I said, 'He *didn't* do it, did he, Clare? He didn't kill that girl?' I asked the question even though I knew the answer. I wanted someone else to say it.

'No. Of course not. He wasn't even there.'

I looked carefully into her face again. The mask was still there and she wasn't saying any more.

A waiter approached. He was a tall, dark-haired and handsome man in his mid-forties, very formally dressed even for a French waiter, with a long apron and big walrus moustaches. Clare spoke to him fluently in his own language and he brought me a beer and her some fizzy water plus a plate with one slice of oily lettuce, one slice of thin-cut French red onion and a hard-boiled egg.

'Do you want something to eat, James?'

I looked at the thin-cut onion.

'No. I don't like eggs. I want to speak to Peter.'

'You can't, I'm afraid. He's off crossing frontiers again. He's trying to put as much space as he can between himself and the people who killed that girl. . . .' Clare had been staring through the glass to the street. She looked at me suddenly. 'I shouldn't have told you that. You won't tell, will you? Of course not. You're his friend. But are you *mine*, James?'

'What do you have to do with all this, Clare?'

'I'm involved with him.'

'How?'

'Oh.' She stared at a beautiful young couple who were passing us. We were sitting close to the glass, the first table in. We could see couples as they passed in the street. Clare sighed. It was one of those involuntary-sounding sighs

75

women use when they want to be enigmatic. 'Involved.'

'Don't lie. I'm sick of all this nonsense.' I grabbed my keys and the car-park ticket off the table and pushed my chair back. 'You two have been using me for a dummy. The idea that you're his bird and all this is a set-up in which you're a pair of victims is a bad joke.'

I didn't know why she would be there if Peter wasn't in Paris. I guessed he was there. I bombed out of the Two Maggots and hung around the corner. She came out after a few seconds, tall and handsome in an autumn suit, a loosely belted coat and a wide-brimmed hat pulled down over her face. She marched a few yards down towards the junction with Saint Michel. I followed as closely as I could. She was walking quickly. Rain began to fall on us. Crowds pushed past us. She's taller than a lot of French women. I could see the wide-brimmed hat still. I just about kept up, fifteen or so paces behind.

Then a late model Citroën swung into the kerb by Clare. It had French plates and was well-used, dusty and muddy despite the rain. I stood behind a couple of Algerian boys who were arguing about something, I couldn't understand what, and peered between them so I could watch Clare get into the car. I noted the Citroën's number and took a good look at the driver. I couldn't see him well in the dark, but he was a big, dark-haired man and he could easily have passed for me.

I turned and set off to find the car park with my car in it. When I found the car I searched it carefully before I drove off. I crawled under it with a handlamp, peering into the wheel arches. I stripped out the boot to make sure there were no dead girls, guns or contraband in it. I just didn't want any more surprises.

Chapter Thirteen

It only took me an hour to find my car and another hour and a half to get out of Paris. I didn't have any maps so I just went out on to the circular road and drove round it looking for an open garage. The first I found didn't have any maps for sale, the second affected not to understand me, the third was frightened I was a robber but when I convinced him I was just a lost Englishman he was very kind and explained to me (in English a whole lot better than my French) that I was on completely the wrong side of Paris but the best thing for me to do would be to keep driving round the circular road until I saw a sign for Saint Denis. That was on the way to Boulogne. Then all I had to do was orientate myself by his map and hey presto! *Alors Angleterre.* I got a phrase book too. I gave the pump attendant a warm smile, ten francs for the map and a hundred and fifty francs for the petrol. Then I gave him five francs for himself. He was a nice man.

I drove about an hour's worth out of Paris once I'd found the sign for Saint Denis, then I stopped on the roadside and tore my excursion ID card into tiny pieces. I drove on, dropping the pieces out of the car window one at a time. I drove through sleeping French villages dropping pieces of ID card. I crossed level crossings dropping ID card. I got rid of the last part two hours before dawn. I was in such a good hu-

mour I even went into a French lorry drivers' café and had
rolls and coffee. My Hillman Hunter looked a bit funny
stuck between all those French trucks, just like me and my
walking stick looked a bit funny squeezing in between all the
drivers dressed in their working blue. But I didn't care. I ate
my rolls, nodded and smiled. They drew on yellow-paper
cigarettes jammed into the corners of their mouths and
looked at me as if I was crazy. I drank my coffee and drove
off. Good old France . . . bye bye.

I made the Channel at dawn. I drove into the centre of the
same old Boulogne I'd left the day before. You come over a
hill and the town's below you and the sea stretches in front.
It looks picturesque-fishing-port. The town doesn't look
dirty and hard-working till you get right down by the dock-
side. I stopped on top of the hill. The day was beautiful and
cold blue. I opened the car window and told myself I could
smell the salt. The sea was oily, battleship-grey with long,
low black waves that showed up as lines, as ripples in a flat
calm from the top of the hill. The sun was behind me and the
journey home in front. I felt good. I stretched and yawned in
my driver's seat and turned the car radio to Radio 4 to listen
to the farming broadcasts. The farmers were already out and
about. I got religion.

I waited until the Boulogne hypermarket opened, then I
went and bought a hundred quid's worth of the garbage they
sell in hypermarkets: fifteen packets of 'generic' French coffee, six bottles of Rosé d'Anjou, some Scotch smoked
salmon and ten boxes full of stubby brown bottles of Belgian
beer. I even bought some frozen smoked Dutch eel. There's
exotic. I hung a couple of strings of garlic over the lot, paid
in English pounds at the check-out and threw the filled car-
rier bags in the boot of my car, not caring. Then I went back
across the Channel on the first boat I could, a Sealink ship. I
was in my own car with my own passport. As far as anyone
was concerned I'd simply gone over to France for pleasure. I
passed the time on the ship playing deck quoits with some

Polo mints I'd found along with my passport in the car. They won.

Dover was like Dover is. Who'd go to Dover if the English Channel wasn't next to it? Not me. Dover's the English Boulogne. I saw the white cliffs, I saw the sun shining on them. So what? I tried to think poetic. All I could think was the Customs and Immigration to get through, the long drive on the motorway before I was home. I stared at the white cliffs for long enough to satisfy sentimentality, then when the announcement came I went down into the fume-filled guts of the vessel and started up my car. The steel screamed, the big chains rattled and the doors dropped. I drove back into England. I saw the queue for the Customs and Immigration posts. I didn't mind waiting. I was in no rush.

Then I saw the two tall men in raincoats walking down the queue. You can always tell. These two were ringers. One was in his mid-to-late-twenties, looked like he might have trained for the church. Pale faced, slim ... almost skinny. He wore a thin, dark tie and an unhappy, cruel face. The other policeman was about fifty, tall, too fat and more than a little pockmarked on the face. The older one had bits of roll-your-own cigarette paper stuck all over his jaw where he'd cut himself shaving. He must have shaved with a cheese-grater. Above the pockmarked face the older man had lizard eyelids that drooped lazily over his cold blue eyes. He was a real beauty. He had white marks on the corners of his mouth where his spittle dried. I know all this because I had plenty of time over the next twenty-four hours to observe him licking his lips. For now he leaned his head right into my car, pulled the keys out of the dash and said, 'Jenner?' His face was next to mine when he spoke and he looked closely into my eyes. His breath smelled like his face looked. He turned to face me and said with his lips almost touching mine, *'Mister* Jenner?'

'What?'

He leaned out again, threw my keys in the air and caught them, then said, 'I wonder if we might have a word.'

Since he was standing next to my car holding the keys and I had yet to pass through the customs post it didn't sound much like a request. I shrugged and said, 'Yeah. Why not? Let's talk.' As cool as I could. 'First of all give me back my keys. Then get polite and tell me who you are. Then show me your warrant card. *Then* we'll talk.'

'I'll keep the keys. I'm Detective Sergeant Timpkins. This young man is Detective Constable Mason. Show him your card, Mason.'

Mason showed me his card. He showed it so quickly it could have been a library ticket or a grocery bill for all I knew . . . but he'd shown me his card. Timpkins threw my car keys in the air again, caught them again and nodded to Mason to open my car door.

'Let's talk, Mister Jenner.'

How can you turn down a request like that? I didn't.

Chapter Fourteen

Unless you've seen the result for yourself, it's difficult to believe how many pieces a couple of really determined men can break a Hillman Hunter automatic into.

There are a few parts which don't break down at all, of course. And a few parts which hardly break down. There aren't many of either of these, by the very nature of car construction. The bonnet, the bootlid, the bodyshell, the windscreen are examples of parts which are either one piece or made of few pieces.

When the police took me back to see *my* Hillman Hunter – two days after I arrived in Dover – someone had had a good go at breaking it down into its constituent parts. I knew how the Hillman Hunter must've felt. Someone had been giving me just about the same treatment.

My car was in a disused commercial garage. I was taken there to see it. I was wearing the same clothes I'd been arrested in, except I still didn't have my shoelaces, my belt or my brand-new, Boulogne-bought walking stick.

Everything in the garage was covered in dust. The Police Inspector with me pushed open a dusty door by turning a dusty door handle and there my car was, waiting for me. Sitting in the dust.

My Hillman occupied enough space on the garage floor to park three or four buses . . . if it hadn't already been full of broken-down parts of my car.

The carburettor was in pieces. The aircleaner was beside it, also in pieces. Even the paper cartridge had been cut up. The sump was against a wall, brutally separated from the block. It dribbled black oil on to the dusty concrete floor. There were some metal pieces near the sump, also coated in black oil. I had no idea at all what these did. I wondered how it would all go together again. A headlamp clanged tinnily against someone's foot as we entered. Something crunched under my own foot. I didn't dare look. My tyres were off their rims. The carpets were hanging on the garage wall, like some favourite Moghul pieces. The underlay was out. The headlining was out. The trim was off the doors and, of course, the doors were off the body. The seats had been unbolted and lifted out of the car and the lining and stuffing was off the seat frames.

My car was a very depressing sight.

When I was taken to pick up my car there were two young men in overalls dismembering it still. One was taking the jack apart in a corner of his own. I didn't even know jacks came apart. The other had a chisel-bit on a hand-held pneumatic drill, and he was committing grievous damage to the underparts of my beloved Hillman. My spot welds were coming undone. The young man with the jack in his hand dropped it so it clanged on the floor, then came over and wiped the hand on a rag before offering me a handshake and a smile.

'Nearly done. Should be finished tonight,' he told me in a friendly way, making me feel as if I'd put the car in for a clutch change. 'Haven't got it yet, though.'

'This is Mister Jenner,' said the uniformed Police Inspector I was with.

The young man in overalls dropped his hand before I could shake it and said, 'We're just in the course of putting it all to rights before we hand back, sir.' He frowned at the uniformed Police Inspector and turned away.

I pushed a piece of torn, bright-cut-metal exhaust section with the toe of my shoe.

'Why have you done this?' I said.

'These are Customs and Excise Officers,' said the Police Inspector. 'They're entitled to search your property if you enter or leave this country. They don't have to give you a reason.'

I could only admire the thoroughness of their search. I said so. Perhaps my tone was a little sarcastic. The Customs Officers and the Police Inspector weren't amused. I didn't care. I wasn't very happy either. I certainly didn't feel like amusing these vandals.

'Get it ready for tonight,' I said, as tough as I could, and turned on my heel. I only cared for the principle, not the car. The car was worth less than a good meal in Langan's Brasserie. A lot less.

The two who'd picked me up, Timpkins and Mason, weren't regular port-of-entry Special Branch coppers. The ones who do that every day would have waited till I was at the Immigration post before they'd have asked me to 'step this way'. The ones who worked at Dover regularly would have known where everything was, too. Timpkins and Mason knew where nothing was. It's hard to maintain your pose as the calm, confident detective if you don't know where the lavatory is, or can't find where you've parked your car.

They blundered around trying to look heavy for an hour or so, then eventually they took me down to an interrogation room somewhere off the Dover port site. I'm not sure where it was, they took me in a blacked-out Ford van. We only went a few miles.

I was locked in the back of the blacked-out van with Timpkins and his bad breath until we stopped. Then I had a brief look at a concrete yard surrounded by a red-brick wall. The wall seemed to be relieved only by some tall, matt-grey gates. Timpkins led me through a smaller matt-grey door opposite the gates and I didn't see the outside until the next day.

First of all Timpkins and Mason did that police thing of

taking away every object you could conceivably damage yourself with. In my case it left me shoeless, shirtless, tieless and one-footed. Why they should think your shirt is more dangerous than your trousers, or your socks more dangerous than your undervest, is beyond me. Perhaps it's for some deepseated psychological reason. Policemen – like nuns – seem to believe that below the waist is more dangerous than above it. Perhaps it's thought a man with no trousers would be intrinsically more dangerous than a man with no shirt. Other decisions are more enigmatic—I don't know why shoes are more dangerous than socks in the self-inflicted-damage stakes, for example . . . you can choke on a sock, but what harm can a shoe do you?

I *do* know there are definite if informal rules governing the order in which a prisoner might be stripped of his possessions and clothing. My state of clothing was a result of the operation of those rules. They're just police station rules. The rules applied. Some of them, anyway.

Timpkins and Mason took me to a small room with a window near the ceiling and kept me there. The room was cold and they only gave me one blanket. There was a radiator but it didn't work. If it hadn't been for the bars on the window, my missing foot and the fact they'd handcuffed me to a chair, I might have tried to escape. As it was I had no choice but to listen politely to a load of questions which started off with pockface Timpkins asking *why there had been these two documents* (and Mason held up my passport and my excursion identity card application form every time Timpkins said 'these two documents' as if he were an iceskating judge giving me marks for presentation and performance) *in existence at one and the same time*.

It was *illegal*. Timpkins seemed personally hurt by the notion of the illegality. Where had I been on the documents? Why did I need two? He was so hurt he screwed his ugly face up to prove it. I wanted to pat him on the shoulder and tell him everything was okay.

'France. I went to France on the passport. I don't know anything about the other.'

Timpkins screwed his face up and looked even more hurt. Why had I been to France?

'Pleasure.'

Did I have much pleasure?

'As much as a man could reasonably expect to get in France. It rained, you know?'

'Tell me, Jenner, why are you in France one day driving your car around, yet you're applying for an ID card in Dover the next day without apparently stirring from France? You're a busy man.'

I didn't answer. Timpkins said quietly, 'Unless there are two of you.'

I said, 'I have never seen the ID card application before in my life.'

Timpkins waved to Mason he should let my handcuffs loose. Mason undid the cuffs and lifted me out of the chair from behind. He kept hold of my elbows even after I'd stood. He was very strong for such a pasty-faced fellow, I remember thinking.

'Tell me again, Jenner,' Timpkins said.

'I have never seen that application form before in my life.'

Timpkins stood, too. He stood before me.

'Never seen it?'

'No.'

'Not your signature?'

'No. It's a forgery.'

Timpkins looked over my shoulder at Mason, who was still holding my arms.

'He's having us on. Don't you think he's having us on?'

Mason didn't speak. Then Timpkins leaned back and threw a punch into my guts. Only the fact that I was being held up stopped me keeling over. The room was cold but I could feel sweat running down my chest. My eyes filled up. My breath wouldn't come. Timpkins waited until I had my breath back and then hit me again. Same spot. I felt sick. Again my breath wouldn't come. Timpkins leaned his ugly mug next to mine again and said, 'You went to see your pal Moody, eh? But you didn't see him, we know. Why? Was he expecting anything from you? What's your involvement, Jenner?'

'I don't know what you mean,' I said. I meant it too. Expecting anything? Timpkins didn't look happy. I obviously hadn't said the right thing.

'Tell me.' Timpkins shook his head. 'You'd better . . . tell me, Jenner. Answer my questions. You'll like the man who asks you questions next even less.' He said the last few words through his clenched teeth.

If I'd taken anything to Peter Moody I'd have told him. I'm not brave . . . but I really had no idea what Timpkins meant. I said so. He didn't believe me.

'Your friend is a dirty murderer and you've helped him. You're going to have to live with that, Jenner. You'll have to answer for it.' He paused. 'You co-operate with me . . . you answer my questions and I'll see what I can do for you, I promise.'

He should have laughed at that point. He should have known what comes next, anyway. I did. I've watched *Naked City*, too. Neither of us laughed, though.

The last time I saw Timpkins he was framed in the doorway. The light was behind him, making a halo around his head.

He said, 'You and me are of the old school, Jenner, I wanted to help you. All you had to do was take a couple of wallops and tell me what I wanted. Then, bob's your uncle. You could've buzzed-off. . . . No grudges. I could've sorted it out for you.'

He paused for dramatic effect.

'The next lot'll come with syringes and tape recorders,' Timpkins said. 'They'll destroy you. You'll wish you'd played along with me . . . instead of helping a dirty murderer like Moody.'

Mason was behind him, nodding sagely, as if Timpkins were some violent Eastern guru, and Mason his chief disciple.

They both stood in the doorway for some time. I guess they were waiting for me to speak. Maybe they expected me to break down. It happens in films, I know, but these two had got me all wrong. If, when I'd been picked up, they'd been straight... if someone had asked me politely had I helped my friend Peter get out of Britain, I might have said yes. If the right man had asked why I'd helped Peter I might have told him that, too. I'd always expected to have to 'pay up' for helping Peter. Depending on whether I thought the man who asked the question was powerful enough, depending whether I believed I could trust him or not, I just might have talked about why I'd done it. Just might. I'd have needed to see the colour of his money, of course. Then I might have told a polite and reasonable interrogator why I'd helped Peter Moody. But not these two dummies. To these I had nothing to say. All three of us knew I'd helped Peter do a runner. What they didn't know was how little I had known about the whole business before they'd begun to interview me. Now I thought I knew what team they were. Timpkins had told me. He'd said Peter was a 'dirty murderer'. I didn't like what I heard. Timpkins was either stupid or he thought I was. Peter was all kinds of things but I knew he wasn't a murderer. I knew it, I had evidence for it. They should have too. Telling me Peter had murdered the girl in his house had tipped their hand to me. They'd got me all wrong. Timpkins had told me all sorts of things in the one sentence. He'd told me they knew about me seeing that dead girl in Peter's house. How did he know? He'd told me they thought I was willing to be an accessory after a murder, all to help my friend 'the murderer.'

Either Timpkins was for real when he'd told me Peter was a 'dirty murderer' or he'd taken me for such a fool he felt he could throw me any old line. Perhaps he'd thought I'd never know the difference. Perhaps he'd thought I wasn't Special

Branch material with a sharp brain and a grasp of all the details like him and Mason. Timpkins treated me like I was a fool, a fall guy for Peter and for them. But I wasn't.

After their interview Timpkins and Mason could have pounded me into the floor and nailed me there, I wouldn't even have told them what date Christmas fell on this year, I wouldn't even have told them where to get the bus home, leave alone where Peter was and whether I'd taken him anything. As for Peter and his real story, I didn't know it. But these two clowns weren't getting it or the little of it I knew from me . . . they weren't even in the game.

Mason – the quieter of the two – had a couple more shots at me during the next few hours. He seemed disturbed by my refusal to answer their questions . . . as if it were so very unreasonable. I had the feeling we were waiting for something else to happen. The questions were just a ritual.

I didn't get so much as a cheese roll during the first twelve hours I was in the little room. They left me alone for quite a time . . . maybe another twelve hours. Then Mason came in, all father-confessor and bearing a little plastic tray with a bacon sandwich and a cup of instant coffee on it. He sat on the little bed and undid the handcuff from my wrist. He left it off. His pasty face looked as if he would just about die of shame for treating me so.

'We've got to know, James.'

I didn't pull him up about calling me 'James'. What was the point? Instead I launched into the bacon sandwich. It was cold. I was cold too, and hungry. I ate. Mason kept talking. He could have been saying anything he wanted. I wasn't listening. . . . I just ate. Then he said, 'It's a matter of importance for the entire state . . . that's a thought, isn't it, James? There's you, police hero, medals, pensions, the works. And you're going to allow yourself to be compromised on a matter of importance for the whole state.'

I smiled at him. What was all this 'whole state' rubbish? 'That's me. Stupid, I suppose,' I said.

He smiled politely, as fitted with his act, then left with the empty plate. A couple of hours later he was back again, only this time it was coffee. The text was the same. My answers were still non-committal, too. The third time he came was much later, at dawn the next day. I'd been with them for twenty hours or so. Mason brought with him a young, clean-looking boy who had very short hair and tattoos on his forearms. He absolutely *had* to be a soldier in civvys, I thought. He was all wrong for a copper. The soldier tut-tutted around me, collected my possessions off Mason, gave me my leg back and then took me out alone to the un-marked, closed Ford van. We drove back to Dover. He locked me – again alone – in the back of the van. All the way to the nick he sat quiet, refusing to answer questions I yelled through the partition. Eventually I staggered back into blinding daylight in another red-brick-surrounded concrete yard, only this time I could smell the sea and see the tops of the ships. This time everyone called me Mister Jenner and treated me like I was made of bone china. And this time I was greeted by a uniformed Police Inspector who smiled and said, 'We've got someone who wants to see you,' as if I were a lonely little boy in a boarding school and an indul-gent relative was coming to take me out for a cream tea.

Chapter Fifteen

When I was taken to the Newport Police Station in Dover it seemed pretty clear the policemen were more than a little embarrassed by my presence. The 'someone who wants to see you' I'd been promised had yet to arrive when the soldier character dropped me off. The Inspector was polite but firm, I could leave but not until this someone came. Was I under arrest? I asked. No, but there are still a few matters to be cleared up, came the answer. It's no good arguing. If they want, they can make the bureaucracy of releasing you take all day – all the while protesting you're just being released, freedom is imminent, of course. I waited. While I waited they had to let me clutter up their most comfortable interview room. I was asked would I like to order a meal of some sort? It's a very strange thing to see a Police Inspector behaving like a maître d'hôtel.

'No. I don't care how comfortable it's supposed to be here. I don't want to choose from your menu. I want my car. Then I want to leave.'

'You can leave, sir. Just as soon as this person comes to pick you up.'

'Good. But first of all I want my car.' I slapped my false leg. 'I'm going nowhere without my car.'

I was being *difficult*, of course, I knew. I wasn't very happy.

'That makes sense, sir.' The Inspector smiled. He wasn't

very happy either, but he kept smiling like a synchronised swimmer.

'I want it now.'

'It may take some time to arrange, sir.'

The policeman was about fifty, grey-haired, grey-eyed and calm. He was using thirty years' worth of experience as a bobby to keep himself diplomatic and gentlesounding. I wasn't going to be moved, though.

'I want my car. I'm not leaving this place without my car. I want my car and I want out. In that order. I want both quickly. Also I want to see someone to complain about being hit. I was hit in the stomach three times by that big booby DS Timpkins. It's not on, you know. It's quite clearly against Judges' Rules. It says there in the rules, "suspects must not be bashed up and must not be kept overnight in cold cells". I was arrested without being told I was being arrested, I was arrested without being told why, I was held without being charged, I was hauled off to some . . .'

The uniformed Police Inspector stood quickly, dragging his chair as he did. The noise effectively drowned my complaint. It was meant to.

'I'll see what I can do about the car, sir.'

'I'm not going without my car, and I'm not going until someone senior hears my complaints. I'm not just any yobbo, you know.'

'I know who you are, Mr Jenner. And I'm sure if someone has been behaving out of turn towards you the matter will be pursued. We both know that.' He shook his head slowly, picked up his papers and left me in the comfortable, modern interview room reading the *Police Gazette*. It's too boring for words. I picked up the police canteen menu. Their menus haven't changed in all the years since I've left the job. I ordered a mug of tea, what I knew would be a damp, grisly-looking ham-and-lettuce-salad and a microwaved jacket potato. A young constable stationed just outside the interview room door took my order. I told the uniformed constable that I wanted my car back too, and I wanted to speak to someone senior. Also I wanted access to a telephone and I wanted to know exactly who was the person I was being kept waiting for?

'Mr Thomas *is* senior, sir. He's an Inspector.'

That's how the catering staff get away with such rotten food. Most policemen are natural conformists. If that's the food available then that's the food we're having, if the Inspector says he's a big wheel then the Inspector's a big wheel. I looked into the young constable's face and remembered myself at that age. It's the way their minds work; all imagined dangers and small victories. I looked into the young constable's baby-blue eyes and decided he was past saving. I said nothing. Mr Thomas was an Inspector, the young constable was one of nature's spearcarriers. Timpkins and Mason were a world apart. I'm a private detective. Peter Moody is . . . well, Peter Moody is whatever he says he is, and something else as well. According to Timpkins and Mason Peter Moody was a dirty murderer. According to me he was nothing of the sort. You pay your money and take your choice.

Inspector Thomas didn't like having me in his police station and I didn't blame him. I was a procedural nightmare. The late arrival of my mysterious visitor and my insistence on being given back my car before I would even consider leaving Newport nick had made me even more annoying and embarrassing for Inspector Thomas. I think it was that annoyance, plus the need to fill in a little time, which had made him take me to the garage premises where the Customs men were reducing my Hillman to very small pieces. I expect he wanted those responsible to pick up some blame. In fairness to Thomas, he'd been lumbered with me. Neither he nor his immediate subordinates had arrested me, yet, since he'd been forced to have me in his police station, he was kind, polite and apologetic towards me. When I discovered how my car had been vandalised he was even more apologetic. As far as I knew he was blameless, but that was no reason to take the pressure off him, of course. I kept up a barrage of demands and accusations all the way from the nick to the Customs garage. On the way back, after seeing my car, I intensified the pressure. Thomas began to look sad-faced and humourless. When we arrived at the nick there was an old black Rover in the yard, a three-and-a-half-litre coupé, the sort government ministers used to swan around in during the 1960s.

A grey-haired woman climbed out of the car. The woman grunted. She was short and quite fat, so her climbing – even out of a car – was clumsy.

'Jenner. Hey, you must be Jimmy Jenner!' She's the only adult I've ever seen get shorter as they leave a car. She called across the bonnet, 'I've got your stuff.'

'Who are you?'

She waddled quickly across the car park, looking like a small and ancient terrier who's spotted some quarry.

'Your lawyer.'

'I've got things to...' I began. She waved down my complaint and began pumping Inspector Thomas's arm and assuring him that we believed this incident had only been a case of mistaken identity, and, presuming no more would be heard about the business of the passport mix-up... blah blah blah lawyer-talk.

Then she stood quite close to me.

I could hear the wheeze in her chest, see her powdered skin, smell the lacquer in her mane of grey hair. Her glaucous grey eyes stared into the Inspector's face. I felt as if she owned me.

'Your wife rang and asked me to come and fetch you,' she said. 'I'm pleased we've been able to sort this little lot out.'

She smiled hugely. My victory would be her victory, only she would get the fee. I didn't even seriously *want* to be set free. I wanted the situation to mature.

'My wife?'

'That's right.'

I decided to let her run the business of the car; after all,

Thomas was hardly going to write a cheque there and then for the seventy-five quid my Hillman Hunter was worth. He said I'd have to take the car up with the Customs people. He said he was hardly in a position to order a top-level enquiry into my treatment overnight, either. He would make a report.

When I pressed my complaint a little further Thomas claimed to know nothing of the second premises used by Special Branch in Dover and said that he'd been under the impression I'd been kept in a port detention cell all night. I looked into his clear grey eyes and got nothing, no faint glimmer of embarrassment, no shiftiness. Maybe he was telling the truth, maybe he wasn't. Maybe he did think I'd been in a detention cell all night. Maybe Timpkins and Mason hadn't told him. It didn't seem very likely, but how was I to know? I gave up puzzling. It was a waste of time.

Half an hour later I was out in the car with Emma Johnson, my self-appointed solicitor. My freedom *and* my passport had been restored. Even though I had enjoyed the embarrassment at Newport nick and even though I would have liked to have found out more about the machinations going on around me there, I swore to myself I would never part company with either again. Emma was about as forthcoming as everyone else.

'How did you find me, Mrs Johnson?'

'Phone call.'

We were breezing along the A20 at about eighty. She leaned over to my side of the car, dipping her head below the walnut fascia, and groaned loudly.

'I can't reach. Open the glove box.'

I opened it.

She waggled her hand impatiently.

'Go on, go on . . . cigars.'

I lifted out a cigar box. It was full of dainty-sized cubans.

'Want one?'

A lorry driver waved his fist at us as we swung wildly round a roundabout. I said no. I said I didn't smoke. I said it quietly but distinctly, so as not to break her concentration on driving.

'Cutter,' she ordered.

I reached into the glove box and fished out her cigar cutter. It was a thick gold job, the kind you might find in the waistcoat of a member of a Jermyn Street men's club. Only when Emma Johnson was all lit up, with a window half-open, clouds of foul-smelling smoke billowing out of the cigar (and her) and with the speedometer needle touching ninety, did she say, 'I had a phone call from your wife. She was missing you.'

'I don't know why she was missing me. We're separated.'

She nodded reflectively, as if this was some new trend of which she disapproved.

'Well, your separated wife rang me and said she'd had a strange call from a young woman. . . .' She screwed up her brow to remember. It was not a pretty sight. 'I don't think she gave me the name.'

'Could it be Clare?'

'Mm. Well, whoever this Carol was she had called your *estranged* wife to say she thought you had been picked up by the police in Dover.'

'Nice of her to tell me beforehand,' I muttered.

'What?'

'Nothing.'

'Anyway, your wife checked up on you and found out you weren't anywhere you were supposed to be. Then she phoned the police in Dover and they said they'd never heard of you. Then she phoned the ferry company in Boulogne and asked did you buy a ticket. They said you had. They remembered you.'

Emma Johnson gunned the motor. She had seen a motorway sign. I wondered what the top speed of a fifteen-year-old Rover was. Quite a lot, I thought. Maybe I should wait until we had stopped before I talked any more.

'So your wife phoned me.' She corrected herself. *'Estranged* wife.'

'Why you?'

'Her caller had suggested me. I'm a very good lawyer, you know. One of the best.'

She was a very good something.

'So after your wife called I phoned Dover police and asked after this one-legged detective who'd gone missing travelling back from France. I said we were certain you'd got to Dover and equally certain you hadn't got any further. They said they'd never heard of you.'

'It was true.'

'Then I phoned someone I know at New Scotland Yard and told them I thought Special Branch had hold of you at Dover somewhere and I wanted you released. I said I was going to slap a habeas corpus writ on the Commissioner of Police for the Metropolis unless you were released or charged within the hour. They rang back fifteen minutes later and said they weren't obliged to tell me anything but unofficially this friend of mine said you were being held as a suspected person under the Prevention of Terrorism Act. Then I made it official... I told them to get lost. You're not Irish. I said if they didn't release you I'd ask a judge in chambers for the writ anyway and then when it wasn't granted I'd make sure the newspapers got the full story of how James Jenner, police hero, was being held under the Prevention of Terrorism Act after entering the country at Dover. I put in a lot of work on you, Jenner.'

Emma puffed the cigar some more. She spotted the sign for Farthing Corner Services and banged the Rover's brakes on, throwing the car across all three lanes of the motorway. Once we were in the sliproad to the services she said, 'Ten minutes later they called back. Deputy Assistant Commissioner this time, as well. He said the Commissioner's people *really* weren't holding you but to give him twelve hours to come up with an answer.'

'What "Commissioner's people"?'

'The DAC didn't say. I think he probably meant that some

other outfit than Special Branch was holding you. Does that make sense?'

She slammed her foot on the brakes again and we stopped dead between two parked cars. It was just as well, there was a third parked car in front of us. I didn't answer Emma Johnson's question. She knew as well as I did that there were no 'outfits' in the Metropolitan Police that weren't the Commissioner's people. If there were, I didn't want to be the one to find out.

'He said "please",' she said, 'the DAC. They must either like you, Jenner, or you've touched a raw nerve somewhere.'

I didn't answer that one either. There was a long silence which Emma was waiting for me to fill. I just stared at my hands. She might look like just a mad old lady, but I thought then she was probably a very smooth-operating lawyer.

She tutted impatiently at my silence and said, 'Eight hours later, just before dawn, someone rang to say I could come to Dover Newport Police Station and pick you up if I wanted. So I did. I thought it better not to send your ex-wife. . . .'

'Separated wife.'

'Yes. Separated wife. Are you going to sue the police?'

'Was there no name? Or was it your mysterious source in NSY who rang?'

She frowned. 'No name. They rang off quickly and I was half-asleep. *Are* you going to sue them?'

'I don't know.'

'Perhaps you'll make friends by not doing it. They'd look pretty sick if you did. Perhaps you should consider suing them and then let them talk you out of it. That would be a good move for a private detective. It would make you a lot of friends.'

'I don't need any friends, Mrs Johnson. I've got all the friends a fellow wants. Too many.'

'*Professional* friends, Jenner.'

'Not even professional.'

She held her hands up and let the half-smoked cigar drop out of the window. 'You needed me.'

I raised my voice. '*You* came to me, remember? Not me to you. *You* sought me out, Mrs Johnson.'

'I believe your ex-wife felt sorry for you. She understood you were badly off. She rang me and asked me to help you. She offered to pay.'

'She's not my ex-wife.'

'But she was right in thinking you were badly off? Wasn't that part true?'

She didn't expect an answer. I didn't give her one.

'Anyway, all that's in the past tense now, Jenner, isn't it? You've had a very successful couple of days. You've turned your finances round, I believe.'

I closed my eyes and counted to ten.

'I've put in a lot of work on you, Mr Jenner. My fee will be five hundred pounds. It's cheap at the price to get you out of there.' She paused and smiled at me coyly. Money seemed to be the only thing that touched her heart. 'I'll put the bill in the post today.' Again the coy smile. 'If you get out now, Jenner, you'll find your wife in the restaurant.'

I got out of the Rover. I slammed the door a little harder than I needed to.

'Were we followed?' I said.

'A light-blue Vauxhall Astra. I thought you might not want to be followed so I lost them a couple of miles out of Dover. That's why we were driving so fast. Go on up to your estranged wife.'

She loved that 'estranged', as if the very sound of the legal-type word appealed to her. Emma Johnson ran her hand through her mane of grey hair, started the motor and was gone.

I looked around the car park for any suspicious types. Driving very fast down the A2/M2 is no technique for losing professional followers. The trouble is, once you start looking for a tail everyone looks suspicious. I've never seen so many suspicious-looking lorry-drivers and travelling salesmen in my life. I went round the car park on foot twice, then I went and checked out the lavatory. Then I came out and checked the car park again. Who knows how many men they'd have available? Once I'd satisfied myself that everyone in the car park was following me I went upstairs to look for Judy.

Part Three

Full Moon and Empty Arms

Chapter Sixteen

I have a wife called Judy Jenner. She was until a few years ago a sergeant in Criminal Intelligence at New Scotland Yard. Judy was destined for the top. Then she married me, threw up everything and came to Spain to run a bar with me. It didn't work out and she blames me. Nowadays we're separated. That's my half of the story, anyway. I suppose she'd want to add that I'd lost all our money in the bar, that I can't even go to it because I'd get arrested, that I managed at one point to get Judy locked up by the Spanish police and that even now we are both *persona non grata* in Málaga. My excursion into the licensed victualling trade was exclusively of the non profit-making variety. We gave up Spain or Spain gave up us ... the net result was that we came home. We came back skint. Judy rejoined the police service and moved into a big flat in Acton with some girlfriends; all policewomen, too, all recently split from some fellow like yours truly. And none enamoured any longer with men as a species or with their particular 'ex' as an example of the species. For my part I rented a flat in Stoke Newington, North London, just a few yards from where I used to own one. And I was lucky enough to rent my old office back in Canning Town, so I was able to go back into the private detection business. This last was a move of which Judy did not approve. She thinks my work as a private investigator is a vain fantasy. Luckily, Acton is in West London, some little way from

Stoke Newington, which means that Judy and I don't have to meet at the Safeways delicatessen counter every Friday night and discuss how well or badly our lives are going. We don't meet and discuss what a heel her bitter-and-twisted divorcee and similar flatmates think I am, too, which is just as well.

Nowadays Judy is back in the bosom of her all-seeing and all-knowing (at least that's the view of the people who work there) electronic machine intelligence in NSY. The boss is meant to be a Commander, a senior rank in the Met, but really he plays second fiddle to their computers. It must be like working in the Vatican ... knowing your boss is never wrong. The only real difference between Judy's present job and her previous (before Spain) arrangement is that she's only holding the rank of constable. When there's a vacancy she'll make sergeant. Judy will need to pass a promotion board again, too, but I think that'll be a walkover for someone like her. All she'll have to do is cross her black-stockinged legs, flash her lovely blue eyes and start talking peek, poke and megabyte. Especially 'megabyte' ... way she says the 'b' in megabyte sends shivers down strong men's backs. Judy'll have the bossmen coppers on their knees. Unless she's unlucky and gets one of the hatchet-faced lesbians who turn up on those boards every now and then my Judy will have her sergeant's job again. Soon.

When Emma Johnson dropped me I went up to the restaurant part of Farthing Corner Services. There was Judy, sitting among the routiers. She was drinking coffee from a mug and had an entire table covered with an outspread copy of The Times newspaper. She was reading it, too. She was wearing her 'no-bullshit' outfit – black slacks, thick roll-neck sweater, the barest touch of make-up, small black wallet-style handbag. She wore no rings nor indeed any jewellery except a watch and her jaw was set and her brow furrowed. I thought maybe I was in for a rough ride.

'Hi,' I said.

She smiled, stood and kissed my cheek.

'Hello, Jimmy. How are you? Coffee? Do you want to stay or go?'

'Go.'

We went downstairs and crammed into her Mini. I'm not Mini-shaped. I don't fit them – either around the elbows or around the knees. If I were only four inches shorter and had retractable elbows a Mini would suit me fine. If I could only take both my feet off and tuck them under the seat a Mini would be perfect. But just one foot won't do.

'Okay, Jimmy?' She plugged my seatbelt in.

'All bruises.'

She smiled again. We were both nervous. It had been a couple of months since we'd met.

'Let's go.'

She fired the engine and we rolled back down to the motorway. We drove for a long time before she said, 'You'd better give me the story.'

'The whole story?'

'Is there any reason I shouldn't know the whole story?'

'No. There's no reason why *you* shouldn't.'

She ignored the emphasis.

'Then tell it.'

I told it. I started off with a description of Moody – my relationships with the two of them had barely overlapped – and a rough and ready description of how we'd been close once. I told her even about Clare and about me finding Peter dead drunk in the street once when I was on my way to see her. I told her about the recent contact, the phone call asking me to go and see him. And I told her about how, when I'd got there, I'd found this stiff. A young naked woman of Middle-Eastern origin.

'That must've been nasty.'

'It was.'

'And you didn't just pick up the phone and call the police?'

'No.'

'Why not? You had a duty to. Why didn't you just report the murder and leave it at that, Jimmy? It would be everybody else's first response.'

I shrugged. I tried to see her face. It's hard to judge someone's emotions from the side while they're concentrating on driving. Nothing less than a grin will convince you they're happy. I didn't need Judy to be outright happy . . . just the faintest sign of approval would have done. She didn't approve of me, though. I sighed and went on.

'I didn't report a murder because I didn't find a murder,' I said. 'I found a stiff but it was a surgical specimen done up to look like a murder victim. That body I found in Peter Moody's flat was as fresh as week-old milk. It was fresh from the cold-store. The lividity was all wrong. The girl was sitting on a dressing stool and had bled to death from wounds in her belly and chest, we're supposed to believe. But the only stains I saw were where her blood had settled under her skin . . . and they were in her back and backside. They were all wrong. The way *her* blood had settled she must have died lying down. From the cut I saw in her gut she might even have died under the surgeon's knife. None of it worked. We were expected to believe she'd been "murdered" with a big knife. There were big wounds in her breast. But she hadn't bled . . . I mean hadn't bled from the breast, Judy. It's a bit unlikely, don't you think? The only people who don't bleed from massive wounds in the chest are dead people. Dead already people. And then her body temperature was miles out for the room. Someone had turned on a load of fires to warm her up – they'd even brought a fire with them, a portable gas fire, one that clearly didn't belong to the house. That puzzled me. I supposed at first the idea must have been to make all that "time of death" stuff difficult. But then I thought "why bother?" A first-year medical student could've told anyone and his brother that that girl was already dead before she went into the room, that she died lying down not sitting up, and that no one of her body-weight could have spilled four or five pints of blood on the way upstairs and even made it upstairs, leave alone bleed another four or five pints' worth while she was in the room. She'd have to have weighed sixteen or eighteen stone to carry that much blood . . . and she didn't. She weighed nine stone or something like that.'

Judy had slowed the Mini because she wanted to hear it all and it's hard to speak in a speeding Mini. I couldn't gauge any response from her yet. I went on.

'Also someone had written the letter "P" in blood on the dressing-table mirror. They'd made it look enough like an "R" that we'd have to do some deduction . . . you know. It was all too neat and it all stank. I've thought about this a lot, Judy. The cut in her guts might even have meant the girl had had a post-mortem examination started on her. Now there's a thought. That's where she might have come from. Some sort of mortuary. But not a public one, surely? Where could they have started a p.m. and then took the stiff to Peter's house? And why?'

Judy said nothing. She took the turn for the Dartford Tunnel, so we'd come into London at the right point for my flat. You can go through the Blackwall Tunnel but she has a prejudice against it. I've never been able to figure out what. Maybe she just likes paying tolls.

'So why did you think you were helping your friend by not reporting the crime? What possible profit could there be for him in that, Jimmy? Leave alone for yourself.'

'It seemed pretty obvious someone was fitting him up. I reckoned the best help I could give him would be to put a spanner in the works and keep my mouth shut. At least I'd be giving him a couple of hours in which to sort himself out, and at least I'd have put the mockers on someone's well-turned plot.'

Judy took an exit. She parked the Mini on the motorway flyover, got out and leaned against the steel railings overlooking the motorway. Traffic roared below. I got out too and joined her.

'Middle Eastern?' Judy said.

I looked across at her.

'Yes. I suppose she could be Jewish. Just. I'd have thought an Arab woman, though. She could be anything really . . . second generation English. Anything.'

'Why do you get involved like this?' she said. 'Why always you?'

I said nothing. The motorway fumes blasted us as lorries ploughed along the M25. We both leaned on the rails and looked out on the traffic.

'I've gone the wrong way,' she said and stood suddenly. 'This is the way to Orpington. I should be going the other way for Dartford.'

I said something rude about Dartford, put my arms round her and kissed her. The warm blasts of air and noise continued to rock us. Judy said, 'That's your answer to everything, Jenner. It won't do.'

But she didn't push me away. I was glad she didn't. I didn't let go. I held her in my arms and kissed her and touched her black hair. Holding Judy was safe and secure. Holding Judy was like touching base.

'What do you want, Jimmy? What are you up to?'

I held her for a long time and she repeated it several times. Eventually I said, 'I've a list as long as my arm of things I want. What about you?'

She laughed and held me even closer. My stomach muscles ached from Timpkins's attentions. I didn't tell her though.

'I've lots of things I want.'

We stood quietly for a long time, then Judy said again and seriously, 'What do you want?'

I said quietly into her ear, 'I want to know which department a DS Timpkins and a DC Mason work for. I want to know which department dear old Peter Moody worked for.'

'Department?'

I nodded against the side of her head, her soft hair on my brow.

'When?'

'Up till a week ago, I guess. I want to know where Clare Fisher lives. She's told me once she lived in Essex but that was a long time ago. I want to know who phoned you and who put you on to this Emma Johnson person. I want to know who this Emma Johnson *is*.'

'I don't know. The person who called just gave their message and rang off. They didn't give a name. It was all very mysterious.'

'Man or woman?'

'Woman. Young.'

'Refused to give a name, or you didn't ask?'

'I asked, okay...but she ignored it. I asked several times. She just told me to pay attention and carried on with her story.'

'Is that it? Then you phoned this Emma Johnson?'

'That's it.'

'Got a piece of paper?'

She gave me one. I pulled a pencil stub from my pocket and wrote on it.

'That's the index number of her car, you know.'

Judy nodded that she knew what I wanted. I said, 'Why did you offer to pay?'

'I thought you were in trouble and you didn't have any money.'

'You didn't have any money either.'

'I've got a little saved now...what do you expect from me, Jimmy?'

We were quiet again, and I shoved my mouth close to her ear again and kissed her through her hair and said, 'I want you, Judy.'

I pushed her hair back and she pulled away. I could have sworn she was crying. I couldn't tell very well, she kept her face down. For tuppence I'd have cried too. I looked at the roofs of the lorries passing under us, then I turned Judy and myself and took her in my arms again and looked back along the motorway we'd left. A steady stream of traffic was on the tarmac and concrete strip. A solid phalanx of steel horses. A car was out of the stream of traffic, parked on the hard shoulder with its bonnet up. Two men were leaning over the engine. The car looked very much like a Vauxhall Astra to me. It was the right size and light blue, anyway. The two men were tall and dressed in dark clothes.

Chapter Seventeen

An hour and a half later Judy dropped me off in Stoke Newington. I couldn't see any Vauxhall Astra. Maybe I had imagined it. I stood around Stoke Newington Church Street and just let the dirt and bustle blow past me. I needed it. After Boulogne and Dover the city felt like civilisation again. I felt as if I could have gone up and down the street, shaking everyone's hand, telling them what a good job they were doing.

My first move when I arrived home was to take a shower. I stank of prison cell and old clothes. It's something when you get to smell so bad even *you* can't live with it. After the shower I ran a bath and lay in it for a long time, then I had one of those twenty-minute shaves where you pamper yourself out of sight, all brand-new blades, long, careful looks in the mirror and hot towels from the radiator. I finished off with talcum powder and clean clothes – a cotton shirt and an old pair of baggy cords. I felt better.

I went into the living room, put some civilising influence on low on my record player and poured myself a good-sized whisky. I made a few phone calls. The first was to the answering machine in my office. My most hi-tech possession is an answering machine you can operate remotely with a little gadget. I love it. I call it my mechanical secretary.

First of all I heard the answering machine equivalent of junk mail, a man asking me to join the Professional Investigators' Organisation (a week before I'd had his letter, too, telling me I could become a 'Chartered Enquiry Agent'). Then there was a copper I'd done some work with once asking me to come and have a drink. The copper, a Detective Inspector called Denis O'Keefe, was so sharp you could cut yourself on him. Deviousness had become a way of life with the man, so much so that he could do nothing without having something else in mind. 'Do you take sugar?' is suspicious when it comes from Denis. 'Come and have a drink one evening, Jimmy' calls for a full investigation.

The next message was from Judy asking after my whereabouts, then a call from Emma Johnson, introducing herself and doing the same. The last message was only left an hour before I'd got home – the caller had given the time and date of her call – and came from a lady who was so difficult to understand I had to run the tape back. She was some sort of Yank, and she managed to stick a 'y' in the middle of all her words.

'Hayllo, Miyster Jeynner. My nayme's Parts, Eysmareylda Parts, aynd Ah'm a viysiter hey-a in yowah cantry. Ah'm in trouble.'

On the second run-through I discovered that Esmerelda was called Potts, not Parts, and that she came from Atlanta, Georgia. She was staying at Brown's Hotel. I apologised both to Bach and Casals, turned the player off and rang the hotel. The pronunciation was obviously catching, because a very English telephonist said, 'Mrs Parts's line is busy. Can I take a message?'

'No, I'll call back.'

Five minutes later I tried again and got her.

'Mrs Potts?'

'Speaking.'

'Jenner, here. James Jenner. You called me.'

'I did. I need a good enquiry agent and you were recommended to me. Are you free?'

'What for?'

'I'm in trouble and I need some help,' she said.

'Do you think you could explain a little, please?'

Mrs Potts giggled at what she called my old world politeness, told me it was the thing she enjoyed most about being in England and that she'd never been here before, that she was going to recommend all her friends to come here and to stay in Brown's Hotel and that if it wasn't for the sad and worrying purpose of her visit coming here would have been the most perfect treat. Eventually she explained, but even that took time.

She repeated that she was indeed a visitor to our country, as had been George M. Potts III, her husband. She told me all about George, including his heart condition and his many operations. As the conversation went on it became clear that it wasn't Mrs Potts who was in trouble, it was George.

The problem with George III was that he'd gone missing. George had come to England without his wife a month before. The plan had been he would attend an Allied Aircrew reunion in Clatford, a village near Bury St Edmunds from whence George III had once flown to do battle with the Hun. Good old George. I saw him as a man who would wear a Legionnaire's tassled hat, and would be found waving his hands and talking loudly in the saloon bar of some country pub. He'd go into the Bull and Bush (or whatever the local boozer up there is) and insist on recognising people who probably weren't born until 1950. I know all about former US servicemen who come here for nostalgia's sake. They get drunk and cry a lot. Because they can't recognise anybody they recognise everybody. I was once accused by a former Sherman tank commander of being his boatmaster on D-Day. We were in the Lamb and Flag and it was towards closing time. He spilled his last pint on his Burberry mac, which upset him no end. I was born in 1951.

So George III overstayed in Suffolk. Not many people do that. He came for three days and stayed for a month. Not only did he stay in Suffolk, but he hadn't contacted Atlanta,

Georgia. Naughty George. Mrs Potts had come to England in search of her missing George, got no joy out of the cops and the immigration service (George's father was English and he had right of domicile), and was told to try the Salvation Army. They were sympathetic but slow. Mrs Potts wanted some action. A man she'd met in the Serpentine Gallery had recommended using an enquiry agent.

'Did you know him?' I asked.

'No, but he was very nice. He knew so much about British Primitivism. I felt I absolutely *had* to tell him my story. I just knew I should trust his opinion.'

I came out of the woodwork, so to speak, on the recommendation of an aesthete and in the expectation of a quicker service than the Sally Ann and a politer service than the police.

'Of course,' said Mrs Potts, 'you have to pay for that, I know. And I'm able to.'

Even though I had Peter's money sitting in my office, I'm not so well-briefed as to turn work away. Good, clean, honest missing-person work especially. I don't mind earning a few quid the simple way.

'Where did you get my name from, Mrs Potts?'

'Can you come here? Or should I come over there, Mr Jenner? I don't know London at all well, I'm afraid. You'd better come here. Can you come today?'

'No. Tomorrow at lunchtime.'

'Good. We'll have lunch and I'll tell you all about it. I feel so relieved already simply because I've spoken to you, Mr Jenner.'

'Mm.'

'I'll see you here tomorrow at one, then. Bye now.'

The next call was to a fellow I know on Fleet Street.

'Tony? Jimmy Jenner here. Did your paper cover that girl who was murdered in Kensington a couple of days ago?'

Tony Tennyson, known at his office as Tony Takeaway for his eating habits and definitely no relation to the poet, groaned into the phone and said, *'What* murder in Kensington?'

'There was a girl murdered Thursday night in a mews house down there.'

'Oh yeah, gotcha. That was domestic, the police are saying. They're seeking someone to help in their enquiries and all that toffee. No percentage there, Jimmy. No story for us. Whatever you've got on it will have to go to some other mug journalist. No ping-ping from round here. You skint?'

'I don't know any other mug journalists, and what's the good of complaining to the likes of you if I'm skint? Other people used the murder story.'

'Not us. We had a Bingo Special prizewinner that day, plus our Bevy of Beauties in colour, plus a double page feature of *Jeanette Says*. We didn't have no room.'

'We didn't have *any* room, Tony. Jeanette says what, anyway?'

Tony giggled and then coughed into the phone. He had a cough like a dying horse. One man who shouldn't smoke.

'Don't you ever read our rag? You've got a bit of a sauce plugging honest working journalists like me for information if you can't even be bothered to sample the fruits of our labours.'

'Jeanette says what?'

'Jeanette Gemini, our hatchet girl. Actually she doesn't exist. She's a team of journalists. Four of them. This week she's got the knife out for *Dynasty*. I'm afraid we wouldn't have had no room for news. What do you think we're running here? Try the *Standard* . . . hang on.' He put his hand over the mouthpiece and yelled at someone across the room, then coughed again. The coughing went on for some time. 'Sorry. Er . . . or better still, I know a bloke on the local rag. Ewence. Tim Ewence. Send him my regards, will you?'

'Of course. If you don't give up smoking you'll end up in a hole in the ground.'

'I have given it up. Now sod off.'

'Number, Tony?'

'Oh yeah. Number. Hang on.'

A minute later I was introducing myself to Tim Ewence. He sounded young.

'Jenner? The bloke in the Regent's Street Blast?'

They even talk in headlines.

'Himself.'

'Well, hello there, Mr Jenner. What can I do for you?'

'Jimmy. Call me Jimmy. I wonder who covers your local crime beat?'

'You're talking to him.'

'I wonder if you covered the murder in St John Mews last Thursday?'

'"Covered" it is a bit of an exaggeration,' he said. 'There was nothing to cover. This bloke does in his bird. Domestic, the local constabulary reckoned. They won't give out his name, but they gave a description.'

'The description that was in the *Standard?*'

'That's right. One of his neighbours said to me he looked nothing like that, but then they never do, eh?'

'Maybe. Who was the officer on the case?'

'Not a local. A Superintendent Leigh. Scotland Yard bloke. Pressure of cases I suppose. That's what I was told to suppose, anyway.' He laughed at his own joke and said, 'I haven't seen hide nor hair of the man.'

'So?'

'Well . . . that's a bit funny. They all love having their names in the papers usually.'

'And he doesn't. Anything else happened?'

'They've opened the inquest.'

'That's interesting.'

'Not very. It was adjourned immediately. Why are you interested in the story? It's a real dud. It's sick to say so when someone gets murdered, but it's routine.'

'Personal reasons. Not work. Did you say you didn't know the name of the man they were looking for?'

'No. I said they weren't giving the name out. It's Moody, Peter Moody. Did you know him?'

'Why do you ask?'

'Because he's an ex-copper, too. My editor won't let me print that. He says it's unjustified.' There was a silence, then he said, 'What have you got?'

'Nothing.'

'Sure?'

'Yes.'

'Then why the interest? *Did* you know him?'

'Personal, like I said. Is your editor very right-wing?'

'No more than most. You coming over this way, Jenner?'

'Maybe.'

'Let's have a drink together. You can buy it. Get a pencil and I'll give you my home number, too.'

Tim Ewence sounded like a man with a mission. Young and eager, set the world on fire. He was sharp, too. Why *just* have a drink with someone when you can have a drink, pick his brains, empty his wallet and raid his address book all at once? The other way, life would be so boring.

Chapter Eighteen

I was all set to spend the evening watching TV and rubbing tincture of arnica on my bruises. I sat there with my shirt off, feeling sorry for myself, thinking of ways I could torture Timpkins and get my own back. I had him eating semolina pudding made with water while watching Open University Social Science modules on the TV; Tina Turner and Princess Di (to cover all eventualities) were stripping off and talking alluringly behind his back. 'Come on, DS Timpkins, gimme gimme gimme.' He could wriggle wriggle wriggle, but he couldn't turn round. Later on I would probably have them both nearly but not quite touching him, groaning and panting into his ears all the while. And he *still* wouldn't be able to turn round.

Then the phone rang.

'Jimmy! Long time no see. Denis here. Did you get my message?'

'Just, Denis. I've been out of the country.'

'*No*? Where? Anywhere nice?'

'Boulogne. I've been to Boulogne. And Paris too. I've been to Paris.'

'Sounds nice. I like Paris.'

'I don't.'

'And Boulogne too, eh? Business?'

'What do you want, Denis?'

'A meet. See me tomorrow night for a drink.'

'No.'

'Wednesday then.'

'Denis, you're selling something, and whatever it is I don't want to buy. Right? Good night.'

I put the phone down. A few seconds later it rang again.

'What?'

'Touchy, aren't we . . . write my number down,' said Judy's voice. She gave me the number. 'Now add. my sisters' ages and your sisters' ages to it and ring me from a phone box.'

I dressed quickly and went down to ring her. I had to wait while two girls giggled into the phone for five minutes. At least I knew the box would work. I got Judy on the second try, owing to my arithmetic being a bit of a washout. I haven't got a sister and hers are nineteen, twenty-one and twenty-seven, which comes to rather a lot when you're tired.

'Where are you?'

'In a coin box at Victoria Station. This is my supper break. We'll have to hurry. I didn't know if you'd have eavesdroppers.'

'Should I?'

'Probably. Wait till I tell you and you'll see why. First of all I can't find anything concrete on your Timpkins and Mason, but I can tell you there's no DS Timpkins of the age your bloke is supposed to be anywhere in the Met, let alone Special Branch. There are only three Timpkins, one's a River Policeman coming up to retirement and the other two are both uniformed PCs.'

'Couldn't be on loan from a county force?'

'Yes, of course he could.'

'And Mason?'

She sighed. 'Have a heart, Jimmy. There are over four hundred of them.'

'Sorry.' I should have thought of that. I was tired.

A man and his dog stopped next to the telephone kiosk.

The dog peed on the door and the man sneered at me, inviting an argument. They moved on. 'What about Moody?' I said.

'I've no idea which department employed Moody recently, but I can tell you he was some sort of "funny" in Ulster before you knew him.'

'When before I knew him?'

'Just immediately before. Seventy. Seventy-one. I don't know what he was exactly because his computer file is double-locked. Two separate senior officers have the passwords to it. There's no chance of seeing it, Jimmy. I found the girl, too. Clare.'

'Where?'

'Fobbing. Near Corringham. She was in the voters' register, you so-called detective.'

'Thanks. Is there a station there?'

'Not for miles. It's a bit remote.'

The dirt and the stench of the telephone kiosk was just beginning to become unbearable. I noticed I was holding my handset as far as I could from my mouth.

'How do you know Moody was in Ulster and when if you can't read his file?'

'The usual thing with a bureaucracy. We've neat minds. Too neat. The personnel file headers also contain a list of cross-references to incident files. Numbers for incident files are given out in strict numerical sequence. The files also have a code to show which force's area the incident took place in. It doesn't work the same with personnel files because they're only flagged for the force inputting information . . . the Met, in Moody's case, which you already knew.'

Inputting information? Flags? File headers? This wife of mine sounded as if she needed a glossary. I tried to backtrack her a little, so we'd end up in the world.

'Tell me about Ulster again. How did you find out he was in Ulster?'

'Easy. Even if a file's locked you can read the cross-reference numbers. They're in the header, right?'

'Right.'

'And they have force codes on them . . . in your pal's case, almost always Royal Ulster Constabulary. To get the dates when they were issued you just look at files with numbers numerically adjacent to the files on your subject's personnel file header. The numbers are arbitrary, allocated as the files are first created, just day by day. *The file numbers* aren't treated as any special security risk because in themselves they're not. There you have it. It's a weakness in the system. Got it?'

'No.'

She sighed.

'Does it really matter?'

'It does to me.'

'Okay . . . last time, Jimmy. If Moody's file has a cross-reference to incident files on it and those incidents have RUC file numbers we can deduce Peter Moody has been in Ulster.'

'Yes.'

'Finding out when is just a question of looking out when this or that particular range of file numbers was being distributed. If you want a precise date you look at the file with the preceding number to the one you can't read. It's unlikely to be more than twenty-four hours out.'

'So Peter Moody was in Ulster in 1970. But doing what? Was he there as a policeman? Soldier? SAS maybe?'

'I don't know. Certainly not necessarily as a policeman, though. On the 6th or 7th of June he was there on a police-related activity. He may or may not have been a policeman and I have no way of telling what the police-related activity was.'

'Well, he wasn't a School Crossing Patrol and he wasn't running the staff restaurant in Belfast nick.'

'No, he wasn't. Jimmy, don't make jokes. This is big stuff.

Dead bodies that aren't and secret squirrels in Ulster are out of your league. Why don't you forget it and find some nice, simple client to do a job for?'

'Thanks, Judy. The same thought occurred to me today. Maybe I will. Maybe I already have one. Thanks for all this. I know you're sticking your neck out.'

'Yes, I did. But I haven't told you all. There's more. There are even better reasons to butt out, Jimmy.'

'Like what?'

'Like RUC isn't the only flag on the incidents in his file header. Some of them are marked with a seven and some marked seven-uncle. That means military intelligence and US military intelligence, in that order. I'm not supposed even to know they mean that. You had better never mention it, because it could only come from one source.'

'I won't. I'd never tell anyone you've helped me.'

'I know you wouldn't want it. But you might without meaning to. Just keep it in mind.'

'Okay, I promise.'

'You'd also better either find that nice quiet simple case or take a holiday. Got any money?'

'I have a bit.'

'Well, take my advice and go on holiday for a while. Not Spain.'

'Not Spain. No . . . thanks, Judy, anyway. Thanks a lot. I mean it. Did you get anything on this Emma Johnson?'

'I did. The car's not registered to her. It's registered in a company name. Kauner Limited. I'm going to see what I can find out about it and let you know.'

'Well done.'

'One last thing, Jimmy.'

'What?'

'I'm seeing a lawyer tomorrow. We can't go on like we are, and we're not going to get together again.'

'Can't we talk about it?'

'No.'

'What about you sticking your neck out for me?'

'I was worried for you. I guessed it would be something like this. I did it for guilt.'

'Well, let's talk.'

'Bye.'

And she went, just like that. There was nothing I could do.

I minded about the second phone call from Denis O'Keefe. It came at about half-twelve the same night, and I was tired – in bed, half-asleep – and he was gabbling that he had this wonderful deal for me.

'What sort of deal?'

'A deal deal. Meet me tomorrow.'

'We've been this route once tonight, Denis. I'm busy.'

'Well, when? Come on. Wise up. This is a nice quiet simple deal that'll earn you money.'

I thought for a while. It had gone through both Judy's and my mind today that I could use a simple, quiet job. Coincidentally, I'd been offered nice quiet deals twice in the same day, once by Denis O'Keefe and once by Esmerelda Potts. That was two nice quiet simple deals more than during my entire career heretofore. I don't believe in coincidences.

'Tomorrow night. The Founders, Bankside. Eight.'

This time he just put the phone down.

My doorbell rang at three. I pulled on a dressing gown and my leg. The bell kept ringing.

'All right, keep your hair on. I'm coming.'

The light was on in the communal hallway. It's one of those timer jobs, you push it when you come into the flats, it stays on for a minute or so. Just long enough for you to put your bags down and lose your key. You'll trip over the bags looking for the light switch to punch it a second time, too.

I could see a man's figure through the wire-reinforced frosted glass of the door. I could only see his shape, not who he was. He was a big fellow. And he was still ringing my bell.

'Lay off!' I yelled. 'I'm coming.'

I didn't switch my hall light on. When I opened the door Timpkins was leaning on the jamb, leaning heavily like a drunk. I just had time to glimpse his pock-marked face, then the communal hallway light went out. Timpkins didn't lay off the bell, either.

'What do you want?' I said to the dark shape he'd become. He slipped a little, as if he really were drunk. He didn't answer me. 'What do you want?' I said louder, 'Get off my bell!' and shoved him.

Timpkins keeled backwards into the communal hallway. His head hit the ground with a sound like a coconut breaking. I turned my hall light on. A sore head wouldn't be his only problem. Timpkins's shirt was soaked in blood. I felt his pulse. There was none. Timpkins was as dead as a kipper. The downstairs communal door slammed. I looked out and saw a running figure, a man. I wasn't going to chase him. Some yards down the street I could see the figure of an old man walking. It was a funny time for an old man to go for a walk. I turned back, went inside and rang the local nick.

'I'd like to report a murder.'

The sleepy constable woke up and took my name, address and phone number. He asked me did I know who the victim was. I told him I believed it was a man named Timpkins and that I believed he was a policeman of some sort. I'd found him dead on my doorstep. I could hear the young copper's throat tighten.

'A policeman?'

'I think so.'

There was some muttering with the constable's hand over the mouthpiece, then an older man's voice came on the line. I gave the story all over again. Then I added, 'Can I have your name, please?'

'Why?'

'Because it's a serious matter and I'm frightened and I'll be asked lots of questions. Your names'll be a starting point.' That wasn't the real reason but it would do for them.

A wariness came into his voice.

'Okay. I'm Sergeant French.'

'And the constable?'

'PC Gregory.'

'I wonder if you'd be kind enough to both make a note of this call and the name of the man who made it in your pocket books.'

'We keep a log of calls, sir.'

'I know you do. But please put it in your pocket books too.'

'Are you frightened of some funny business? Because I can assure you . . .'

'Assure me of nothing, Sergeant. Put it in your pocket book.'

'Our car will be outside in a second, sir. They're just talking on the radio now. I can hear them.' He obviously thought I was hysterical and was trying to keep me calm.

'Write it in your pocket book,' I said. I didn't want any cover-ups or funny business over this one.

Chapter Nineteen

I didn't make my lunch date next day with Mrs Potts of Atlanta, Georgia, which was hardly surprising. I didn't get any more sleep that night, either, which also wasn't much of a surprise. I spent the night in my local police station, telling and retelling what had happened. I told it to every rank of copper imaginable – except for police-dog and cadet, and they were probably busy. Meanwhile my flat, I knew, would be full of size twelve feet and electronic flashlight.

About dawn the capo came from New Scotland Yard, a Detective Chief Superintendent Palmer. I was drinking tea in a tacky, sea-green-and-grey room, and when Palmer came in I was being babysat by an unhappy, baggy-faced young uniformed constable who didn't want to talk to me because he'd been told not to. He hadn't wanted to talk to me for an hour and I'd gained some small entertainment from devising ways to make him talk to me ... enigmatic statements like 'could it all be true?' addressed to the ceiling. If you do enough of them even the most unwilling conversationalist would say 'what?' The constable had resisted the temptation to say 'what?' ... but only just.

Palmer came in alone and he dismissed the constable. He smiled and sat across from me. He was a squat fellow in his mid-to-late-forties, too small – I would have thought – to have been recruited as a copper in the first place. Maybe the physical standards had changed between my generation and his. Ten years can make a lot of difference. Palmer had a dark, greasy, balding head over a dark, greasy hairy face. He was one of those men who need to shave four or five times a day, and when I first saw him Palmer had missed a couple.

Palmer wore an old check shirt that had been washed too hot so that the collar tips had turned up, and he had on a tie he'd knotted when he'd first bought it and had kept the same knot on since. The tie was Thames mud brown, *Vogue* magazine Color of the Year – only the year in question was 1950. His suit was Thames mud brown too, to match. The tie knot had grown shiny from being always exposed. The suit had grown shiny from being worn for too long. It was like a loose brown second skin, only with lapels, vents and buttons. It should have become his allotment garden suit a long time ago. Palmer might be a big wheel in New Scotland Yard but in Jermyn Street and Savile Row the tailors wouldn't spit on him.

Palmer and I had a big grey metal desk between us. He wriggled on his wooden seat and shuffled some papers on his lap. When he'd done that he wrung his small hands for a couple of minutes while he fretted about how to ask me to tell my story again. That's how it seemed to me anyway. That's how it was meant to seem. You don't get to the rank of DCS by worrying about making witnesses (or anybody else) repeat their stories time after time . . . making out you find it difficult is just a way of depicting yourself. The polite approach is a classic interrogator's gambit and I never saw anyone open any better than Palmer.

'Ah . . . Mr Jenner, isn't it? I wonder if you'd be so kind as to let me know – in your own words – about all the events leading up to last night and then exactly what happened during the evening until you found the . . . er . . . *body* on your er doorstep. I know it's the most awful bore going over and over with different policemen, but I'd been led to believe by a Seargeant . . .' he shuffled through the sheaf of papers on his lap, 'Sergeant . . . er, well, I've been led to believe you felt a certain sense of . . .'

He broke off and looked over my shoulder for a long time. His eyes weren't quite focused, I thought. The silence paced round us, then suddenly Palmer said loudly, '*Déjà vu*. I believe you'd felt a certain sense of *déjà vu* about the man.'

'I had seen him before,' I said. 'No mistake. No possibility of one. I'd seen him less then twenty-four hours before.'

'Quite.'

I waited. Palmer smiled over my shoulder again. This business of looking over my shoulder made me feel nervous, as if there were someone else in the room who'd slipped in quietly and was managing to stay just out of my view all the time.

'Tell me. Tell me all,' Palmer said.

I told him. I told him the truth, too. But not all of it. I didn't tell him that Timpkins had belted me, for example, and I didn't tell him that Timpkins had been worried about getting something off of me and that I didn't know what the something Timpkins had wanted was. I certainly didn't tell Palmer that I didn't know what the hell Timpkins had been interrogating me about. That would reveal my entire hand . . . all fours and fives, I was going to give away as little as possible. If Palmer wanted to give me a motive for killing Timpkins he'd have to go and find his own. I wasn't making them a present of one. I told him I'd gone to France on a pleasure-trip and that when I came back Timpkins and a DC Mason had picked me off the immigration queue and asked me politely would I like to come with them. So I did and they took me away in a van and questioned me closely about a man I used to know. A Peter Moody. Another former policeman.

'And?' Palmer's eyes were still over my shoulder. He looked like he was thinking about whether he should have one rasher of bacon or two for breakfast.

'And I was unable to help them because I hadn't clapped eyes on the man for eight or nine years. And they kept me locked up and questioned me inside-out and upside-down for some twenty hours, I guess. And they let me go when a lady lawyer came and said she wanted me released. They released me.'

'Just like that, Mr Jenner?'

'Just like that. Don't you have a written record of all this from Dover?'

He didn't answer. Of course he didn't have a written record. I'd been picked up by a couple of enterprising Special Branch coppers, given the once over and set free once it became clear someone knew they had hold of me. Emma Johnson was the someone.

'The lady lawyer,' said Palmer. 'Tell me your story. We'd got as far as the lady lawyer who came and told the policemen what to do.'

I chose to ignore the sarcasm.

'Yes. She's a very firm lady lawyer. Timpkins and his sidekick also had the Customs service take my car apart and they also appropriated a load of shopping I'd bought in France.'

'They didn't,' Palmer said.

'Well, I arrived in England with a perfectly healthy if ancient Hillman Hunter. Now I own a pile of scrap metal in Dover.'

He shook his head.

'I mean the shopping. They didn't appropriate the shopping. Detective Sergeant Timpkins had it in the back of his car. We found his car parked outside your flat. He was bringing the shopping to you. Before it went off.'

I stood and walked round the room. I read some posters on rabies and swine vesicular disease. Palmer kept shuffling the papers on his lap, stopping every now and then to make a pencilled note on one.

'Mr Palmer, you must take me for a charlie. A right charlie. I'm charlie. I'm the man who's expected to believe that a Special Branch Detective Sergeant came to my flat in the middle of the night to deliver my shopping? Okay, Mr Palmer. I believe you. I'm a charlie.'

Palmer smiled wryly, but still over my shoulder.

'I'm not very keen on sarcasm, Mr Jenner. At my school we were taught it is the lowest form of wit.'

'At my school we weren't taught anything. You must've been a fee-payer.'

He sighed. Maybe I was getting to him. He said, 'Your shopping had been in the boot of your car when Timpkins questioned you at Dover. Correct? He was coming to London, knew your stuff was perishable and offered to drop it off and get a receipt from you for it. What do you think of that?'

'In the middle of the night?'

'It was perishable. He was coming there, that was the time he was coming at.'

'Didn't ring first to find out if I'd be there?'

Palmer smiled. 'You said yourself it was the middle of the night.'

I sat down again.

'You're joking with me, mate,' I said. 'You're expecting me to believe this bloke Timpkins broke all the rules about possession of a prisoner's property, drove to London in the middle of the night and tried to deliver the stuff to me on the basis that I *might* be there? Only might, mind. I thought he was supposed to be an experienced copper, detective sergeant and all that. Where did you get this story from?'

Palmer smiled again and raised his hands like some greasy balding Buddha. 'It's what he told his colleagues. And they told me. Now what about your story, Mr Jenner? Can I take it you're sticking to this line about being in France for the day trip only?'

'Not a day trip. I was there for three days. I was on a pleasure-trip.'

He leaned over his sheaf of papers and wrote something on one, saying slowly and loudly enough for me to hear, '*Not* day trip. Three days.' Then he looked up at me and smiled and said, 'Good. *Good*. I like to know what story people are committing themselves to. Will you sign a statement to that effect?'

Then I saw it. As if someone had parked a bus in my front room and I'd never noticed.

I said, 'You've not been sent out here to investigate the murder of a policeman, have you? You're not interested in the truth at all. You've been sent to find a reasonable way of explaining an inconvenient and nasty death away. You'll be telling me next it was suicide.'

'He was mugged,' Palmer said. 'Obviously mugged. Clear MO, it's happened round there before. Follow a drunk home and mug him. That's what they do. Usually it's the Negroes that perpetrate such crimes.' He leaned forward and dropped his voice to give a confidential tone. 'Though if you quoted me I'm afraid I'd have to deny saying that. We think he was carrying some booze from your shopping. There are a couple of bottles missing from the inventory the Customs took in Dover. Maybe the muggers saw the booze bottles and thought he was a drunk. Maybe he looked like easy pickings.'

'And why should Timpkins bring a couple of bottles upstairs without the rest of the shopping?'

'Maybe to have a drink with you. Maybe there was something he wanted to discuss. We'll never know now. My guess is that he came there with the intention of discussing something with you and that he was bringing a couple of bottles upstairs to oil the discussion. My guess is that some mugger took him for a drunk and tried to hold him up. Only Timpkins wasn't a drunk and it all went wrong. They struggled and Timpkins ended up being stabbed.'

Fifteen times, I thought, they struggled and his mugger stabbed him fifteen times. I didn't say it.

'Don't tell me,' I said, 'and your guess is that the mugger saw what he'd done, was upset by it, asked Timpkins where he'd been going, carried him upstairs to my door, leaned him on the jamb, all to make sure Timpkins was found before he died. It's important to die among friends. Maybe the mugger was a philosopher. He was a clever bloke if he did all that, I'm certain of that much at least.'

Palmer screwed up his face as if he'd been sucking lemons, then ran his fingers through his greasy hair.

'No. I'm not suggesting that. But we did find a flick-knife on the floor near your front door, and the flick-knife is the classic mugger's weapon, as we all know. Either he was staggering to your door after he'd been stabbed or he was dragged there. Forensic tests will show. I think there might be something in the second. It depends whether he was alive or not when he got to your front door.'

'Rubbish. Of course he was alive. How did he ring the doorbell if he was bloody dead?'

Palmer seemed to discover his stubbly chin, suddenly. He frowned and sat back in his chair. He caught the chin in his hand and rubbed it vigorously.

'Of course . . . *you* could have done it. Maybe that's why we found the flick-knife. I mustn't leave you out of our picture. How would it go? That you didn't have a chance to get rid of the knife, Mr Jenner. Or you lost it in the struggle. How about that? Flick-knives do usually come from France, don't they? Maybe you bought it and killed him. Who were you seeing in France?'

'Motive? And why should I report the crime if I'd done it and lost my knife?'

'So it was your knife?' he said. I didn't even answer. He knew it wasn't, I knew it wasn't.

'As for motives . . . oh I'm sure you'd have plenty of motives, Mr Jenner. I'm always confident of finding a motive in a murder. It's finding the strongest one that's the problem.' He rubbed his chin again and focused his eyes on mine. 'I think I could find you a motive. I think I could find all sorts of motives. You certainly had the opportunity. If we knew why he was coming to see you we'd have more of an idea whether you'd want to take up the opportunity. We know you had access to the murder weapon because we found it at the scene. I might be able to make a good case for you . . . you're the only one who says they saw these mysterious figures. We only have your description of the people

132

running away and we have no one else's word that these figures existed at all. You're the only person in Stoke Newington who had prior knowledge of the victim, as far as I can tell so far, anyway. I suppose there's always an outside chance we might find the old man. But then there's an outside chance we might find all sorts of things, don't you think, Mr Jenner? Isn't the surprise discovery which comes through diligent labor what police work is all about?'

I didn't answer. We were both silent. Palmer pursed his lips for a time, then grinned suddenly and banged his flat hand down on the grey desk-top.

'I don't like it. I don't like that theory at all. It's too neat. It sounds as if he was trying to incriminate you by committing suicide on your front doorstep.' He laughed. '"*I don't like Mr Jenner so I'm going to stab myself on his front doorstep. That should get him properly into trouble.*" No, I don't like that one. The alternative would be that it was you. That you murdered a man you knew to be a policeman on your own doorstep. That's nearly a domestic, and domestics are normally *crimes passionnels*. I would have to indicate that you had some sort of relationship with Timpkins.' Palmer shook his head. 'I don't fancy that, Jenner. Smearing a dead man's name. I don't like dirty washing and I don't like that sort of dirty washing most of all.' He pursed his lips again. 'Even if it were true, I think I'd want to find a way not to say that. I think we should have some sort of solidarity between policemen, don't you?'

I said nothing. It was all bull and he knew it. I was waiting for his real pitch. I thought it would come soon. Palmer was waiting too. He waited a long time, then he said, 'Even between policemen and ex-policemen . . . you were a policeman for a long time, Mr Jenner, eh?'

'Long enough.'

'And you think maybe we owe each other some . . . some what? Loyalty? Well, I'm in favor of giving you the benefit of the doubt. I'm in favor of treating you as if you were still a policeman. I certainly wouldn't like to go through all the dirt that might come up if I tried the "relationship" angle. I *want* to believe your story. All in all I prefer the mugger theory. You said yourself you saw a youngster running away. He wasn't black by any chance, was he?'

'I couldn't see. It was dark.'

'No . . . but dark is their time. Sometimes you can tell blacks by the way they walk. And they wear those funny hats. Bit hats. Woolly ones with lots of colour, all that business. Did he have a funny hat?'

'No. Not that I saw.'

'But you couldn't be sure? You didn't *not* see one?'

'I didn't see a funny hat.'

Palmer slapped his knee.

'You see, there's a strange thing . . . and you're sure he wasn't black?'

'I couldn't say whether he was or he wasn't. What about the old man?'

'I don't think we can seriously suspect him of mugging, do you? It'd be a turn up, eh, Mr Jenner? Old-man-mugger. Nearly as good as man-bites-dog. The popular press would love it, I know, but I think it's a bit unrealistic. I think I'm going to have to stick with our running-Negro-mugger. Or with you.'

He took a sheet of paper from the sheaf on his lap. He laid it and the sheaf separately on the grey desk-top. The single sheet was blank.

'I'm going to take your statement if you wouldn't mind, Mr Jenner,' Palmer said. 'Then you can go home with our sincere thanks for your assistance and our sincere apologies for keeping you so long.'

He wrote the statement. I sat opposite him reading it upside-down. It's very rare for a policeman of that rank to take your statement. Palmer must have thought it a very important statement . . . if not for what it said then for what he could prevent me putting in it. He prevented me putting almost anything in it, and it was all I could do to stop the running figure in the street below my flat from becoming a

Negro. I think if Palmer had had his way the figure would've stopped under the street lamp and sung 'Minnie the Moocher'. I managed to fix it so that we just got a running male figure. He'd have to add his Negro fantasies to it in his own time.

There were no lies in the statement (I could hardly call it *my* statement), no outright lies anyway, and I guessed it would fit into the picture Palmer wanted to build up. Halfway through writing it the baggy-faced young constable popped his head round the door.

'There's a phone call for you from NSY, sir, and there's a Special Branch fellow here for . . .'

'Shut up!' Palmer screamed. He had stood from the desk with a screech of metal chair and table legs. His fists were clenched and the veins stood out on his neck and on his temples. His papers had all fallen to the floor.

'. . . the car,' the unhappy young constable said. I almost felt sorry for him. He'd sat there in silence with me for all that long time, just like he'd been told to. Then the first time he opens his mouth he manages to put his foot right in between his teeth. Poor boy.

Palmer stood glowering at the young PC for a few seconds longer. A pencil rolled off the grey desk between us, clattering on to the floor with all the finesse of a dropped plank, then the constable closed the door with the lightest of touches, with an almost inaudible 'click'. Palmer composed himself and sat opposite me again.

'Excuse me, please,' he said, 'I can't stand being interrupted. Especially when a witness has been kind enough to cooperate in writing a statement. It's the height of rudeness to interrupt statement-taking. My sincere apologies to you, Mr Jenner.'

He looked at me long and hard. Unsmiling, no emotion in his face at all. My move. I'd heard what had been said clearly enough, though. No matter what Palmer did I'd heard it and he couldn't bluff his way round it and he couldn't empty it out of my head again and he couldn't have what the young PC had said unsaid. The baggy-faced young policeman had said that there was a Special Branch policeman outside. No doubt he'd have gone on to say he was waiting to pick up Detective Sergeant Timpkins's car.

It took until two p.m. before Palmer finally let me go, despite his 'just sign this and you can leave' promise. By the time we'd written the statement I knew Palmer and he knew me. I'd say we both felt a little cagey about each other. I felt he needed watching, that he was as tricky as a barrelful of monkeys. He didn't let on about how he felt about me. He just kept ordering me more tea and offering me cigarettes. I don't smoke and neither did he, but he kept the cigarettes in the pocket of his old brown suit and about every fifteen minutes he'd offer me one.

When I came out of the station I walked for about twenty minutes, then stopped at a phone box. I rang the New Scotland Yard switchboard.

'Metropolitan Police.'

'Special Branch Admin, please.'

Even if Special Branch doesn't have their office at NSY – and I don't know where their office is – I'd always brag a pound to a penny there will be one clerk sitting at one desk in New Scotland Yard doing administration work for them, just as there is at least one clerk in NSY doing administration work for every other department of the Metropolitan Police. At least one clerk.

There was.

'Hello,' said a man's voice, thin and watery. He sounded like a bad chicken soup tastes. I decided to go brash.

'That's no way to answer a phone. Give your name . . . who are you, man? Then give your extension number.'

'Who's speaking?'

'My name's Wakerham. Customs Waterguard Office i/c special operations, Tilbury Dock. I've got a lot of clobber here that a Detective Chief Superintendent Palmer from Special Branch wants kept. Or at least he did the last time we spoke a couple of weeks ago. Now I want this stuff out, pronto pronto fashion, because it's jamming the place up. I'd send it to Palmer but you people are such secret lovers I can't even find out what office he's in to have it sent to him. Got an address I can send it to?'

'What kind of "clobber"?' said the watery voice.

'Clothes, assorted. One Japanese motorcycle, rusty. A couple of motorcycle crash helmets, well worn. Got the picture? And a pair of binoculars for the spotting of villains through. That's the kind of clobber I'm talking about and it's blocking up our offices. Some of your mateys used it on an op down here and asked us to store it. I did so willingly. Well, I mean I'm a patient man but this stuff has been here since . . .'

'Give me your name and number.'

'Wakerham.' I spelled it out for him. 'Tell Palmer to look me up in your book, secret lover. I'm not doling out my number on the phone. Tell Palmer to phone me as soon as. Preferably yesterday.'

'We're lovers of secret, not secret lovers,' the voice warbled.

'Suit yourself. Your private life's not my affair, Johnny. I want to get rid of this clobber. And I want to know why it's been left here. Just get Palmer to ring me, right? Tell him he's abusing our hospitality and have him ring me.'

'I'll have him ring you, Mr Wakerham.'

'Thanks.'

I felt like cheering. *That's* what I wanted him to say. I wanted him to admit Palmer was one of theirs. I was elated. I went over the top.

'Cheer yourself up, too, when you answer the phone. Don't forget you've a secure job with a good pension all paid for out of public taxes. Try to sound a bit more cheerful and business-like.'

'Thank you, Mr Wakerham. Hang on . . . here's Mr Palmer's colleague Mr Leigh, if he could answer your questions.'

'No, I don't want Mr Leigh. I want Palmer in person.'

Well, perhaps I'm as tricky as a barrelful of monkeys too, but you have to be. At least I knew for certain who Palmer was and had some idea where he was coming from. Leigh's name rang a bell in my memory, too. I'd heard it some-where . . . a Detective Superintendent? I called Tim Ewence from the same phone box.

'What did your Detective Superintendent from Scotland Yard call himself?'

'Uh . . . Leigh. Why?'

'Did he say what part of NSY he came from?'

'Never spoke to him in person. Press conferences were run through the Press Bureau. I've never clapped eyes on the man.'

'Has anyone else?'

'I'll find out . . . why?'

'Can't say now.'

'Oh, that's a bit rich, Jenner.'

'Ewence. If I get a story, you'll be first in line. First re-fusal goes to you, no doubt whatsoever.'

'So what have you got?'

'Nothing. I said "if". Wait and see. See if you can't find out something about this policeman you never met; what he looked like, that sort of thing. Then give me a bell on my office number and tell me what you've got. Be discreet about it. You never know who's listening nowadays.'

'What do I get out of it?'

'First bite of the cherry.'

Chapter Twenty

Apart from the deviousness which all senior policemen seem to suckle at their mother's breast, Denis O'Keefe couldn't be more different from DCS Palmer. Denis is flashy. Sartorially speaking he comes from another planet. I've known Denis for a long time, since I was a young uniformed constable and he was a detective sergeant in the East End of London. He's never changed. He always considers himself the senior partner in our relationship. He always thinks I'm naïve and easily fooled, and that somehow he's protecting me against my own naïvety. Denis wears clothes which cost far too much, a fat gold ring with a big diamond set in it on the little finger of his left hand. He fiddles his hair around his head like Arthur Scargill so he won't look bald. That's about all he has in common with Arthur Scargill. All I know of, anyway.

Denis likes money. There's no way round it. He's already gone through a couple of retirement points without retiring because he can't find anything more lucrative than being a bent copper. He has sad but confident brown eyes, eyes which might convince the unwary that Denis isn't bent . . . but he is. He just likes money too much.

When I went into The Founders Arms on Bankside I saw him perched on the edge of a barstool and being careful how he sat. The latter activity was partly so he looked as if he cut a dash with any girls who happened to come in, partly so he could concentrate on avoiding getting beer-soaked in the elbow of his too-expensive mohair suit. When I approached he was peering with those sad brown eyes at a beautiful young office worker who in turn only had eyes for her boyfriend. The girl was in her very early twenties, dark, slim and with long hair. She had the kind of legs that went all the way up to wherever they're supposed to. She was wearing a formal blue women's business suit, too, which made her legs look even better. The boyfriend was an unshaven hunk of rippling flesh with a pip on top for a brain and one of those bullet-head haircuts. His clothes were scruffy and looked as if they had recently graced a building site. The youngster looked grubby but only honest-work-grubby.

'Hi,' said Denis. 'Want a drink?'

'Orange.'

'Orange. Cop an eyeful of that bird . . . what's she doing with an underage ape-man like that?'

'She's nice, Denis. Bit young for you.'

He smiled.

'I could do with a turn under the blankets with a nice young bird like that, Jimmy. It'd rejuvenate me, know what I mean? Half-an-hour of that every morning would be better than a hundredweight of ginseng for breakfast.'

'Only half an hour?' I said.

Denis nodded agreement.

'Before breakfast, anyway. I musn't be boastful.' He smiled. 'I've been sitting here wondering whether I could arrange it. Get the boy arrested for breathing in a public place, something like that, then give the bird the opportunity to widen her horizons with a man of true taste, style and experience. What d'you think?'

'Stop worrying about birds, Denis, and order my orange juice.' I put my hand on his arm. 'How are your daughters?'

'Prig.'

He sucked his teeth, waved a fiver at the barmaid and ordered the drinks. We went to a corner. We settled in some chairs before a huge glass window overlooking the Thames.

Men and women ghost figures moved across the surface of the thick glass before us, then there was the white flood-lighting and then the river. I thought of my childhood and the tugboats and the dockers. I remembered the Bankside of cobbled streets and Albion motors, swinging crane jibs and men who wore leather sapper's jerkins on their backs and steel hooks on their belts. It was just a flash, a dream, an insight. Then I saw the riverside through the glass. I saw it as it really is, with pubs run by the licensed victualling equivalent of chainstores, with buses bringing foreigners to gawp, with the floodlit concrete of the river frontage stretching before us and the floodlit mass of St Paul's squatting, hunkered down, on the city. I could see a train moving over Cannon Street railway bridge. I knew the sound should be clanks and clatters and angry metal screams. I couldn't hear it through the thick glazing, of course.

I sipped my orange juice and forced my attention to Denis's whisper.

'How do you fancy Australia?' he hissed.

'Australia?' I said out loud. I don't know what I'd expected, but it hadn't been that.

Denis scowled, rubbing his cheek nervously. He sipped his vermouth and played with the ice-cube in it.

'*Quietly*. This is only between you and me. I have got a dead simple job lined up and it involves spending the winter in Oz. We are now in October. You should be back just about in time for Feb, know what I mean? You're going to have brown knees, the Bondai rub and a floozie on each arm while the rest of us silly billies are flogging our guts out here. You are a lucky chap. You are even going to get paid for lying around Australia pulling your plonker.'

'Denis!'

'Well, whatever you do. I have got you a peach, my son. A peach.'

I turned away from him and watched the river again. I saw the lights and the black mass of a tug going up river. What the hell would a tug be wanting up the river nowadays? It was probably on some government-sponsored Job Creation scheme. Full of long-term-unemployed single-parent families. I waved at the government-sponsored tug. One up to the single-parent families. They were a service industry . . . keeping London looking like London.

'Know them?' Denis said.

'Tell me about the job.'

'It's a peach. You've hardly got to work at all.' He held his hand out and waggled it towards the tugboat. 'Some matey's gone and sunk a boat out there. . . .'

'Boat? You want me to investigate a sunken boat?'

'*Ship* then. Some matey's sunk his ship out there and it all looks a bit dodgy. More'n a bit. This geezer I know of is an adjuster and he's after a legman. Someone he can trust. Know what I mean? Some Englishman who comes with references as an insider . . . that's you, Jimmy. Eleven thousand smackers, six months getting your tan touched up and all you have to do is the leg work for some claims adjuster.'

'One leg work, Denis?'

'Eh? Oh . . . yeah. Very funny. You know what I mean. You're getting expenses, too. It's a reputable outfit. Could be a big breakthrough for you. Better than all this poxy stuff you do here. All this writ-serving cobblers and finding lemons who've lost themselves.'

'Thanks.' I drained the orange juice. 'Thanks for all the advice, Denis, and thanks for rating me so highly. I used to think you were bent but you were my mate . . . you know? Who put you up to this . . . Palmer?'

'Palmer? Never heard of him. This bloke who asked for you is all right.'

'A regular, Denis? Some old pal, eh? Hasn't ever been in the army by any chance? . . . How much are you getting for this?'

'Nix. Have another drink?' He touched our glasses together. They were empty. I shook my head.

'I get absolutely nothing,' he said. 'You get paid direct. Nothing to do with me. I was just asked by the insurance underwriters to make an approach to you on behalf of their investigator. Seems he'd heard of you . . . that's not impossible, Jimmy. People have heard of you.'

I shook my head. No, it was not impossible the underwriter's investigator had heard of me. Nothing was impossible. But Denis's offer was improbable.

'Do you know the adjuster?' I said.

'No. Nor the investigator. I was passed them by a friend of a friend. They wanted to find the right way to approach you.'

'The right way to approach me is direct, over the phone. I'm in the book . . . are you sure you're getting nothing out of it? Not a penny?'

He smiled sheepishly. 'I might pick up a head-hunting fee. We've yet to discuss it. I suppose it depends whether you'd agree to take on the work or not. You'd be a mug not to.'

I looked at Denis smiling his used-car-salesman smile. If it weren't for all the mugs he'd put in the nick with that smile I'd have said Denis had missed his vocation.

'Do you know the name of the brokers, Denis? Do you know the name of the underwriters? Do you know the name of the claims adjuster?'

'Course.'

'Well, check them out. There is going to be a dodgy one in there somewhere. Someone's tried to pull a flanker on you. My usefulness in shipping claims adjusting would be strictly limited to operating a pocket calculator under someone else's instructions. That's not worth eleven grand of anyone's money. I only know the sharp end from the blunt end of a boat . . . that's it.' I sighed. The approach had been so crude . . . and using my old friend Denis of all people. I looked at him. He was staring into the vermouth glass, waiting for my next word. I wondered if he really meant it. I wondered if he'd just been used. It was possible. I gave him the benefit of the doubt.

'As for using me because they fancied me,' I went on,

'I'm afraid not. Your friends, somewhere along the line, are having you on. Look at me.'

He looked into my eyes. I thumped my chest and said, 'Who'd honestly want a berk like me clogging up their lines in Australia? I only just about know where it is on the map. The country's full of mugs like me. Why import one from England? There's no logic in it. The reason I'm being offered that job is to get me out to Australia for a few months, not because of how useful I'll be there.'

'You're paranoid.'

I didn't answer.

He said, 'It's a lot of dough, Jimmy.'

'I don't like any of the Bankside pubs now. They've all lost their atmosphere.'

The Founders is new. Any atmosphere would be a struggle and the brewery's interior designers had struggled, but I still resented whatever was missing. I knew it was unreasonable to feel that way.

We went outside. There'd been a rain shower while we were in the pub and the dark streets smelled of flushed sewers and fallen leaves. Windswept rubbish. Autumn decay.

'It's a lot of cobblers, that's what it is,' I said. 'No one wants me in Australia. No one *would* ever want me to go to Australia except to get rid of me. Did you know someone killed a copper outside my flat last night?' He didn't answer. I went on, 'A detective. It's not a little thing, that, Denis; dead detectives in the center of London. Normally you wouldn't be able to move for flatfeet. The street would be full of them. Anyone who'd ever been on that street would normally have been taken down the nick and questioned. If there'd been two people on the street they'd have been questioned separately . . . and so on up to a hundred. And so on until they'd got their answer. They'd have grilled me for days if they'd thought it necessary. You know the score, Denis, and I know it. But though I'd had a copper knifed outside my own front door I was offered none of that aggro.

144

Nothing. Can you believe that?'

Denis still didn't speak. I answered myself

'Of course you can't. Who could believe it? I had a polite morning with a DCS in my local nick chatting about how awful it was for this poor sod to get stabbed, what a pity it was that I didn't seem to know anything about it. All terribly polite. Wanted to keep me till my story checked... they said. *I didn't have a story, Denis!* I could've still been there now for all they needed to let me go. You'd have kept me there.'

Denis stopped walking, arched his back and stretched his arms. His face twisted into a grimace as he stretched. I couldn't work out if it was for physical or psychological discomfort.

'You should've given my name,' he said. 'Or any of us that knew you. We could've sorted it out, Jimmy. Rumour I got was that that geezer had been mugged. News travels fast, eh?'

Denis was proud of his network of contacts, loved to have the inside track on everything.

'Too fast,' I said. 'News travels fast when someone wants it to, know what I mean?'

We'd reached Denis's car, a big new Ford Granada. The metallic paint job glittered under the yellow street lighting.

'Doesn't it smell here?' he said. He leaned against his car roof and turned and grinned into my face. *'Something* smells. You reckon what I've told you smells, I reckon the street does. I have the evidence of my nose to rely on... what have you got, Jimmy?'

I realised Denis really wanted to know the answer. I saw that the grin had been a nervous one. Denis had been fooled and didn't like it.

'It's the rain,' I said. 'It's the rain that makes it smell. It flushes out the drains.'

Denis suddenly stopped grinning and scampered back from the car roof as if it had stung him. He twisted his coat sleeve round to see the back of it in the street lighting.

'Ugh. I've leant in something.'

'It's rainwater. Why don't you listen?'

'Why don't you?' he said, still examining his sleeve. 'Just because some bloke gets mugged in your flat . . .'

'Not "some bloke". A copper. And murdered on my doorstep, not mugged. Stabbed. After he'd interviewed me about the disappearance of an ex-copper friend of mine. The bloke who got stabbed was coming back for more.'

'Still mugged, it could be,' he said and frowned. The frown could have been for what I'd said or it could have been for his jacket.

'Fifteen times, Denis,' I said. 'Stabbed fifteen times. Some mugger, eh? Bit overactive, wouldn't you think? Know a Detective Chief Super Palmer?'

'No.'

'Special Branch. He was trying to convince me it was a mugger as well. Who has Special Branch investigating murders, even the murders of coppers? What do they know about it? You might as well ask a traffic cop to investigate a murder.'

Denis walked away a little, still twisting his sleeve. He stopped under a streetlight.

'I think it's bird's,' he called back to me.

I shrugged.

'I can smell something,' he insisted. 'Ammonia or something. I can smell it on my sleeve.'

'It's the sewers.'

'How do you know he's Special Branch . . . did he tell you?'

'No. I found out.'

'That woman of yours'll get caught one of these days, Jimmy. You're not fair to her.'

'Not Judy. I found out on my own. I didn't fancy him as a regular divisional detective Chief Super, so when they let me go I phoned Special Branch and asked for him. They said he was out of the office.'

Denis took a tissue from his pocket, wet it on his tongue

146

and began to rub his sleeve vigorously. His face looked angry.

'Bird's. I knew it was . . . bloody hell.' He rubbed again, even harder. 'You're too fly, you are, my friend. You're too clever for your own good. You'll get your fingers burnt.'

'Rainwater. Find out who's really offering this dough. Who's putting them up to it. Find out if anybody in the chain has strong links. MOD, Special Branch, army, anything like that. Any of those links. Anything funny. Find out for me and let me know. That's the best thing you could do for me, Denis. And next time they ask you to run a message tell them Jenner's being a bit moody.'

'No.' He shook his head to emphasise it. 'No. Even if you were right I wouldn't look into it any further. Neither should you. If you were right your best bet would be to take the dough and go to Oz. And if you were wrong the best thing to do would be to take the money and go to Oz. Either way your best bet is to pick up the dough and get a suntan. Why fight it?'

Denis O'Keefe climbed in his car and started the engine. He wound open the window. A trickle of water ran down the door surface. Watery fumes flooded from the Granada's exhaust.

'It probably is rain. It's soaked right through.' Denis held his sleeve up. He lowered his arm again. 'If you're right – and I'm not saying you are – you should definitely be doing just what your Special Branch friend has arranged for you to do. I don't think you're right, though. I've made you the offer I was asked to make you. I don't know about any soldiers or Special Branch or none of that caper. An honest citizen asked me to make you an offer and I've made it. What's your answer?'

'Find out who they are for me, Denis.'

He shook his head again and said, 'I've made you the offer. If you don't take it it's your business. Whatever happens, I don't want to know any more. I'm not going digging around for secrets because I don't want to find any. You'd do well to have the same attitude, Jimmy.'

I stood by his open window. He gunned the engine. The smell of burnt hydrocarbons drifted up to me. Then the revs dropped and I could hear water hissing as it dropped on to his exhaust.

'Just find out if someone with a security background put you up to this,' I said.

'No.'

'Denis?'

'What?'

'That stuff on the roof was definitely birdshit.'

He leapt out of the car, narrowly missing me with the outswinging door. I walked away, leaving him standing in the beams of his headlamps. Almost dancing with agitation, he was twisting his coatsleeve round again.

As I walked back to my car I saw the beautiful office worker and her boyfriend again. What did they know or care about Denis and me? Denis was wrong and so was I. The good-looking girl was better off with her hunk. She wasn't wasted on him. She would be on us. You never believe you're going to get any older, then you see some young bird and realise she's going to be wasted on a mug like you, that the gawky kid squiring her round town suits her better than you ever could. Then you're older. Maybe Denis didn't feel like that.

I walked slowly and I took a long way round. It looked like rain again. The towering chimneystacks of Bankside power station were above me, great black columns in the sky. I felt as if they should be belching steam, but they didn't. They just stood like guards over my quiet, dark street.

The rain came. It fell around me in big, thundery drops of water. It hit the pavement with the splat, splat, splat sound of summer evening rain. It wasn't summer and there was no thunder. It wasn't thundery weather, just that type of rain. It soaked into my clothes but I didn't care, I still walked slowly. I wanted the dark and the quiet of the streets. I wanted the sensation of the rain, both the feel and the sound.

When I reached my car I sat in it thinking about the cadaver in Peter's house and thinking about Peter himself. I don't know how long I sat there for, but it was a long time. As I drove past the spot where I'd seen the beautiful girl with her boyfriend I noticed they were still there. I wished I'd had Denis with me. It would've driven him mad.

Chapter Twenty-one

The police who'd been at my flat that morning had been thorough but neat. There was no bloodstain outside my front door, just as there was none of the mess I associate with the scenes of serious crimes inside. The communal hallway didn't look like it had recently had a dead detective in it, just as my own hallway didn't look as if it had recently had a crowd of policemen scrimmaging in it. The atmosphere was unreal and unnatural – maybe as unnatural as Peter Moody's house had been. I was soaked through from the rain. I went into the bathroom, peeled off my damp clothes and dumped them on the floor. Then I put on a dressing gown. The wool scratched my skin, but I liked it. The physical sensation was something I could rely on.

I poured myself a whisky, sat on my cheap old sofa and tried to work out whether anything wasn't back in its right place. My possessions seemed to be all there, only they'd been moved and dusted. I didn't have any collections of Chinese jade or English seventeenth-century silver to check up on ... just my junk. I looked around the room without stirring from the sofa. My junk was safe, only it was as if everything had been shifted one-sixteenth of an inch to the right.

I'd been given the once over, twice over and three times over by absolute experts; none of your run-of-the-mill scenes of crime detectives had been here. Whoever had gone through my junk had treated it as if it was the Chinese jade I didn't have.

I took a long pull at the glass of scotch. I closed my eyes and laid my head on the sofa's back while the liquid burned in my throat. Even that fierce sensation couldn't stop my head feeling dull and my eyelids heavy. I thought about Peter. Why had he involved me in it? And why had I allowed him to? I knew it wasn't the action of a reasonable man to go on ferreting around in Peter's life. I knew I was going to do it, too. The last thing I thought before I went to sleep was that an unreasonable, ferreting man like me had too much to do and mustn't go to sleep.

I woke at five the next morning with an empty whisky glass by my side. I had cold feet, an aching neck and itchy skin from the dressing gown. The only surprise was that I'd slept so long while I had been so uncomfortable. I'd been tired. I still was. I dumped the dressing gown and climbed into bed. I ignored the phone when it rang. Eventually it rang on for so long I had to get up and pull the plug. By eleven a.m. I was ready to get up. By twelve I'd had coffee and a shave (in that order) and felt ready for anything. I'd decided I needed to have a long talk with Clare. I needed some straight answers. The way I saw it, I reckoned she just might be in England. She wasn't running from anything. I wanted to go to Essex and find out, anyway. At four minutes past twelve my doorbell rang.

The man on my doorstep was about twenty-five, with short, cropped hair and thin, pointed features. He had hard grey eyes and very pale skin. He wore a plain grey double-breasted suit under a crumpled, off-white 1940s-style rain mac and he was shaking an umbrella as I opened the door. He looked enough like another of those Special Branch coppers to have me worried. Any unannounced visitor would have had me a little worried. At least this one wasn't dead.

'Mr Jenner?'

He held his hand out and smiled. I took it, mentally scratching the possibility that he was a policeman.

'Tim Ewence. We met on the phone, so to speak. I rang a few times this morning but I thought you must be out.' He laughed and scratched his head. 'So I came over to see you ... that doesn't make sense, does it?'

The grey eyes didn't seem so hard, suddenly. I stepped back from the door.

'No, it doesn't. Come in, Tim Ewence. A trip across London deserves a cup of coffee.'

I gave him some coffee and a seat on the battered sofa. He gave me his story.

'Well, after you were asking yesterday afternoon about who investigated the death of the girl in Peter Moody's house, I started worrying.' He stared into his coffee cup for a while, as if to show me what he looked like worried. 'And I began to think of all the unusual things to do with the girl's death. First of all we still haven't been given the girl's name. The police say they have their suspicions as to who she was but want to confirm it first.'

'Yes?'

'Irregular?' Ewence asked.

'No,' I said. 'You shouldn't need to ask. It's absolutely regular. Imagine the hurt that could be caused if they doled out names without being sure if they were right.'

'Then there is the business of this Superintendent Leigh you phoned me about. You see, no one seems to know him. I don't know him. I know all the detectives in my part of the world and none of them know him, either. That's strange, because they're all as nosey as hell. Also I keep wondering why none of them has been given the job. They're busy, but not that busy. If there were to be another murder tomorrow I have the feeling a local chap would be given the job. Do you see what I mean?'

'Yes. But you're never going to get an answer on that one. I don't suppose for one minute that New Scotland Yard will discuss policing decisions with you or anyone else. They're entitled not to,' I added. It sounded pretty weak when I said it, but I knew that was the answer Ewence's enquiry would bring from NSY at this stage.

He nodded. 'That's what I thought, too. I haven't asked.' He put his cup down and stared at me with those hard grey eyes. 'But I did ask about the p.m. The man who carried out the post-mortem isn't regular, either. He's a Home Office pathologist, okay, and well enough known as such. But he hasn't done anything other than push bits of paper around for ten years. He's a policy man, not an active doctor.'

'How do you know?'

He smiled.

'I have sources, too, Mr Jenner.'

'Jimmy. Call me Jimmy. I keep telling you. What's this bloke called?'

'Collins. He's a Mister, not a Sir, too. Most of them are "Sirs", but not him. E.W. are the initials and he hasn't stuck his nose outside the Home Office for ten years. Yet last week he was called in specially to do the p.m. on the girl in Kensington. I rang the chap who normally does all that work in our area.'

'And?'

He shook his head slowly.

'Wouldn't speak to me. Just like E.W. Collins wouldn't. His secretary suggested I "go through channels", whatever the hell that means. I presumed it meant go and watch the inquest. So I did . . . or at least I meant to. It was supposed to start at ten this morning. When I arrived it was off. Adjourned. A clerk told me a preliminary hearing had accepted evidence of post-mortem examination via a deposition and that the coroner had freed the body for burial last week. Last week!'

He stood up. I grabbed his coffee cup. He looked as if he might break it.

'There's something here, Jenner. I can feel it. I know what you're thinking . . .' He nodded and held his hands in front of his face in a defensive gesture, palms towards me.

'That I'm only a local rag journalist. But I can tell you, what I'm doing here is what every journalist does. I'm trusting my nose. And my nose tells me there's definitely a big story. Of Fleet Street proportions.'

I suddenly saw the ambition reflected in his eager young face. The magic words 'Fleet Street'. Ewence saw this as his ticket to the big time. I had, after all, been introduced to him by Tony Tennyson. If Ewence played his hand right he too could be putting bingo games, scandal and naked girls into print for a huge salary.

'Maybe,' I said. 'Are you telling me the body has been disposed of?'

'Cremated.'

He paced the room and wrung his hands. Then he turned on me.

'Well?'

'Well what?' I said.

'I've given you mine, Jenner. Now give me the story.'

'I don't have a story. Yours fills in a bit, but not much. I used to know Peter Moody, the man who lived in that house. Now he's on the run. We're supposed to get the impression he killed the girl. But I don't believe he did. In fact I know he didn't.

'How? How do you know?'

'Have some more coffee?'

'No. How do you know?'

'How does your editor feel about this?'

He laughed suddenly.

'He told me to drop it. He says leave Sunday scandal journalism to Sunday scandal newspapers.'

'Good advice. That's my advice too.'

He sat again, smiled and stretched out his legs. His rain mac crumpled against my sofa.

'And if I won't take it?'

'I'd say sit around a while while I phone this E.W. Collins character and talk him through his post-mortem.'

'He won't talk.'

'I'm not a journalist,' I said.

Collins was in the book, a Dulwich number. His wife answered and was helpful enough to give me his extension number on the Home Office switchboard. People are like that. It's what keeps me in business. Collins answered on the second ring.

'Hello, Mr Collins. My name's Jenner. I'm a detective. I wonder if I might ask you about the p.m. you did recently in Kensington?'

'What station are you from, Jenner?'

'None, sir. I'm a private investigator.'

'Oh yes. I think I've heard of you. What's the question?' His voice had hardened. His guard was up.

'Well . . . to what did you attribute the cause of death?'

'That's in the public record, Mr Jenner. To save you a bus ride I'll tell you. The girl died of multiple punctures of the heart and lungs and a massive wound in the carotid artery. In layman's terms her chest was full of holes made by stabbing and someone had cut her throat. She died of blood loss. It's all in the public record, as I said.'

'Did you estimate when she died, sir?'

'No. It was impossible given the wildly varying temperatures in the house and the conditions people had to measure body temperatures under.'

'You didn't do the scene of crime temperature measurements yourself?'

'I did not.'

'Were there any other wounds, sir?'

'Other wounds?'

'Yes, other wounds . . . were there any other wounds in the body?' I could have added 'like surgical incisions in her abdomen' but I didn't.

'No, Jenner. There were no other wounds. Now I was given to understand that the person police seek in connection with this is a friend of yours. Is that so?'

'You know a lot about policing for a surgeon, sir.'

'I spend my life with policemen, Jenner.'

155

'Then you won't expect an answer. When was the last post-mortem you held before this one?'

'What's that supposed to mean?'

'It's supposed to mean I'm not a dummy, Collins. You won't get away with holding a spoof p.m. and cremating the evidence. That's for starters. That's for the benefit of you and your friends listening. Goodbye.'

When I put the phone down it rang again immediately.

'Mr Jenner?'

'Yes.'

'Esmerelda Potts here. You don't answer your answering machine's messages. I've been ringing you for over twenty-four hours.'

'Oh yes. Mrs Potts. I'd forgotten all about you.'

'Well, I know. That's what I thought *must* have happened. But we had an appointment, Mr Jenner. Appointments are important, don't you think?'

I sighed. Tim Ewence sat by my side waiting patiently.

'I couldn't make it. I'm sure you and *your* pals know why.'

'I don't have any pals in England, Mr Jenner. That's why I was advised to contact you.'

'Yeah. Well, you contacted me. How did you get my home phone number anyway?'

'You're in the book. I looked you up. Could we make another appointment?'

'A week from today. Lunch.'

'That's a long time.'

'I'm a busy man, Mrs Potts. Lunch a week from today at your hotel is the best I can offer. If you need anyone sooner try another detective. There are plenty in the Yellow Pages. Now will you please get off my phone line.'

I hung up. I could do without 'Mrs Potts' and her coincidental offers of employment.

'What was that all about?' asked Ewence. I'm afraid my mother wouldn't have liked the reply. She'd have said I've spent too much time mixing with coarse people. She'd have been right, too.

Chapter Twenty-two

I was rid of Ewence by half-twelve. By one I was in the public library reading London local newspapers dated for the week before Peter had done his runner.

By half-two I had what I wanted, a report of the discovery of the body of an Iranian woman in a bedsit in Harrow. She had come here to escape the ayatollahs and gassed herself when she'd heard that the revolution had overrun her family. They were now part of the general gore in Iran. She was part of the general gore in England. Charming for them.

I cross-checked the death of the Iranian woman in a dozen newspapers. She turned up on page ten or so of a couple of North London suburban papers, and in one report there was a tiny, passport-type photograph of her. It was the woman I'd found in Peter's house. I had no doubt it was her. The same report, the fullest, said that an inquest had been opened and adjourned and a post-mortem report was expected. *Police are not seeking anyone in connection with the death*. A story told a hundred times a week in every big city, in one form or another. No doubt if I dug a little further I'd find the guy who was post-morteming the girl would be none other than Mr E.W. Collins. I almost didn't want to find out. I waited till the library woman wasn't looking, then tore the piece out of the paper. Tearing quietly in a library is hell on the nerves. When I got up to leave, a tramp hiding behind the *Economist* winked at me. I winked back . . . what could I do?

I went down the road and I hired a Ford Granada automatic, then I drove out to Essex. The car was so big the bonnet seemed to stretch for ten feet in front of me. I felt as I drove that I would crash into everyone. If they'd had another auto for rent I'd have taken it, but I was offered the Granada or nothing. It took me half an hour to drive out to Grays and what seemed like another half an hour to park the car.

When I finally managed to settle the Granada down I walked over the road, pulled open the door of a rusting blue Mini parked at the kerbside and said to Tim Ewence, 'Don't follow me. And if you do be kind enough to be good at it. You're the sort of fellow who could lead to a decline in the standards of tailing. Anyway, where's your false moustache? Don't you have any work to do? Doesn't your boss pay you wages to go about his business?'

He shrugged inside the off-white mackintosh. 'Which do you want answered?'

'This one. Are you going to stop following me?'

'Not that I can promise it. What did you find in the library?'

'So it was *you* reading the *Economist*?'

'*Economist*?'

'Don't lie, o master of disguise. Don't make out you don't know what the *Economist* is. Are you going to let me alone?'

'I'm afraid not . . . at least tell me what you found in the library.'

I shook my head. 'Do your own research. But if you're going to insist on following me hang on, buster. You can chauffeur me and save us both some petrol and some trouble.'

He pointed at the Granada.

'I'm not insured to drive that heap.'

'Then this heap'll have to do.'

Another Mini. Another sore-elbow-and-knee session. I resolved to mix with a more affluent class of person.

I looked up Clare's address in the local council offices and then Tim Ewence and I pottered around on the marshes for an hour, getting lost and finding ourselves at my direction. There are an awful lot of big hedges and narrow lanes around that part of the world, and not too many road signs. The lanes all look the same and seem to have been designed to let the visitor see as many hedges as he or she would like from the comfort of his or her own car. The lanes don't *go* anywhere. Every now and then I'd manage to bring us to a point where we were facing marshes, the river, a council estate, a farm or any combination thereof. Then Ewence would have to make the reverse gear earn its living.

Eventually we came by Clare's house via a mixture of good luck, divining and serendipity. Navigation never entered into the matter.

It was late afternoon, becoming autumn dusk. The house was a big red job with herringbone brick, antique doors, carriage lamps and pink gravel. Just the kind of place and just the kind of style for the successful businessman/woman. There was a view across the River Thames estuary, just as she'd promised all those years ago. It was a pretty house okay, but remote for a single girl. There were reeds behind the house and hedges before it and then farmland. A big new blue tractor was bashing across a field near the house. No doubt the driver was hoping to look as if he was doing something rural.

'Drive straight past,' I said.

I hadn't had a plan. I suppose I'd originally thought to just go and knock on the door and ask for her. When we had come upon Clare's house I'd dumped even that rudimentary plan. I'd found myself looking at one of the most clumsy stake-outs I'd ever seen. First of all there was the tractor being driven by a man who clearly didn't want to go far from the house. Why? How much furrowing can one chain of earth take? Then there was a British Telecom tent, a red-

and-white nylon job stretched over steel hoops. Any boy scout could tell how you always face the door of a tent away from the prevailing wind. Any detective using one as a cover, however, needs the tent door to face whatever he wants to watch. That meant the 'Telecom engineers' had to huddle in their tent with the door facing into the prevailing easterly and their little blue faces peering through the flaps. Tim Ewence drove slowly by. I felt like sticking my tongue out at them.

We drove on. I had a problem. Anyone with two legs would've come back across country, wriggling up to the house so they could see what was going on. Not me, though. My wriggling days were over. Same for my cross-country hiking days. That was the problem. Ewence was going to be the answer.

'I wonder if you'd do a bit of yomping for me, Tim?'

'What's yomping?'

The correct answer, the answer of a prudent man, would have been 'no'.

I sat in a lane a couple of miles away, holding his coat and listening to Radio Essex. I made him walk that far because you can't just park round the corner. It's got to be a realistic distance. So Ewence had a nice country walk while I had to listen to the car radio. Now I know all about the personal and private problems of housewives in Grays, Basildon and Billericay . . . and they've got some steamers.

Ewence came back a couple of hours later. I was standing next to the car and getting blown around by the wind. It's always windy in that part of Essex. I was surrounded by darkness. There wasn't a house in sight. Ewence staggered up from the gloom, like some marsh spirit. He was muddy and he didn't smell too good, but he was pleased with himself.

'It was even better covered than you thought, Jenner. There were men all round the house and they all seemed to be armed. They weren't making an obvious display of the arms, though.'

'Describe them.'

He described a lot of detective clones. I didn't recognize any, or I recognized them all. He described a woman, though, and I recognized her. Clare.

'Anyone else?'

'No.'

'Did she seem to be under arrest or held there in any way?'

'No, she seemed free. Quite the opposite to being under arrest, I would say.'

He pulled open the car door and flopped inside. I went and sat in the driver's seat.

'Why's that?' I said.

'They seemed to be protecting her. When she came out of the house they walked around with her but they weren't watching her. They were watching everywhere else.'

'What was she walking around for if they were so scared?'

'Ah . . . this is the *pièce de résistance*.'

'English please. I'm off frog at the moment.'

'The best bit. She was getting in a car. That's what she was walking for. They all got in cars and drove off. They're not there any more.'

I turned the courtesy light on. I wanted to see this boy. He sat beside me grinning. With his mud-smeared face and his now filthy clothes he looked like a mudlark might under the old Waterloo Bridge.

'All of them?'

'Even the telephone men. The place is empty. We can drive round there and have a look if you want.'

'Yeah. We'll drive *near* there, then take a look. I don't want to be caught parked in her drive.'

The wind buffeted his little Mini and Tim Ewence sat there looking as gung ho as a man ever would. A woman on the radio complained about her husband. A newspaper on the back seat of the Mini proclaimed Fun and Frolics with Our Very Own Fiona if I could only get this question right. I never can understand the question, let alone get it right. Fun and Frolics with the Fionas of This World are Off the Menu for Me.

Clare's friends seemed to be playing for keeps and I didn't really feel like driving up to one of their safe houses and having a nose-around. I might get the nose bitten off. I had to do it, though. I had to have a look.

I was scared. I controlled my voice, otherwise it would have given me away.

'Okay. Got a torch?'

He pulled an old-fashioned black rubber lamp from under his seat.

'You drive, Ewence,' I said.

He just grinned again and leapt out. The wind pulled the car door against my hand as I got out. He drove.

Chapter Twenty-three

We made sure again that we didn't park too close to Clare's house, but we didn't crawl across any fields either. I got Tim Ewence to put his Mini in a field entrance with the lights turned off. I didn't see any reason to expose him to the wrath of either Clare's minders or her possible employers so I told him to relax his body for half an hour, tune into the local radio and have a good listen. I would be back soon: meanwhile a man could apprise himself of some very interesting bits of information by listening to the radio hereabouts, I told him. Tim Ewence turned the machine on, got an earful of supermarket music, then an ad for disinfectant, and gave me a funny look.

I left him with his muddy clothes, his grin and his rusting Mini. When I looked back from the lane Tim Ewence had his Mini's courtesy light switched on again and was busily scribbling pencil marks in one of those spiral-bound reporter's notebooks they all use. He wasn't just some chancer, Ewence. I reckoned he'd been to journalism school and he'd bought the whole ticket. He really wanted to be a proper journalist. If manners maketh a man, tools form the artisan.

I plodded along the dark lane. The air was full of the smell of bio-degradables and the noises animals make while they're getting their nightshirts on. I hate both. Clare's house was in darkness, too, then some celestial lighting technician arranged for moonlight so that the pink gravel drive shone brilliantly for just a second. Then the light was gone and the gravel was crunching lightly under my shoes.

I walked round the back. There was a locked double garage with a security padlock. The downstairs windows were all sashes and they had pretty serious locks on them, too. The back door had mortices and the front door was like the front door of a bank, only it didn't seem to have a letter-box. I couldn't see alarms. There's not much point in having alarms when the nearest neighbor is getting on for half a mile off, and anyway, Clare would not have found it convenient to have any unwanted visitors discovered by regular police.

There were French windows at the back of the house, old-fashioned ones made of lots of little panes to match the sashes. I went for those. They're impossible to make really secure without a steel bar across them, and anyway I wasn't subtle. I just leaned my shoulder where the doors join. A couple of good pushes, then when that didn't work I took a couple of paces and gave it the same treatment. The wood splintered and I was on my hands and knees on Clare's drawing room floor cursing my false foot and my lack of balance.

I picked myself up and listened. There was no sound. I switched on Ewence's torch and sneaked around the ground floor. Clare's minders had been thorough. They'd even taken the rubbish with them. I went through kitchen cupboards, around the back of the gas stove, through every drawer on the ground floor . . . nothing. About when I was finished on the ground floor Ewence came along and half-scared me to death by poking around outside the house.

'What are you doing?' he called to me through the broken French windows. 'You've been twenty minutes.'

'I have broken into someone's house and I am in the process of seeing if there's anything worth stealing. Now if you want to have the rest of that journalist's career, why don't you go and write up your notes again? Otherwise stick around and get six months in Pentonville with me if I get caught.'

'You mean it, don't you?' he said. 'Would you really steal from here if you had to?'

I couldn't see his face. I wanted to. What I was doing had scared him. It scared me too, only I wasn't allowed to show it.

'Go back to the car, Tim.'

'What would you do if you were caught?'

'Go back to the car.'

He went.

I turned my back on him and made my way upstairs. The stairs creaked, even though they were thickly carpeted. I pushed open the door of the first room I came to. Heavy curtains had been drawn. I was in utter darkness. I ran my lamp over the room. It was a bedroom. I stopped the beam on a man's face. He was sitting absolutely motionless in a small armchair. His lips were drawn back in a snarled expression. A click behind me, the light came on and strong hands held my arms, one man on each side. The man in the small armchair relaxed his face and said, 'Jenner. What the hell are you doing here?'

'I was just going to ask you that, Mr Palmer.'

Detective Chief Superintendent Palmer waved at the men by my side to free me.

'Waiting for someone. As you can guess the person wasn't you.'

I heard the engine of Tim's Mini start up. It was muffled by the curtains and closed window, but distinctive.

'Who's that?' Palmer said.

'I don't know,' I said.

The man on my right spoke. 'There were two men with you, Mr Jenner. I think Mr Palmer wants to know who they are.' He was a tall, dark-haired man in his early thirties with the clothes and mannerisms of a minor bank functionary, and he took hold of my elbow in a grip like a mechanic's vice. 'I think you should tell him.'

The elbow hurt. I said nothing. I was looking at the fireplace. The grate was painted matt black and someone had put dried flowers in there. On the mantelpiece were some china figures, a 1930s clock which had stopped and a small framed photograph of a woman and a man.

The grip tightened. He had a nerve inside my elbow.

'I said I think you should tell him. It would only be polite,' said the dark-haired man.

The man and woman in the photograph were somewhere foreign and they were sitting on a wall in front of a big castle. It wasn't a very good photograph. The sun was behind the castle and behind the couple, so their features were unnaturally darkened and difficult to see. The man could have been anyone. At least, he could have been any North European or American male over sixty. The woman was Clare. They were arm in arm. The castle was like castles are. Made of stone. Big. Impressive. Impregnable. That's the point of them. The castle, like the man, was North European.

'Who?' repeated the man with the grip. He sounded angry. The elbow hurt too much. They'd find out soon anyway. I told them.

'Ewence. Tim Ewence. He's a journalist. He doesn't know anything. And it was just one man, not two.'

The man at my side let go of my elbow.

'Two,' Palmer said with conviction. 'We saw them.'

'Mine was young, blond with short-cut hair, cheeky-looking and wearing a white mac. He's the only person I brought with me. What was the second like?'

'Bring the car round,' Palmer said softly into a small radio. There was a crackle for a reply. I couldn't understand it.

'Now,' Palmer said. 'Do as I say. Do it right now. It's all gone wrong here. And where's Martin?'

The radio crackled unrecognisably again.

Palmer said, 'Couldn't see him properly. It was dark. Turn the lights off please, Jenner.'

He stood and pulled the curtains. We could see what I took to be the Mini's lights in the distance, moving fast along a country lane. Palmer threw open the window. We could hear the Mini's engine clearly now, carrying across the marshes. Then the lights disappeared. The sound didn't for a few seconds more. I could hear Palmer's two men scuffling around in the road outside.

A voice came from the lawn below us. I recognized it as belonging to the man who'd held my elbow.

'No one. Not a sausage.'

I sat on the bed. My elbow ached.

Palmer said, 'And Martin?'

'No sign, sir. He's not where we left him. His car's gone, too.'

'Find him. The chap in the white mac . . . what's his name?' He looked at me.

'Ewence,' I said. 'Tim Ewence.'

'Tell them he's a journalist called Tom Ewart,' Palmer called.

'Tim Ewence! Are you bloody deaf?'

'Keep your shirt on, Jenner. Don't know the index number of the Mini, do you?'

I shook my head. He strode across the room and turned the lights on again.

I said, 'This boy's a journalist, Palmer. He knows there's a story here and he wants it. You'll have to come up with something good. You'll have to convince his paper. This is about to go public.'

'There's no merit, Jenner, in telling people things they already know.' There were bags under Palmer's eyes and his morose, hang-dog expression looked tired suddenly, instead of just calm.

'That's right. But you people seem to think there's no end of merit in plain lying. You think there's no end of merit in corrupting judicial procedures and in spinning yarns to blokes like me and Ewence. You think we're all mugs. Maybe we are . . . but you, mate, are about to come unstuck in a big way.'

He rubbed his bristly jaw. 'I don't think you would have done very well if you'd stayed on the job, you know. You've no sense of the diplomacy a policeman needs from time to time. I think you were well suited to walking the beat.'

'I'm fine. I've come to terms with my lot, Palmer, but how will walking the beat again suit you?'

He smiled sourly.

'Not even remotely funny.'

A big car crunched the gravel below us. It was showing no lights. Palmer went on to the stairs and held a muttered conversation with one of his assistants. He came back and waved at me impatiently, as if I'd been in on the conversation. 'Come on, then. We'll go and make a housecall.'

We went downstairs. Palmer slipped into the back seat of the car and waved that I should do the same. He seemed totally relaxed. Once inside I tried my doorhandle and found the 'childproof' buttons had been pushed over. It could only be opened from the outside. The windows were electric too, controlled from the driver's position. There seemed to be a dozen men milling about on the lawn and in the road outside. I wondered where they'd come from. The big car was the only one I'd heard drive up. I realised that I'd been blundering around Clare's house earlier in full sight of a lorryload of coppers. Perhaps Palmer was right about me. Maybe I was well suited to walking the beat. Once.

The driver turned on the lights and pulled away with no command from Palmer. Rain began to fall heavily before we'd gone a mile. Palmer closed his eyes as if to sleep before we made it back to the main London/Southend road, the A13. If he wasn't sleeping he was acting well. I tried a bit of light conversation with the driver but he was one of nature's surly types. He wouldn't even co-operate when I asked him would he turn on the radio, so that instead of listening to Humphrey Lyttelton's jazz program I had to make do with whistling a lot of tunes I reckoned were appropriate. Eventually, when we'd come into the yellow-lit streets of the great metropolis, he put the radio on. By then it was too late, though. So we had to listen to a so-called 'news' station rambling on about gardening and cooking. No doubt if they'd kept going we'd have got to the inevitable phone-in. Instead we got to St James's Park, turned into a side road off Birdcage Walk and pulled up outside a Queen Anne terraced house. Palmer opened his eyes just as the car stopped and within a few seconds was on the pavement brushing down his crumpled clothes with his flat hands and straightening his tie. For some reason unknown to me I found myself brushing my clothes down in the same way, as if we were going to meet a cabinet minister or an archbishop. As if I was embarrassed to be me.

I followed Palmer into the Queen Anne house. There was a brass plaque on the door and the names of lots of companies, dozens of them, were inscribed on the plaque. Inside a highly polished commissionaire sat behind a highly polished desk; a small, fat, grey-looking man I just knew was the prototype commissionaire. He was pompous and self-conscious as pompous men are, pulling at his cuffs and straightening his tunic. Once he might have been a Company Sergeant Major in the British Army. More likely he'd been a pay clerk and claimed to be a CSM. Nowadays he would be a church warden and inspector of persons like myself. Nothing would go past this commissionaire. He had a highly polished desk, a highly polished radio and a highly polished but very small TV set. I had the impression the TV set was tuned to the outside of the house, not the BBC.

The commissionaire looked me over as if I were a non-too-recently-dead fish, then nodded at Palmer. Neither man said a word, both men seemed to share a sneer at my expense. The commissionaire pushed a buzzer and a young fellow came rushing along a corridor behind him, clack-clacking in steel-tipped leather shoes as he walked.

'Chief Inspector Palmer, so pleased to see you.'

Palmer didn't even correct him. The young man had sticking-up mouse-coloured hair, a wan face and a too-ready smile. He wore a chalk-striped suit, a sharply pressed white shirt and one of those ties that are only for the knowing, covered in stripes and indicating the wearer has either been a Major in the Brigade of Guards or a Pom Pom organiser for the Dagenham Girl Pipers.

'Winter. Charles Winter. You're Mister Jenner, aren't you?'

I smiled and shook his hand.

'It's my limp,' I said.

Winter smiled his smile, somewhere between an estate agent's and a politician's. The lips bared and the grey eyes stared straight into my eyes. 'I haven't seen you walk,' he said. 'No doubt I shall. Let me show you upstairs to our appointment.'

'Are you an MP?' I said. You don't have to be wearing a fancy tie to tease.

'Me?' He looked quizzically at Palmer. 'Good heavens, no. I'm a servant. Just a servant . . . a mere *apparatchik*.'

'What's that?' I said, though I knew. You can buy the *Tribune* even round our way.

'It's Russian,' said Palmer. 'Like Kulak and Tovarich.'

'Come this way.' Winter led us towards a grand staircase. An enormous chandelier sparkled above us. 'I don't look Russian, do I? Jolly good cover.' And he laughed. It sounded as a dying donkey might. 'Russian . . . *Russian*.'

'You'll have to slow down,' I said. 'Someone's stolen my stick.' I'd left it in Tim Ewence's Mini, though I wasn't telling them.

Winter marched on to the head of the stairs, then turned and said triumphantly, 'You'll have to see a policeman about that.' He brayed again. 'Ask the Chief Inspector.' Then he clacked off to a pair of huge double doors. The doors were polished mahogany, old and blackened varnish, crazed from years of cracking. The walls around them were painted in light blue with a dark blue oil-drag. Another, smaller chandelier shone above Winter. He opened the doors wide and said to someone I couldn't see, 'Messrs Palmer and Jenner are here.'

Part Four

The Lush Life

Chapter Twenty-four

The room beyond the double doors was much as I'd have expected. Its floor was covered in a plain, grey-coloured, wool carpet. The walls, like the walls of the hallway outside, were painted in the blue paint – only this time without the oil-drag. There were some badly drawn but old English horse paintings on the walls. A cheap chandelier shone above us. Along one wall was a long, folding Indian screen with an electronic whirr coming from behind it. At the far end of the room tall French windows – half as tall again as a man – led only to the darkness of the house's garden and then to St James's Park. The chandelier, Winter, Palmer and myself were reflected in the glass of the long windows. So was a large oval mahogany table with papers spread upon it and dining chairs of the same wood drawn up around it.

At one of the dining chairs sat a woman. I hadn't expected a woman.

'I believe you know Mrs Black, Jenner,' said Winter.

'Er . . . in a way, yes.'

'Jimmy, Jimmy Jenner. Pleased you could make it.'

Emma Johnson ignored Palmer and Winter, half-stood and held her hand out to me so that I might shake it, then changed her mind and used the hand instead to indicate I should sit on a dining chair. I sat. So did the others. Palmer immediately seemed to allow his attention to drift out of focus. It was only an impression, I was sure, and it was an impression we were all meant to get.

Emma Johnson tossed her head of grey hair and smiled. Charles Winter made an answering, polite smile to Emma's. Then his gaze drifted down to the polished table-top and the smile faded. Emma cleared her throat and both men looked up, sharply. Emma was in charge. She was wearing the same sort of formal business suit as Charles Winter, only hers was a skirt suit, minus the chalk stripes. She wore it as if she'd been born in it, and her relationship with my companions was the relationship of one who gives orders and is used to giving orders; that much was clear. She was their boss. Yes, Emma was clearly in charge.

'Let's talk, Jimmy.'

'Yes,' I said. 'Let's talk. First of all, what should I call you?'

'Black. The other was . . .' She paused, then smiled. 'A deception. A necessary one. But to business . . . I think our friend here, Detective Chief Superintendent Palmer, was both surprised and upset to find you trampling down his flowers, if you see what I mean.'

Palmer nodded almost imperceptibly. No, he hadn't liked finding me in Fobbing. I can't say as I was over the moon about finding him there.

'I think we all feel it's turned everything into a bit of a pig's ear, hasn't it?' said Emma Black.

Nods from both Winter and Palmer this time.

'When I heard what had been going on in Essex, I thought you'd want to talk. I expect you'll be wanting what's known as a "full and frank conversation" with us. We'll certainly want one with you.'

'Good,' I said. 'Something like that's called for. I think you or some of the people in your department might end up having what you're pleased to call full and frank conversations with other people, too. Newspaper editors. Members of Parliament. Maybe even non-spooky parts of the Metropolitan Police. I'm sure the Commissioner would be very interested to know of the activities of some of his boys.'

She frowned. Palmer was impassive. Winter stared at his hands. Emma tossed a padded envelope across the oval table-top to me. 'We'd better start with this. I would have had it delivered to you tomorrow anyway.'

My name and address were on the front of the padded envelope. Inside was a clear plastic bag and in the clear plastic bag was my blue handkerchief; the handkerchief I'd used to swab down the mirror in Peter Moody's Kensington home. There was a typewritten laboratory report in the padded envelope, too, and a bill for services rendered. The lab report ran to two closely typed pages. It was written in the usual gobbledegook scientists use but I'd expected that. I'd also expected one clear phrase. I got it.

'The subject seems to have been soaked at some time in a substance which our analysis indicates appears to be pig's blood.'

Seems, indicates, appears. Don't stick your necks out, boys.

'You've been reading my letters,' I said.

Emma said nothing. I threw her the bill.

'You can pay that for the pleasure of reading my report. By the way, does this ring any bells?' I pushed her the newspaper piece on the dead Iranian girl.

Emma read the piece, gave me an uncomfortable smile, stood and said, 'Very good, Mr Jenner...Charles, I expect Mr Palmer hasn't eaten. Why don't you treat him to one of your watering holes? I'm sure he'd like it.'

Palmer nodded solemnly to indicate that he would like it but said nothing.

'It's a bit late, Mrs Black.'

'Well, find him somewhere.'

It wasn't a request. They left quietly. The electronic whirring was the only sound in the room for a few seconds after they'd gone, then Emma stood and padded up and down the carpeted floor.

'Drink?'

'Scotch.'

She disappeared behind the Indian screen, came back with an amber drink for me and a clear one for herself.

'Water?'

I shook my head.

'Where shall we start? Where would you like? With the handkerchief?'

'No. Start in the Metropolitan Police. Start with two young coppers in 1973. Start by telling me whether Peter was one of yours then.'

Emma sipped her clear drink and sat.

'You obviously think I look older than I am. Nobody was "one of yours" in those days as far as I was concerned. I was a very minor character. A slip of a girl.' She allowed herself a smile. 'When you met Moody first he was genuinely a policeman . . . have you signed the Official Secrets Act by the way?'

'Yes.'

'Recently?' she insisted.

I sighed. 'It's not a tetanus booster, you know? I've signed it. I understand the implications. Have you read the law on perversion of the course of justice? Has your pet pathologist Mr Collins read the law on perjury?'

Emma sorted through the papers on the oval table and came up with a small green one.

'I fetched this up especially for you this evening, once I knew you were coming.' She pushed the form and a black ballpoint pen before me. I ignored them.

'What was Peter genuinely before he was genuinely a policeman?'

'My understanding is that he had been a soldier. Really, Jenner, you knew him better than I did when he was younger. Why ask me?'

'Was he some sort of funny in Ulster?'

'I don't think so. I think before he left the army he was a desk chap in Military Intelligence. It's a common job for soldiers.'

Lie, I thought. What about Judy's researches in the police computer?

'And after?'

'I imagine that Her Majesty's Government decided it had better use for the young Mr Moody's talents than keeping order on the streets of East London.'

'And the drinking? The theft of the smoked mackerel?'

'Smoked mackerel?'

'All right, shoplifting.'

Emma raised an eyebrow and took back her unsigned green Official Secrets Act form. She tapped it with her forefinger.

'What I'm more interested in is what you're up to, Jenner. Why were you in Clare Fisher's house?'

'Visiting.'

'Did you find the person you were visiting?'

'No. I found Palmer. Who was he looking for?'

'You'll have to ask him, Jenner. Why were you in Moody's house that night?'

'The night you people put the cadaver there? Simple. Because he asked me to go and meet him. Before then I hadn't seen or heard of him for years.'

Emma shook her head. 'If you'd only picked up the phone and rang the police . . . like anyone else would have done. There'd have been no problem if you'd just done that.'

'For you.'

'For anyone except Moody, and he's made his own problems. You were a nasty shock. We didn't know who the hell you were and we didn't know what you were up to. You should have just dialled 999.'

'Too fast,' I said. 'Go back. Was all the drinking after Peter left the police an act?'

'I believe so. You've finished your whisky. More?'

She went behind the Indian screen to pour it. I thought of Peter sitting on the little wall of the piazza outside Fenchurch Street station, surrounded by his school of drunks, and I thought of me 'bumping' into him. Who'd asked me to travel out via Fenchurch Street? Clare, of course. Clare. Who just a few days ago asked me to get Peter out of England? Clare. Clare who met me in Paris.

'So I was set to provide a cover for him . . . what about Clare Fisher? Is she his case officer? Recruiter? Just what?' I called.

'No water, right?'

'Right. And Clare?'

'Clare was an outsider. Worked for and with Peter.'

'And how about Peter now?'

She was silent. The whirring behind the screen became clear again. She tapped the green form again.

'I don't have *carte blanche* you know, Jimmy Jenner.' We both laughed. Then she cried, 'Oh damn!' And leapt up. Emma rushed behind the screen and clicked a switch.

'Tape recorder,' she said when she came back. 'Reel-to-reel job. We use it to record all our conversations in here. It's a lot of nonsense really. Started with the last holder of my post. I bet you'd think we'd use very sophisticated stuff, bugs and all that nonsense. Would you like a cigar?'

'No. No cigar and no I didn't know what sort of stuff you'd use to record these sorts of conversations. Or even that you would do it.'

She pulled a cigar from her handbag, lit it with a match from a truly enormous box of household matches, then puffed angrily for a few seconds.

'I'm giving them up. It puts me in a foul mood. Here.' She pulled the Indian screen back to reveal an ugly little government issue side-table. The table supported coffee mugs, an electric kettle, a jar of instant coffee and the squalid detritus which goes with instant coffee-making in an office. Beside the side-table was a truly massive Tandberg reel-to-reel with a bottle of scotch and some glasses perched on top.

'There's our high-technology super spy kit. One old-fashioned tape recorder. Half the time the tape breaks, the other half the machine's broken. Pathetic, isn't it?'

I thought that the big reel-to-reel was pathetic, but that it was for show. Switching off an old tape recorder while another would be silently recording behind a wall, say, would be well within Emma's range of mendacity.

'How about Peter Moody,' I said. 'Are you in charge of him?' I meant 'Are you at the root of this mess?' She must have known I meant it, too.

'Uh . . . Moody. Yes. He was working for us in America.' She puffed at the cigar in silence for a few seconds. 'We brought him back to Europe and had him run the same sort of operation for us here. Then things went wrong.'

'How?'

'The first thing was he started making a thing with Clare Fisher.' Emma Black's brow furrowed. She didn't approve of 'things'. 'Very unprofessional, that. It lasted for about eighteen months. Then he began to drink. I'm afraid drinking wasn't half of it, though. Our people began to suspect him of working on his own account. That wasn't the nature of the bargain he had with us, Jimmy. He had a whole operation of his own going, and his only loyalty appeared to be to money. We don't run things like that. We were about to close in on him when two weeks ago Moody jumped.'

She puffed her cigar. I said into the smoke, 'Where did he go?'

'Nowhere at first. Just went to ground somewhere in England. London, I think. Then you helped him to France. That was no problem. We wanted to follow through his trail of contacts. Then he went to Germany.'

'Which?'

'Since we'd lost him it didn't matter. I imagine it would be first West and then East. At some stage he was going to end up in the East. People like him do. East Germany, Czechoslovakia. Maybe Hungary or even Austria. Austria's a good place to run a business like his. If he went to the East proper, everything would be organised to go on as before as far as the subject is concerned. The only difference would be that his dealings would be organised for the benefit of the host country.'

'Where did you lose him?'

'France, Strasbourg.'

'Has he taken anything with him?'

'Yes. His head and what's in it. His contacts. A few million dollars and a lot of our self-respect. In our business it's probably the last which will end up being the most expensive. We want him, Jimmy.'

'And the "murdered" girl? The one I didn't ring 999 over ... what on earth was all that supposed to achieve?'

She smiled briefly. 'One of our people's ideas. And a brilliant idea, too, considering the timescale. I can't say that I went willingly into the Burke and Hare business, but you know this one was good. It was meant to make him look like a common criminal, a man with fantasies about being involved in defence and intelligence work. The idea was that, if it looked as if Moody was a habitual drunk, a man who'd been thrown out of the Metropolitan Police for theft and finally had had to run out on his own country because he'd murdered a girlfriend in a drunken rage, maybe people ... maybe he would be discounted as a lunatic with delusions of grandeur. With a stinking record, quite a bit of dud information and a weak cover story, you can make the best of people look totally unreliable. That's what we were doing. We were trying to make Peter Moody look, as our transatlantic cousins would say, "totally out to lunch".'

She blew smoke out and stared into the plume wistfully. 'We had him bang to rights, as I'm sure you and Detective Chief Superintendent Palmer would put it, and we had England tied up tighter than a duck's arse. Nothing would go in or out without our knowing. It was wonderful. We had a team of tame coppers all ready and waiting for the off as soon as someone discovered the body and reported it. All we needed was someone to find it and call the police. Moody must have known.'

'How?'

'I think he must have observed. He certainly has no contacts here now. Just Palmer and myself. I certainly didn't tell Moody and Palmer has no reason to. No, he'd seen what we were up to and used you as a spoiler . . . a spanner in the works. You were especially a spanner in the works when you simply buzzed off without reporting what you'd seen. Up until then I thought we'd done well. We'd had to have something that would turn up in a minor way in press reports. We'd had to have something that would convince his friends across the North Sea that Peter Moody was just a drunken slob who'd murdered his girl. Well, we had it, we made it happen. And we achieved it all within twenty-four hours. Then, courtesy of you, it turned into a débâcle.'

'Hang on a minute. Don't blame me.'

'No. Blame fate and Moody. In that order. Only two types of people would have smelt a rat in that mews house. Doctors and policemen. Moody arranged for you to stumble on it, fate was that no one beat you to it.'

'And I presume you knew Clare contacted me the next day?'

'Of course. He wouldn't contact you direct. It had to be through his girlfriend. We wanted to find him. That's why Palmer was at Clare Fisher's house tonight. Palmer had convinced her Peter Moody was dirty. She told Palmer that Moody was due to come and see her there. I'll find out later how we fluffed it . . . *except*, Jimmy Jenner, except *you* turn up again, spoiling it all and frightening Moody off. What I need to know tonight is, was that a coincidence?'

'Yes. You must know no one's phoned me. . . .'

Emma stood abruptly, interrupting my sentence. She threw open the huge French windows and stepped on to a small balcony, guarded by iron railings. A cold blast of air burst into the room. It seemed even to shake the chandelier. It shook me. I stood too. Without our reflections and those of the lights inside the room I could see into the darkness of the garden and then the park. The rain had stopped. Headlamps of cars skimmed along the slick surface of the road, shining light back up into the trees.

I drank my whisky and went over to Emma. She rubbed her face with her hands, turned to me and said, 'I don't care a damn about your phone. Your arrival at the mews house put the cap on any chance of our plan working. I can take it that he was using you the once, in Kensington. It set us a problem but one we could solve. Who were you? An entire night in the files gave you a clean bill of health. I can take that. I can deal with it. What Moody did to you there he could have done to anyone. But then suddenly you're helping Moody export himself to France. Is he using you or what? I'm forced to wonder. I decide for the moment that Jenner's okay, Jenner's just been fooled by Peter Moody. So have lots of other people. I put you out of my mind, so to speak, as a coincidence. Next thing we know, one of Palmer's fellows is murdered on your doorstep. Let's be *really* charitable, Jimmy. Let's say "well, that fellow Jenner's been running with a rough crowd, and they chose him, not him them. Let's decide to give Jimmy Jenner the benefit of the doubt for a third time." There's nothing in your past to make us believe you hadn't been simply used in each of those situations.'

She walked back inside, shaking her head slowly. She turned and spoke to me with a raised voice. I wondered if she'd gone back in to make sure microphones picked her up clearly. 'Until tonight, Jimmy Jenner. Tonight you walked straight into a trap we laid for your friend, springing the trap and scaring him off. Another coincidence? It would be a dereliction for me to believe that. I think you have some arrangement, some relationship with Moody. What is it? What's the basis of your work for him? Does he have a debt you owe him, some hold . . . what?'

'We have none. I haven't laid eyes on the man for years. The business of me being at Clare Fisher's house tonight was a simple coincidence.'

Emma shook her head.

'No. Not coincidence. Not the slightest chance. The kindest light I can put on you is that you're too straight to be anything other than Moody's dupe. Someone he was using. He sent you there, right? To find out if the coast was clear. On the subject of using, Jimmy Jenner, I should point out that he has done that to you several times to my certain knowledge. I think that's something we've demonstrated here tonight.'

Using. When Emma Black said that word it sounded as if it was the purpose of the whole conversation. Using. She hadn't really been interested in my answers at all. Only in arriving at that word. Using. It could have been true, I thought, but there's more than one way of using a man. It might suit someone to have me believe Peter was using me. The same thought, that Peter was 'using' her, must have been sold to Clare for her to tell Palmer that Peter was coming there.

'If you thought I was one of Moody's intimates, why did you get me out of the chokey in Dover?'

'Because Timpkins and Mason really thought you were the opposition. They thought that you must've been more than a mere victim of Moody's duplicity. They're not as kind as I am.'

'Timpkins isn't so *anything* now. Why did you come personally to free me?'

'I wanted to make sure Timpkins and Mason weren't right. You *just* might have been. But you and that cute wife of yours...no. And with your record? You were the real thing. A small-time private detective who had the misfortune to have acquainted himself once with Peter Moody. Hard luck, Jenner.'

'And Clare Fisher?'

Emma walked back to my side on the little balcony before she answered, and when she did she spoke quietly and intimately. 'She has flown the nest with him. When she didn't run out with him at first I thought they'd lost contact. But tonight cleared that up once and for all. Clare Fisher's in it with him. No doubt about it now.'

That part of Emma Black's story was rubbish, I knew. When I had arrived at the house Clare had gone, and Palmer knew it. He was waiting for someone else. If he knew she'd been waiting for Peter and had gone away with Peter he'd hardly have been staking out the house on the off-chance that they'd come back having forgotten something. What would it be, a toothbrush? A forgotten Visa card? That part of Emma's story, a story which was already full of inconsistencies, was too silly for words. Palmer had been waiting for Peter and Peter was not with Clare.

Emma stood close by my side and we both stared across the park towards the luminous aura of the night-lit Buckingham Palace. Standing next to Emma, looking at the top of her grey head as she stared into the night, I almost believed her. She had managed to make her face seem so hurt by all this deviousness going on around her. As if, somehow, she had no part in it all. As if this woman who had introduced herself first of all as my self-appointed solicitor and saviour, as if this woman who appeared to have control of a state security department and openly admitted to using and abusing people to its ends, as if she was utterly incapable of displaying the kind of deviousness with which she was surrounded. I was a more likely liar than her. I was a more likely spy. She was honourable. We were in England. The centre of the democratic universe, the centre of fair play, the centre of non-lying and non-cheating government.

Some hopes. Emma Black was a poker player, and the only hand she certainly *wasn't* holding was the one she was telling me about.

And I almost wanted to believe her. Emma's story almost held water. It would have been the quickest and neatest solution to what was already an ugly and messy situation. But 'almost' leaks, though it might leak a little more slowly than a story that doesn't hold water at all. It leaks.

The doorlock clicked in the room behind us and Winter came in.

'Hello. Urgent message, I'm afraid, Mrs Black.'

'Of course. We've just about finished here, Jimmy Jenner, haven't we?'

I said nothing.

'So you can see,' Emma went on, 'what's required. From you and your journalist friend. A little self-control is called for. Matters of state are very delicate, and a real problem could develop for no good reason except that people were being indiscreet. People who, unlike you, hadn't signed the Official Secrets Act, journalists, those sorts of people. Just the ones you were threatening me with having to explain myself to when you first arrived here, Jimmy Jenner. You can see why Charles and I have been concerned.'

Emma Black guided me to the door. At the top of the staircase I said, 'What about Timpkins? How do you explain that?'

'Very tragic. We think he was killed by one of your friend Moody's new colleagues. We don't know, of course, only think. We can't have it getting in the papers in that form, that's for sure. Not until this other business is all cleared up, anyway. For the moment Timpkins was killed by a mugger. Palmer's seeing to it, I believe.'

Emma Black waved goodbye from the top of the stairs, cigar in the waving hand, enormous black handbag in the other. She looked like a mother waving her son off to school. I walked slowly downstairs, head spinning, stomach empty except for scotch whisky, confused and alarmed. Emma had had a good shot at giving me a story. Some of it might have been true, but I wasn't sure how much . . . and I was sure her story was in essence a lie. It didn't leave me any nearer an answer to my questions than before.

Chapter Twenty-five

When I left the house beside St James's Park the night was cold, the first night of winter. The black-painted iron railings were cold to the touch of my fingers. White light from old-fashioned street lamps shone at me, reflected by still water in puddles. A policeman shrugged his shoulders inside his great-coat a few doors down. A car passed down the narrow street, a Jaguar with big tyres rolling slowly along the kerb-side, crunching small stones and dirt beneath rubber. The young men inside the car looked me over carefully but they didn't stop. A middle-aged man and a woman stood at the street corner, half in darkness, tightly embraced. Some politician, no doubt, making sure his secretary would arrive home safely. I walked past them, then down some old stone steps to Birdcage Walk.

Detective Chief Superintendent Palmer was waiting in the cold night. Clouds of steamy exhaust poured from the rear of a big unmarked police Rover he was leaning against.

'I thought you'd come this way,' he said. 'I waited for you.'

'Are you offering me a lift?'

'Certainly.' He slipped behind the wheel. The door clunked softly behind him. I got in too. The inside of the car seemed strangely silent after the night street.

'Where's your driver?' I said.

'Home in bed, I hope. Just like we should be. Where to?'

'Essex. Grays.'

Palmer rubbed his stubbly jaw and smiled. 'It's a long way, Jenner. I thought you lived in Stoke Newington?'

'It certainly is a long way, and I've left a hire-car there courtesy of your lot and your secret conferences. Take me to Grays or leave me right here, Mr Palmer.'

He took me to Gray's, I knew he would. Palmer wanted to speak. We drove across the city in a polite professional silence, a silence penetrated only by the rumble of the rubber tyres on the tarmac and the soft 'drawing' sound of the big engine. We were each waiting for the other's opening gambit.

Palmer stopped at Spitalfields Church and bought me a revolting instant coffee and a worse hamburger from a greasy and unhygienic-looking stall there. The white, flood-lit stone spire of the church loomed above us. Soaked and frozen drunks reeled about us, cursing each other over small sums of money, snatching swigs of booze and fighting for the favours of equally derelict women. I was very hungry but the food seemed to stick in my throat. The sight of my fellow men grubbing around in the dirt made eating impossible.

Palmer locked the Rover, then said, 'Let's take a walk.'

'I don't have my stick. Anyway it's about to rain.'

'Then we'll go slowly and if necessary you can lean on me.'

We walked. Once we were out of sight of the derelicts I threw the half-eaten hamburger into the gutter and followed Palmer into the bright lights of Spitalfields vegetable market. Spanish and French lorries sat at the kerbside, growling. Their drivers either hid in curtained cabs or stamped their feet at the kerbside. The Mediterranean fruits the lorries had brought were being unloaded. Cockney salesmen ticked sheets on clipboards and gave orders to blue- or brown-coated porters. A security man in a uniform halfway between an English policeman's and a South American general's stood by the lorries. He drank steaming liquid from a Styrofoam cup and pushed pieces of a burst pumpkin in the gutter with the toe of his shoe. In all the quiet city night these markets, these sudden flames of light never fail to surprise me.

'Can't you speak in your car?' I said.

Palmer shrugged. He wasn't sure. 'What story did you get, Jenner?'

'That Moody belonged to Emma Black's outfit, whatever that is. No doubt you know more precisely. She gave a hint that he always has been her man. The story was that he was operating some large-scale private enterprise operation on her firm's time, that he has been caught out and is now going east, presumably to sign up with the Red Army. She said that fitting up the body in Moody's flat was a spoiling tactic they'd organised when they'd realised he was doing a runner. That my coming along spoilt the spoiling tactic. She told me tonight that when I helped Moody get to France, far from spoiling things further, I was doing exactly what she and presumably people like you expected, almost *wanted* from me. How am I doing so far?'

'I didn't want anything from you then. I'd never heard of you, at least not in connection with this Moody business. Runner where?'

Lie. A man from his own office, Superintendent Leigh, had been involved in setting up the fake murder at Peter Moody's house. Leigh had certainly been involved in the 'investigation' of it. That Leigh was unaware of the identity of the man who went there that night – me – was beyond belief. Special Branch were in this up to their necks.

'East. Don't tell me you didn't know that?'

'Yes I knew it. But where east?'

'I've no idea. Why does it bother you?'

'It doesn't bother me. It's not a police problem . . . not in the first instance. A man's allowed to travel just where he wants. But I want to make sure we've both been given the same story. What about Timpkins? What account did she give of that?'

'None. None worth taking seriously. You appeared to know all about Timpkins's death, Mr Palmer. That was the impression you left on me in Stoke Newington nick. Why ask me about it? I thought all you had to do was find some black kid with a knife in his hand and bob's-your-uncle ... no more mystery.'

'I know nothing about it. I came in ostensibly to run a holding operation on a crime that had most likely been committed, it was felt, by agents of a foreign power. It was understood we needed time to get our act together.'

'But you knew about Moody?' I said. 'You knew about him getting out to France and the attempt to fix him with this make-believe murder? You knew that was related to Timpkins and that I was one common factor?'

He didn't answer. Of course he knew. Palmer and I walked on, travelling into dark streets and shadows, surrounded by black looming buildings; then we came to the corner of a row of half-demolished houses. In the middle of the row was an open space and in the open space was a fire, a big fire built of broken pallets and tomato boxes. Derelicts surrounded the fire, huddled as around a prehistoric camp-fire. They sheltered under soggy cardboard and scraps of abandoned tarpaulin. We went near, near enough to hear the hiss as occasional raindrops hit the fire. Near enough to hear the tramps grunting and moaning and turning over in their cardboard boxes, but not so near that they would notice us if we spoke quietly. The fire flickered orange and yellow light over Palmer's face and figure.

'What did Timpkins want from you?' he said suddenly. 'What did he want so badly that it made him want to come to your house?'

'Nothing that I know of. Wanting something from me intimates a deductive process going on in his mind. From my brief experience of him I'd have thought that was a bit unlikely.'

'But you *do* know something. He might or might not have understood what you had in Dover, but later, when he came to your house, he was certainly coming there with a purpose in mind. And that purpose worried someone enough to have Timpkins killed.'

'No mugger then?'

Palmer paused, then said, 'What was it? Some physical object? Some information?'

'I don't know anything. You can't be serious, Palmer... he worked for *you*, not me! He must have told you he was coming.'

Palmer shook his head. 'He spoke to our office and said he was coming to London, that he wanted to talk about something important. He never mentioned you, Jenner. And he didn't speak to me. You knew something – still know it probably – and Timpkins wanted it from you. He couldn't use a phone and he needed it urgently so he came to get it. He came all the way from Kent expecting to find you. And he was going to talk to us about it afterwards. *Talk*... you see? He didn't want to use the phone, even a secure phone. Did you have any contact with him?'

'Certainly not. I didn't ask him to my house and I didn't want him on my doorstep, dead or alive.'

'Well, he wanted *you*, Jenner. He must have been followed. When it looked like he was about to get whatever he wanted from you he was murdered. What is it?'

I shook my head. Palmer went on, 'He was murdered but you weren't. Why? If you have this information why not deal with the source of it?'

'I don't know. Do you know who killed him?' I said.

'I'll have the answer to that when I know what he was coming to you for.'

I shrugged. 'What you have to face up to, Palmer, is that someone amongst your people will have arranged for Timpkins to be met. Or met him. If you can find out who talked about Timpkins's meet to an outsider you're home and dry.'

'*If*,' Palmer said. 'A big word.' But his voice had changed, and he fell silent.

A man's silhouette emerged from what appeared to be a

pile of rubbish, tipped some more pieces of broken pallet on to the fire and then was one shape again with the rubbish. The smell of singed, rain-soaked wool reached me from him, reminding me of classrooms and schoolboys and blazers and flannel trousers. Tramps and schoolboys smell the same in the rain.

I shook my head again. 'I don't know anything. If I do have a secret I don't know what it is. And even if Timpkins had figured something out, it still doesn't mean that what he'd worked out was true and accurate. But it was enough to frighten someone.'

'So there is something . . . what?'

'I don't know. I think you're suspicious of everyone. Maybe there's no need to be. Maybe when I say to you "I don't know" it means just that. Did you ever consider that possibility?'

He said nothing.

The flames danced, flickering light over us and the desolate scene. Palmer stood by my side, silent. Then he sighed. 'I'll trust you. I have to, Jenner. Look . . . there are suspicions against more than one person in this business. You tell me, do you really see Peter Moody as the man he's made out to be in all this?' His voice was now intense, choked.

Then I saw it. Palmer had spoken to Moody since he'd done his bunk. Palmer thought someone was framing Peter, just like Peter had said. Maybe Palmer felt responsible for Timpkins. Maybe he'd done something he now regretted, something to endanger the man.

'Lost, gentlemen?' a deep voice said.

'No, constable. We were just out walking,' said Palmer.

A handlamp shone in my face, then moved on to Palmer's.

'Particularly unsalubrious area for walking, this, sir. I'm going to Bishopsgate. Shall I show you the way?'

'No. We're okay. We're parked in Spitalfields, anyway.'

I couldn't see the constable's face. I could hear a forced, polite smile in his voice, though. 'Spitalfields is that way, sir.' He pointed with the beam. 'About four hundred yards. Right, left and right again. I expect you'll want to be getting back to your car now, gentlemen.'

He clicked the torch off and moved away without another word. At first I couldn't see at all, then we slowly made our way from the fire back to the market and then to Spitalfields Church and Palmer's car.

'Grays,' said Palmer.

'Grays. It's a car park near the Town Hall. Just drive to the town centre and I'll show you . . . by the way what's my chance of a firearms permit?'

'Join a gun club,' he said. 'Small bore. I'm sure there are plenty around. You don't even need to own your own gun. Use theirs. Got no form, have you?'

'I mean for the street. I might be in danger.'

'You can't legally come by a gun like that, Jenner. This is England.' Palmer sounded outraged. 'I'll tell you what I'll do for you. I'll put a man on to follow you everywhere you go . . . only if you want,' he added, and laughed. 'I wouldn't want to interfere with your human rights.'

It was the first time I'd even seen Palmer amused, let alone laughing out loud.

'Or then again,' he said, 'perhaps you might be lucky enough to find someone who'll offer you a nice juicy job as an ace private eye, something that'll take you out of the way for a while. I would think the other side of the world would do famously, Jenner. The sort of place that's just about to have its summer. I reckon somewhere like Australia would fit the bill just right, don't you?'

When I didn't answer he said, 'All you'd need to do is sit at home and wait for an offer like that to roll in. It does happen, you know.' And then he laughed heartily. 'People do get offers.'

'Thanks. Just what I wanted, some good ideas from an expert.'

I settled back in the thick luxurious seat of the Rover. Soft music played on the car radio. A woman with a warm, reassuring voice told me the news headlines were due in ten minutes. The derelicts were, thank God, somewhere else. Palmer switched on a second radio and spoke into a telephone-type handset. He spoke in cryptic phrases and I guessed the message was that he was going to Essex. I don't know why he couldn't have just said 'Palmer here, on my way to Essex.' I don't know why the codes mattered. I think it's just that policemen love codes and secrecy and insider knowledge. Nothing pleases them more than knowing something everyone else doesn't know. It's both their strength and their weakness.

By Poplar I was asleep. My sleep was full of guilt, though, and of fear and bottomless pits. By Dagenham Palmer was shaking me to wake me. He still held the telephone handset of his car radio in the hand that shook me.

'Your journalist friend's car's been found.'

'Super.'

'Guess where?'

My mouth and throat felt awful. I could still taste the cheap hamburger and ketchup. I could still smell the tramps round the fire. The whirling pit of my dream was still all too close to the surface of my mind.

'I give up, Palmer. Where?'

Multi-storey car park at Heathrow. Long-term, too. What do you say?'

'Not much.'

We stopped at traffic lights.

'What do you know about it?' Palmer asked.

'Nothing. Absolutely nothing.'

We passed huge car parks containing hundreds of brand new Ford cars. Steam and smoke bellowed from the brightly lit interior of the factory. The still unpolished cars looked dull and grimy. Movement inside the factory made it look like a devil's kitchen. Palmer just sat there grinning.

'How about that for a turn-up? *Heathrow* Airport. The car park for terminal one, though that means nothing. He could have got a plane anywhere from any terminal.'

'He could have got a tube back home.'

'Yes. Where's he gone?'

'I don't know.'

'I wonder why he took off in such a hurry?'

'My crystal ball's broken.'

'I don't suppose his editor will be all that pleased with him tomorrow morning when it comes to making up their paper and the ace reporter's gone missing. Your crystal ball really is broken, Jenner ... far from explaining myself to him, I should think I'll be directing your friend Tim Ewence to a dole office.'

'I don't know about that,' I said as neutrally as I could manage. I felt like saying 'when you're back on the beat you'll be able to, clever clogs.'

'You don't seem to know very much about the entire business, Jenner. To be a detective you've got to be able to give yourself the overview.'

Three a.m. and I find myself a philosopher. Just my luck, a stone cold sober philosopher. I wondered what he was like drunk. Worse, I imagined. DCS Palmer slapped himself on the thigh and put his foot down on the Rover's accelerator. The engine revved and buildings flashed past us.

'That's the way detection is,' he said. 'It's like an ant that sees a pie. The ant's not a man so he doesn't get the overview. The ant only sees a huge cliff of pastry. If he's lucky he might get up that cliff and see a plain of pastry stretching before him, with boulders of sugar. He'll see all that but he can't ever see the pie. It never occurs to him that his cliff is just a tiny piece of pie, because the whole is outside of his grasp. And it never can be inside his grasp because he can never get the overview. He isn't intelligent enough. Do you follow me?'

His face was deadpan. Then he was rubbing his unshaven jaw enthusiastically. Grinning mischievously. DCS Palmer was having a joke at my expense. He was taking the mickey out of me.

'Are you telling me I don't have the intellectual equipment

194

to see what's going on around me? Are you telling me that's why I can't answer your bloody questions, that that's why I don't know what it is Timpkins wanted from me? That I don't know what it is I'm supposed to know?'

'It's certainly one way of looking at it.' He laughed out loud again.

'Like an ant?'

'That's right.' He laughed again. I thought Palmer would make a formidable chess player. I mentally stuck two fingers up to Palmer, the too-clever-dick. Stuff the overview. I had a lead . . . even if the lead was only that an old man had once had his picture taken in front of a castle with Clare.

'Like an ant and a pie.' Palmer chuckled again.

I laughed too.

'You know, Mr Palmer, for a detective of such obvious intelligence you seem to know an awful lot about the internal workings of an ant's mind.'

To his credit, Palmer kept laughing.

Chapter Twenty-six

I drove the Granada back to Canning Town, then went up to my office. It showed all the signs of the same expert search as my flat had, but considering what had happened to Timpkins I would've expected that. I even expected a mess. A tidy but thorough search was a nice surprise. Peter's money was still where I'd left it in the filing cabinet, an equally pleasant surprise. I apologised out loud to my liver, poured a scotch and played the tape-recorded messages from my telephone answering machine.

beep

Judy's voice. 'I'd like to talk to you soon, Jimmy. Face to face. Give me a call please.'

beep

'Hello, Mr Jenner. It's Esmerelda Potts here. . . .'

Click. Fast forward.

beep

'Jimmy. Denis. . . .'

Click again. Fast forward again.

beep

'Judy again. It is fully twenty-four hours since I phoned you and you still haven't got back to me. I want to talk to you. Please call me, Jimmy.'

beep

'Hello, Mr Jenner. It's Esmerelda Potts here. . . .'

Click again. Fast forward again.

beep

'One in the ay em, English time. That is, at night, Jenner.
Plenty plenty news news, bwana, from foreign parts. I will
speak to you at the poet's desk tomorrow, two pee em English time, which is during the day. And I can tell you it will
be worth your while attending. Bye now.'

Ewence's voice. In foreign parts, eh? No surprise there.
But where? I thought of the photograph of Clare with her
castle and A.N. Other. Maybe there – wherever *there* is –
maybe there is the foreign part. And the poet's desk? It
could only be in the office of his friend and mine, Tony
Tennyson. Ewence had – probably rightly – presumed I
would have listeners on my phone. But Tennyson wouldn't
have listeners. With any luck he wouldn't even know what
we were talking about. I wouldn't trust that kind of luck.
Tennyson's kind could smell a story at five hundred yards.

I poured some more scotch, took a clean sheet of paper
from a drawer, then began to write. I wrote down all the
people I'd met since this business began. I added Peter,
Clare, Judy and myself. Then I tried to link them up, one
with another, describing all the relationships in some detail.
I Sellotaped more sheets on to the first when I needed them,
and I needed quite a few. The descriptions got longer and
longer as the relationships and possible relationships became
more complex. The chart grew quickly, but I didn't need to
finish it to see what I wanted.

I have a little Moka Express machine in my office. As the
dawn broke I was grinding high-roast continental coffee
beans to go in it. The sound of the grinder would make a
strong man weep . . . all over the world people's teeth are set
on edge at breakfast time by coffee grinders. I used the same
match to light the stove under my coffee machine and to
burn my chart. The yellow flames ran up the channels of
celluloid which held the pieces of my informal chart together. I had turned my desk lamp off, and the yellow
flames illuminated my furniture, Chardray's washing

powder packets, my hand, my desk top, the face of my cheap alarm clock. The clock said seven.

I dropped the still-flaming chart into a metal wastepaper bin where the flames illuminated only themselves. The room was full of the acrid smell of burnt celluloid and paper. Outside my window the red light of dawn glowed against the concrete of Canning Town flyover. The morning's busy, unself-conscious traffic was building up nicely. In another hour there would be hundreds of men sitting in steel boxes on the flyover, swearing at each other and listening to Capital Radio. They would have no chance of moving more than a hundred yards in twenty minutes. Why did they do it every day?

Chardray was crashing around in his shop below me. He does it every morning. You'd think he was a steel stock-holder, not a grocer and newsagent. I poured myself a coffee from the little machine, then shook my wastepaper bin, mixing the ashes of my chart. I put a lot of gas bills and the like on top of the ashes, poured a splash of scotch on and lit another match. I drank my coffee with the flames of my little bit of detection glowing before me. When I'd drunk my coffee I poured the rest of the contents of the Moka express on top of the pile of ashes in my wastepaper bin, then ground the lot up with the bentwood handle of an expensive-looking umbrella a visiting solicitor had left in my office. I had never liked that solicitor. When I'd finished I reckoned that even Palmer's clever chaps couldn't get anything out of the resulting black, stodgy porridge.

I opened my filing cabinet and took one thousand of Peter Moody's pounds. I wrote a note of what I'd taken so far and tucked it in with the wad of notes. Then I piled a lot of useless papers on top, and locked the filing cabinet. I walked happily downstairs to the car. I didn't mind about joining the early morning traffic jam. I didn't mind about driving a car that was two feet too long in every dimension. I didn't mind that I'd had no sleep. I now knew why Timpkins was coming to see me. I knew what I hadn't known when I'd gone to my office.

Gotcha!

Chapter Twenty-seven

There was somebody in my flat when I got home. A man gets to notice the little signs. I noticed the little signs. If I hadn't noticed the overcoat flung carelessly on my hall table it would've been the fact that the hall and living room lights had been left on. If it hadn't been the lights left on and the doors open it would've been the drained coffee cup on top of the TV. If it hadn't been the coffee cup it would have been the one lipstick-stained glass with the dregs of some red wine in it and if it hadn't been that it would have been the half-empty bottle of Mouton Cadet in the kitchen. My visitor had brought her own wine. I don't like red wine much; not French, anyway.

I put the kettle on.

My bedroom was the clue that gave the game away. Even if I had missed all the clues in the hallway, living room and kitchen, there's no mistaking a pile of abandoned clothes on your bedroom floor and the form of another person lying in what should be your bed. The bedroom curtains were pulled, the room was in darkness; but from the light in the hallway I recognised a blouse I'd bought a woman some time ago, a red silk number, plain but naughty. The blouse, that is. The figure in my bed didn't need any introduction.

'Judy.'

I sat beside her. She was heavily asleep. Her eyes were open at once but she woke slowly.

199

'What's the time?'

'Nearly eight. I'm making tea. Want some?'

She groaned and pulled a pillow over her head. Her muffled voice said, 'Where the hell have you been?'

'Working. No work for you today?'

'No. Go and make the tea.'

I went and made the tea. I didn't want any, but Judy always likes to wake up to tea. She only likes to wake up to it . . . she doesn't drink it. My wife gets satisfaction from having an early morning cup of tea going cold next to bed. True to form, when I took her the cup of tea she wouldn't drink it.

'Put it on the side.'

'Drink it.'

'I'm tired. I'll drink it later. Come to bed.'

'It's later now. Late enough for good people to get up and do some work. How can you be tired at this time?'

'Come to bed.'

'I've a lot to do.'

'Have you been with another woman, you alleycat?'

'Certainly not. I've been out all night working my fingers to the bone.'

'Then you must be tired, too. Come to bed and let's sleep a while longer.'

'What a suggestion! With you suing for divorce and all. It's immoral.'

'How can it be immoral to go to bed with your own wife?'

Well, from the beginning the arguments I put up weren't offered with any real conviction. I didn't take much more convincing. A flash of the blue eyes, a smile. Her hair on my pillow. An outstretched hand. My tea went cold, too.

'Tell me all,' she said while the kettle boiled for the second time that morning. Judy was sitting in my kitchen, dressed in my scratchy wool dressing gown, pushing her fingers through her hair and smiling at me.

200

'You. Yours is bound to be shorter.'

'Okay. I've got some leave. I've been given a place on an administration course at Hendon, three months' worth. The condition was that the leave year finished during the course, so I had to take my annual leave first. I went home two days ago fancy free. I called you. I thought it would be a good opportunity for us to get some uninterrupted time together to . . . well, to discuss things.' She smiled. 'Isn't that nice of me? I've been calling you ever since. When you hadn't called back by yesterday afternoon, I thought I'd come round and wait for you. I've had rather a long wait.'

'How long's the leave?'

'Two and a bit weeks. Two now.'

'You hadn't mentioned the course at Hendon to me. Did you apply for it in the normal way?'

'No. I was proposed by my department head. What are you getting at?'

'Nothing for now. Get dressed and let's take a walk.'

'Tell me yours.'

'Let's take that walk.'

'Denis called me,' she said. 'He said you'd had some trouble here . . . well, quite a lot of trouble.'

'Denis called you.'

'That's right. He's worried about you. I was worried about you when that woman phoned me about picking you up. I was right to be worried, too. From what Denis says there's even more to worry about now.'

'He's worried about his pocket and about staying in with his superiors for a change. Those are Denis's biggest problems.'

She didn't answer. My neck was sore from not sleeping. My eyes were sore from not sleeping. My head felt thick and aching. I munched a piece of toast. I felt as if someone was breaking paving stones inside my head.

'Let's take a walk, Judy,' I said. I held my forefinger over her lips. 'Let's take a walk.'

A thin, watery sun was over Stoke Newington. It wasn't windy and it wasn't raining and the thin, watery October sun was the best we could expect by the way of weather before next April or May. It's so depressing.

We walked through the park towards the public library. Kids who should have been at school were beating each other up in a playground. What are their parents up to? I used to feel like that every time I dealt with kids when I was a policeman . . . 'What are their parents up to?'

I sat on a bench with Judy and told her the truth, the whole truth and nothing but it. If I left anything out I didn't do it on purpose. I started with when we'd last parted company and I went via Timpkins's amazing plan to incriminate me by having himself killed on my doorstep to my visit to Fobbing and my meeting with Emma Black – not Johnson – who was neither a lawyer nor a guardian angel but some sort of security person.

'I don't understand. What's all this about someone having himself killed on your doorstep? I thought the story was that the chap had been mugged. That's how Denis has it.'

'Yes. But there's a DCS Palmer from Special Branch who was responsible for that story. He's got an overactive imagination. He's the one who was sitting waiting in Clare Fisher's house in Fobbing. Given half the chance he'll have this DS Timpkins either committing suicide, having himself killed or being the victim of the world's first spontaneous crime committed by a pocket knife. Palmer has one weird relationship with the truth. He's just beginning to display the tiniest doubt about the value of living in such a double-dealing environment, I think.'

In the playground before us a boy of about ten was trying to garotte what I presumed to be his smaller sister by jamming her head in the safety rail of a child's swing and then closing the rail. The smaller sister appeared to be laughing.

'So why *did* Timpkins come to you?'

'Because he'd worked out that I hadn't actually *seen* Peter

* * *

Moody. That's the special thing that I knew. And it somehow had enormous significance to Timpkins."

'Hadn't seen him? What do you mean?'

'Literally that. Not since day one of this entire business. It could well have been that the bloke I saw mending his car outside my office the day Clare Fisher came there was in fact Peter . . . but it didn't *have* to be. Apart from that I simply haven't seen him.'

'What about this conversation in Soho? You're not saying it wasn't him there?'

'No. Of course it was him. But I haven't actually clapped eyes on him once. He's kept himself completely out of my sight, both in England and in France.'

'What does it mean?'

'It means he was still in England while I was mucking about in France, trying to get my passport off him and thinking of myself as having done him a big favour. It means I was laying a big noisy trail over England and France while Peter Moody was sitting with his feet up in London somewhere waiting to make his move. Look at it this way . . . he'd let me go through this pantomime fairly publicly. If someone had tipped off the Special Branch looking for him at Dover that I was on my way back, everyone would presume I'd got Peter out of the country. It means the watch on ports for him would be called off. He could then leave England having done whatever he was wanting to do first.'

'Clever him. And what will *we* do now, Jimmy?'

'We?' I said.

She smiled. 'I've got two weeks' leave, remember.'

'They've probably fixed that. Seriously . . . they're probably fixing me as well as Moody. And you.'

I had to laugh at myself. The statements were good evidence of paranoia. And even the version of events I'd rehearsed to Judy didn't sound watertight to me. Maybe Palmer had a point in all that guff about ants and apple pies. Now, more than ever, I believed Peter was the victim of something. My guess was that Palmer thought so too.

'We'll go to the library,' I said. 'And then we'll have lunch in Fleet Street. Then I'll go off to foreign parts to do what I can while you take your leave somewhere sunny. Where's still sunny in October?'

'Spain?' she suggested. We both laughed at that. Spain is indeed sunny in October. But not for us.

Chapter Twenty-eight

Newspaper offices are not noted for their tidiness, but Tony Takeaway's was a menace, a genuine glass-partitioned farmyard full of ancient, yellowing newsprint, scraps of journalists' copy, abandoned hamburger cartons and empty Coke tins. Judy and I were shown in by a young man with a sallow, almost jaundiced-looking complexion and sad brown eyes. I put the skin down to the neon lights in his office and the eyes down to an overprotective mother. I didn't like that kid. He'd obviously been to both a public school and a posh university and was equally obviously trying to unload his education and accent. He met us at the newspaper's reception desk and he must have called me 'mate' a dozen times between there and Tony's office.

'In here, mate. Tony said he was expecting you and that I was to make you comfortable. That means offer you a glass of scotch. Har Har.'

'No thanks, mate. We're okay, mate ... know what I mean?'

He gave me a strange look and pointed in the direction of a desk strewn with papers and some chairs occupied by boxes of photocopier paper.

'So, make yourselves at home anyway. He'll be back any minute, I should think. You know Tony ... gone out, mate.'

'I know Tony, mate. Cheers, mate.' Don't be so bloody familiar, mate.

Judy didn't know Tony, and cleared a seat for herself in his mess with undisguised disgust. We watched the newsroom buzzing happily outside the glass that partitioned off Tony Takeaway's office.

'Is he the editor?' Judy asked.

'Of a section. I'm damned if I know what section. Definitely not Sport. Love Interest and Food, I should think, knowing this rag.'

One of the phones on Tony's desk rang. I could see a light flickering in time with the rings on a miniature switchboard outside. No one attempted to answer it. I threw some papers on the floor and sat on Tony's desk to answer it.

'Tennyson's office.'

'Call for you . . . go on, you're through,' said a bored-sounding woman's voice.

'Hello. Is that Tony Tennyson?'

'No, it's not. It's me. How are you, Tim?'

'Jimmy! Fine, fine. Can we talk?'

'Well, let's not go mad. You never know who's listening nowadays. First of all, I think you're in a big town with a castle and a lot of music, yes?'

'That's right. Brilliant guesswork.'

'Good. It's not a guess. Don't name the town. As I said, you never know. I think you must have followed someone there . . . how did you get on about passports?'

'I missed a fortnight's work in Bermuda once when I was a freelancer because I was in London, my passport was in Leeds and the flight left from Heathrow in one hour. Ever since then I've kept it close by my side, in the car. A copper followed me to Heathrow but he hadn't been such a boy scout as me. I left him to hang around the departure gate staring at my back. No doubt he must know where I've gone.'

'No doubt.'

'Is that important?'

'Maybe. Was it a man you followed? Don't name him.'

'It certainly was. I've just left him now. He's your double, very nearly. It's uncanny. He even sounds a bit like you. He's very friendly and has one hell of a story, Jenner. He's here with a couple of other people.'

'A young woman and a man in his sixties?'

'That's it. Only the man's in his seventies. Where did you get all this from?'

'Deduction, Watson. It's what we detectives are good at. Have you phoned your paper? What does your editor say?'

'He's gone ape. He says I'm sacked. I promised him a scoop and he was really foul about it.'

'Mm. I'm not surprised. Does he know where you are?'

'No. I haven't told anyone that. I wanted to wait until we'd spoken. I didn't want to queer the story.'

'You'd better come home, Tim. It's no good losing your job. I'll be there at eight tonight, local time. I'm booked on a flight. Ask him to meet me at the airport, will you?'

'Okay, I'll ask him. But I'm going to get this story, Jimmy. I'm going to sell it to Fleet Street. The *Clarion* can get stuffed.'

'Don't ask him to come, tell him. Tell him I'm friendly too, and won't be bringing an entourage. Got it? And watch out for yourself.'

'I've got it. I don't know whether he will or not. We only meet at his say-so. Different places both times.'

'Well, make it work, Tim.'

'I will if I can. I'm sure he wants to see you, Jimmy. He says so.'

'Okay, Tim. Let's cut it here. You know what I said about listeners. Bye now.'

'Bye, Jimmy.'

'Who were you worried about listening?' said Judy. 'I thought the point of coming here was that no one was listening.'

'The point of coming here was that the *police* wouldn't be listening.'

I waved my hand at the room. Judy nodded but said nothing.

The young man who'd shown us into Tony Tennyson's office was sorry we couldn't stay to meet Tony, wouldn't we just like some coffee? He was sure he'd be back soon. Judy gave him a stern look and he shut up.

On Fleet Street a weak sun hung in the afternoon sky. The street was, as ever, crowded. Judy and I walked arm in arm back to Ludgate. I had a couple of hours to lose. Then suddenly there was a lot of yelling and an extremely tall, fat man in a nylon shirt and loosely knotted patterned tie was running after us.

'Jimmy! Jimmy!'

We stopped. Tony Takeaway took a couple of minutes to get his breath back.

'What's happening, Jimmy?' he said eventually.

'You should know. I presume you were listening.'

'Oh *come on*! You know better than that.'

'Course I do. I'll be seeing you, Tony.

He stood there, panting still, streaming sweat, his shirt tail out and with his wispy hair plastered to his brow. Tony Takeaway was going on for forty-five and he would never make fifty. His washed-out grey eyes gleamed with anticipation. He'd heard Tim Ewence say 'scoop' on the telephone.

'Come on, Jimmy. Give us a break. You expected me to listen in.'

'Yes, but only to my end of the conversation. Not at the switchboard. You were naughty, Tony. Naughty boys get no supper. Naughty boys certainly get no stories.'

'His editor will sack him . . . he said. Maybe I can use him. You owe it to young Tim, Jimmy.'

'Not you? You're sure you don't mean I owe it to you?'

'What does it matter who to? What's all this crap about castles and old men? Where's Tim?'

Judy had stopped a taxi. She opened the door. I got in.

Tony pulled down the passenger's window and leaned in, his big face looking like a sweaty version of the man in the moon.

'Where is he? Where are you going? I'll pay his expenses.'

The taxi pulled forward. Tony Tennyson jumped back sharply to the kerb.

'He said!' Tony screamed. 'He said he wanted to sell it to Fleet Street. I'm Fleet Street! I've helped you both. He should sell it to me.'

The cab driver stopped, alarmed. Cars and vans stopped around us, too. The cab was halfway across the street.

'Calm down, Tony. Don't be silly.'

'I'm Fleet Street. You tell him. You tell him I'll pay his expenses. If it's a good one I'll pay yours as well, Jenner."

'Drive on please,' Judy said. The cabby was doing so anyway.

'You tell him, Jenner, you swine!' Tony Takeaway called after us. I had to laugh. Judy laughed by my side. Tony Tennyson suddenly became aware of himself standing in Fleet Street with his shirt tail hanging out and shouting like a madman. He looked like a man who had found himself naked in public. That's a particularly nasty dream and Tony scurried away in a manner befitting the embarrassment it would cause. He was, after all, well known in Fleet Street.

'Would you have told him if he hadn't been eavesdropping?' said Judy when we reached the beginning of the Strand. She'd just asked the cabby to take us to Waterloo Bridge. Really anywhere would have done. Anywhere away from Tony. We had no appointments. Not until that evening, anyway.

'Of course not,' I said. 'What a suggestion. I just thought he deserved to be told it was his own fault.'

Chapter Twenty-nine

My flight to Salzburg landed in Munich. That was due to the fog in Salzburg and Innsbruck, we were told. It meant I had quite a bit of heel-kicking to do over the next fifteen or so hours.

It was Judy who had figured out Salzburg, thereby allowing me to stun Tim Ewence over Tony Takeaway's phone with my brilliance and perspicacity.

When we had gone into Stoke Newington public library a woman librarian had started on about someone who looked like me having vandalised the periodical section the day before.

'It wasn't me.'

'Of course it was you. You've got the same coat on.'

'Not me. You're mistaken.'

'You tore a page out of a newspaper. We can't be doing with it. The children are bad enough . . . but a grown-up man. . . .' She frowned and folded her arms at the same time. I was impressed. If your average public librarian tried to fold his or her arms and frown at one and the same time they'd probably forget to breathe, or fall over.

'It wasn't me,' I said.

'Of course it was you.'

'It wasn't me. I haven't been here for weeks.'

'He had a limp,' she said. 'And he looked like you. I'm

sure it was you.' Turning to her colleague she said, 'Jane . . . call security.'

Jane, a pinch-faced, unhappy-looking woman aged twenty-five (approx) and dressed fifty-five (approx), called security. I slipped out quietly while security were draining their mugs of tea and putting their official jackets on. I went and fed birdseed to some club-footed pigeons who'd gathered round my park bench in a show of solidarity. It comes to something when a man can't make a visit to the library with his own wife in peace.

Judy was back in ten minutes, brandishing a book on European castles, and within fifteen minutes or so we had it . . . Salzburg. They were being photographed in front of the Hohensalzburg, which is what the castle was called. All I needed now was a book of European old men and I would know who Clare was standing with. I could hazard a fair guess anyway.

'Why was the picture left there?' Judy asked.

'It was a message. I think someone was meant to find it . . . Palmer maybe. Even me.'

Even though Munich is in Germany, it's the nearest decent-sized airport to Salzburg. We passengers were herded on to an airport bus in Munich, then rumbled down the motorway for fifty miles or so until we met the much-promised fog. The airline representative was relieved to see the fog, and walked up and down the bus's gangway pointing it out to us as if we couldn't see it and discussing its qualities as if it were roast beef or a tall blonde or good wine. He told us that through the fog that way was the beginning of the Alps. Through the fog the other way was a plain. Through the fog in front of us was the Austrian border, and through the fog behind us – the only one I didn't have to take on trust – was Munich airport. During the journey I expanded my miniature German vocabulary by one word – *Nebel* – and managed to get in a good hour's worrying that I mightn't meet Peter in Salzburg airport.

I needn't have worried. He wasn't there. Of course he wasn't. He probably never had been there. He'd probably never been anywhere near Salzburg in his life. I took a taxi into the city and put up in a pension in the centre of the town. I had trouble finding a room, too. It's never out of season in Mozart-town.

The next morning I was offered ham, bread, coffee and the *Guardian* for breakfast. The pension's proprietor, a man with a name I hardly dared pronounce so he was simply 'Herr Ober' to me, presented the *Guardian* with a smile.

'A man who knew you was here. He said you like to read English newspapers when you're abroad.'

Since I only speak English I can *only* read English newspapers, whether in England or abroad.

'What did he look like?'

Mr Ober laughed. 'This is a joke, yes? He's your brother, I think.'

'No, he's not my brother. He's my friend.'

Mr Ober nodded knowingly. I felt like kicking him.

'Did my friend leave any message?' I asked.

'Yes. He said he would take a walk in the Getreidegasse and wouldn't you join him there after breakfast.'

'Where's the Ge-doodah-gasse?'

My Austrian host laughed heartily at my ignorance both of the Austrian language and the topography of his home town.

'Eat your breakfast. After, I will show you on a map. It's in the old town.'

The bread was stale. All the bread I ate in Austria was. They must like it that way. I can't face ham in the mornings and the coffee turned out to be hot chocolate. Hot chocolate ... in the morning! It's only slightly better than France. When I asked Mr Ober did he have anything else for breakfast he suggested cheese.

'Just show me where the Ginghamgasser is, sport. We'll give the breakfast a miss. I'll put this one down to experience.'

* * *

The Getreidegasse came off the Something-else-gasse and led down towards the Universitätsplatz via the Durchhäuser, which is nothing more nor less than a load of alleyways. The friendly Mr Ober eventually gave up telling me how to get there and what they were called and lent me a map. The map's easy, you orientate yourself by the castle. Everywhere you go in Salzburg Clare's castle Hohensalzburg is above you. You can hardly get your photograph taken without it turning up in the picture.

I walked down the Getreidegasse. It's an extremely narrow, pedestrianised street with lots of shops ready to take lots of lolly off tourists. In October most of the tourists appeared to be American servicemen on leave from Germany, in which country they spend their time defending Yooroop against Russia and worrying about the military rate of exchange, dollar/DMark.

Getreidegasse has a house – one of the many, I think – where Mozart was born. That Mozart fellow got around in Austria like Robert the Bruce did in Scotland or Charles II did in England. Getreidegasse has olde worlde shop fronts with black-painted wooden upper parts to lend them authenticity, and girls in dirndls inside. The girls seemed to be willing to flirt with anything in trousers, which was just as well because most of the strollers in Getreidegasse were the US servicemen with just that in mind.

I strolled slowly along the street, wondering what the hell Peter was up to now, then I felt an arm go round my shoulders.

'Jimmy.'

It was Peter. He kept his arm round my shoulders and smiled into my face and we kept walking. He wasn't as young as I'd expected. I'd expected too much. He'd shaved the beard off and had lost some weight, but he was still bigger than me.

'Jimmy,' he said and laughed. He was visibly pleased to see me. You can't act that. We went into a coffee shop. It was empty, save for the waitresses. One was a large, slovenly looking girl, the other was a mouse. They were both rigged out to look like a couple of medieval peasant girls, with black dirndls and white blouses which – in the case of the big one – only *just* did the job. Peter spoke to the big one and we took a seat.

'Your plane was late,' he said.

'You could have waited a bit.'

'I did. I waited till your bus came from Munich. I didn't like the people on the bus with you, so I waited till you took a cab, then followed you into town.'

The coffee came, strong stuff with icebergs of cream on top and tiny chocolate biscuits in the saucers.

'What's happening, Peter . . . can we talk in here?'

'I think so.' He grinned. He looked happy and handsome and so full of life. It was like we were both kids again, plodding up the mean streets of East London. I *wanted* to trust him, I realised. No matter what his story was, his was the one that mattered.

'Will you tell me what's going on?'

'I will. What do you know? I'll fill in the rest.'

'What I have is this. You worked for the secret service . . . yes?'

He shrugged.

'And you used me when we first knew each other to help set up your cover occupation . . . *used* me, right.'

He sighed. 'Yes.'

'And then you wanted to drop out of it. So you used me again, thirteen years later, only this time you used our physical similarity to demonstrate to the people you were working for that you'd done a bunk, gone over the wall. Were you that important?'

'Yes and no. The point is I didn't want people to be searching England looking for me, and I felt I was in quite a lot of danger.'

'And I wouldn't be?'

'You wouldn't be. There was no question of risking danger to you.'

214

'Well. I got a good-sized thumping off a detective who picked me up in Dover . . . does that count as dangerous?'

He grinned. 'Not very. Since they claimed the thing they wanted me for was a murder, and since that "murder" wouldn't wash and wasn't meant to, you were in no real danger, Jimmy, physical or legal. Go on with your side of it.'

He waved for more coffee. When it came he leaned back close to me again so we could speak quietly.

'The Special Branch copper cashed his chips in,' I said. 'I suppose *he* felt perfectly safe, too.'

'I didn't know that.'

'No. Well it might not be your fault. As for a pieced-together story, I haven't got much more,' I said, and nibbled the little bitter chocolate. 'I've been given cock-and-bull stories about you by experts; both by a woman called Emma Black, who I guess was your boss, and a bloke called Palmer. Know him?'

'A bit.'

'Peter . . . knock it on the head. You're obviously involved with him up to your earholes. He was waiting in Clare's house for you the other night when I walked in on him. And when I talked to him afterwards he was sweating on something. He's involved with you but he doesn't trust you.'

He laughed and slapped my arm. 'Okay . . . maybe. Mister Detective. Just maybe. You're good at theories, anyway. Did you reassure Palmer?'

'No . . . how? Tell me what's going on around you.'

'It's a long story. Don't worry. I'll tell you.'

Two gigantic black men came into the little coffee shop. They must've been approaching seven feet tall. When they sat they half-filled the shop. Peter stood.

'Let's go. Let's take a walk.'

Chapter Thirty

We took the funicular railway up to the castle. The city below us was cold and drab-looking, despite its reputation for music and art, theatre and sunshine. The fog of yesterday had gone but had given place only to cold breezes and showers. It was a relief in one way to think that the burghers of Salzburg don't get it any easier than we Brits. They will have to freeze all winter too. It will rain on them as it will rain on us.

Peter and I left the funicular and climbed slowly up the remaining tarmacadamed road to the Hohensalzburg's proper grounds. There were high grey walls of the castle on our right and a dizzy view over the city to our left. Peter wore a raincoat but I had none. Neither of us had hats and the rain lay on the surface of our clothes and soaked into our hair. I didn't care. I don't believe Peter did either.

He took my arm and spoke. 'My father was a diplomat. He was English and he spent the years of my childhood living and working in Canada. It wasn't a very tough assignment, either for the man or the boy. I was born and educated there. My father spent the years of my teens living and working in Germany. By the time I left school I spoke both French and German fluently. When I joined the army I was an obvious candidate for Military Intelligence. And I served there. You know that, I suppose?'

'Yes. I know it. But lots of people do that. How did you

get from there to being . . . whatever? A spook?'

He smiled and repeated, 'Whatever.' And then, after a while, he said, 'Those facts, Jimmy, the army and the background, plus my skill as a linguist, made me a certainty for the service. They recruited me while I was serving with you as a policeman, gave me the cover of being a businessman . . . and I really did sell bulbs and flowers as well as guns. . . .'

'For your brother-in-law?'

'No. For me. I had the *cover* of being a businessman. It was a fairly deep-seated deception. At first glance there was all that nursery nonsense. Then, if anyone cared to look a little further they found an arms dealer. Further yet and they found a disgraced policeman. There were lots of layers before you found me being employed by the British government. That was important for the first job, in Canada, but after that was finished we discovered it was useful to keep that show going. So I had two lives running side by side, both under the surface, both dodgy. One in the service of Her Majesty, the other in the service of filthy lucre and gun-running. And my immediate superior – at first, anyway – was Emma Black. As the years went by Emma got some big promotions and became everybody's superior. To cut a long story short, Jimmy, one day – about a year ago – I made the mistake of looking back over her career and engaging my brain. That's how we get to this mess. I realised there were some things wrong with Emma.'

Peter and I moved to one side of the road to let a delivery van make its way up to the castle. Probably a load of cheese and wurst for tomorrow's breakfast, I thought. The bread would have been delivered yesterday and should be ready to eat next week. We leaned against the stone wall, wet and mossy or not, and stood close to each other and continued talking.

'She was a spy, you mean?' I said.

'Crudely, yes. That's what I thought. For the moment I was content to have my observations considered. I brought

217

them to the attention of some colleagues. Senior colleagues. But it came to nothing. If I could see something wrong I was on my own. My colleagues took it seriously in a professional way but eventually they all had to admit "false alarm". The whole thing had been a waste of time. A waste of time for me and for the service. That's how I felt . . . was *made* to feel. It's how other people felt too. They won't thank you for telling them there's a traitor in their midst whether you're right or wrong. Especially wrong.'

He laughed briefly. He was very agitated. The laugh had been nervous. Peter turned to face the castle and let his head drop back on his shoulders. Light rain fell on his face.

'Think for a minute, Jimmy. Think. My complaint had been rejected in the short term, but she must have been aware of it, and she must have known I'd always be there, always watching. How would you deal with that situation most effectively? How would you cover your tracks?'

'I'm afraid your business is a closed book to me, mate,' I said over my shoulder. Then I saw it. Peter turned and looked into my face and he saw the recognition there, too.

'Accuse the accuser. That's right. The next stage, although it didn't happen straightaway, was for her to build up a case against me and claim my earlier complaint was mischievous. I was put on the spot.'

'How?'

He groaned. 'Easily. Too easily. My activities were such as to make me look like a wide-boy . . . I mean they were *meant* to. I was meant to be the sort of fellow who looked like he was into everything. All someone had to do was tell a few lies and reinterpret what I was doing and I could be made to look as if I was a wrong-un. As if it had all been for my own benefit and as if I was selling my services to both sides, to *many* sides, at once. I relied on my colleagues' good faith. If you've got an act going as an arms dealer, as a fixer, as a highly illegal person, you're exposed. If someone suddenly turns up one day and says, "Look at what Moody's doing, we didn't tell him to go *that* far," how can you argue?

There is no book of rules to go by.'

'And that was said about you?'

'Yes. From the top. It came from Emma...I mean the word was put about by one of her poodles but that's where it came from, I'm sure.'

'And was it true, Peter? Leaving aside any interest of hers which might have been served by that, was it true?'

He shook his head slowly. 'No. It was never true.'

'And what about this stuff about you going over to... well, to whom? The Russians, I suppose she was telling me.'

He squeezed my arm and laughed. 'What good would I be to them? I'm not a real spy or a code expert or a scientist. It's a lot of crap, Jimmy. They don't need blokes like me.'

We stood in silence together for a long time. Then Peter leaned off the wall. So did I.

'Is there a bus down?'

'No.'

'We'd better get on back to the railway thing, then. My leg's giving me gyp.'

We began to make our way slowly back down the hill. The city was disappearing under misty rain again. My leg didn't hurt. I suppose I was looking for time in which to digest what Peter was saying.

He went on, 'Recently things warmed up. I was in quite a bit of danger, I knew. Someone had already tried to kill me.'

'How?'

'Explosives on the bottom of my car. Presumably it would have been slipped to the press afterwards that I had had enemies in Ireland for the past seventeen years. Easy, eh? Unfortunately for them I've got a bit touchy lately and have been careful about dark alleyways, unexpected postal packets and the undersides of cars.'

'But would it be true? Do you have enemies in Ireland?'

'Yes, Jimmy, since you ask. It would be true and very believable. Also Cyprus, Greece, Africa, Central America. Other places too. Shall I list them all?'

'No. But your response to this obvious threat was to do a bunk?'

'Not immediately. It would be even more dangerous to rush. They'd be ready for that. But a few days later I simply picked up as much money as I could realise at once and walked out. My plan was simple . . . it was that I would fight my corner best if I stayed alive. I went and parked myself in a hotel in Brighton and travelled up with the commuters every day. I reckoned a couple of weeks' full-time research in London would be enough to have a really watertight case against her.' He stopped walking and clapped his hands against the stone wall in frustration. I stood in the roadway still, distanced from him, while the rain fell around us. Peter leaned against the wall for a long time, then he turned around and said, 'I asked you to go to my house because I had word that Emma Black had set up this murder spoof. You look so much like me, I couldn't resist it. I wanted to send her off on a wild goose chase. I'm sorry, Jimmy.'

'*Using* me?' I said. 'You could have got me killed.'

He gave a wry grin and shook his head. 'Not at that stage. You were safe enough.'

'Why would she set all that stuff going if you weren't a defector or anything like it?'

'She had to. To make it look as if she really was taking my "defection" seriously and to make it look as if I really was as dirty as she was saying. I think the plan would have been to have me killed later, while I was on the run. Then the public story for press consumption would have gone: one, highly dodgy and illegal arms dealer with known terrorist connections murders girl in his house; two, goes on the run for weeks in England; three, is found shot dead presumably by one of his contacts who thought this was all getting too hot. Someone in Eastern Europe would no doubt have been landed with the blame. Among my colleagues, and within her own group, God knows what story she would have given. That the reds found out I wasn't interesting in the end and found me an embarrassment, perhaps? So they got rid of me? Whatever happened they would have been to blame and I would have been to blame. Emma would be whiter than white.'

We began to descend again.

'But Palmer told you what was going on. He trusted you.'

'Yes, he did. He told me they had been convinced by Emma and that I was really being taken seriously as a defector. They were pulling all the stops out to convince everyone – maybe including any possible new employer – that I was just a common criminal. Hence the spoof murder. Once I knew about that I knew I was sure I'd never convince any of the English people.'

'Did they have any other reason to think you'd become a defector? I mean was there anything in your track record to indicate it?'

'Who knows? Emma had had at least a year to cook up a past for me. I'd have thought she'd have had that angle covered.'

Two old women approached us, dressed in modern style with Burberry-type rainmacs and carrying gay umbrellas. Despite the clothes they looked very much to be Austrian peasant women. They walked very slowly indeed. When they reached us the woman furthest called to me, 'Do you speak English?' Speaking slowly and clearly, as if she were talking to an imbecile.

'Yes.'

'Is it far to the top, young man?'

Peter answered. 'Not far at all. A few more minutes.'

She nodded thanks and saved her breath for some more puffing uphill.

I said, 'You people do too much cooking up, Peter. What about Clare? How did you convince her?'

'She's not an insider. I had simply used her as a helper from time to time in the past. Not being an insider she didn't have all the prejudices everyone else had. She didn't know as much. I went and saw her and told her the story. I sat in her living room and told my story and refused to go away until she believed me.'

'And she did believe you, which is why she was in my office the next evening trying to get you out of the country?'

'Trying to get it so it looked like I was out of the country, I'm afraid. Yes.'

'Why did she believe you?'

'It was an act of faith, Jimmy.'

'And why didn't you go back to your former employers with her as a character witness?'

'It was an act of faith! She believed me. The belief was everything. I couldn't expect anyone but my closest friends to believe me.'

'Not even me?'

'Would you have believed, given the choice? If I deceived you, Jimmy, we were both better off that way.'

'Why did you need the deception on getting out of the country? Why did you need me at all?'

'For time. To give me time. I couldn't go back to our people. I wanted to get my story absolutely right. I wanted to get the evidence lined up. Then I wanted to approach someone.'

'Who?'

He didn't speak. We'd reached the funicular. We stood in silence with the other would-be passengers. We rode in silence with them, too. At the bottom he called a taxi from across the street. The driver was old and brown and gnarled-looking, like a blasted tree root. Peter gave him an address and we travelled through the streets in a silence broken only by the car's radio, by incomprehensible words blurting rudely from time to time into my consciousness.

The taxi took us to a housing complex on the outside of Salzburg. The area wasn't rich and it wasn't poor. Just like Austria. The streets were clean and tidy, cars parked neatly at the streetside, and the rain fell on it all like stair rods. I followed Peter into some modern flats and he spoke into an entryphone before leading me upstairs. The flat we went to was modern German kitsch and the woman opening the door was pretty. Very pretty. One might almost say beautiful. Clare.

'My father.' She didn't greet me, she didn't look happy or sad or embarrassed to see me, she just led me into a living room and said 'my father', introducing me to a morose, elderly man who spoke no English and gripped my hand like a drowning man when he shook it. He was the man in Clare's photograph. The atmosphere in the flat was polite but strained, and not just because I'd arrived. I wondered if the old man knew why they were there.

'Is it safe to stay here?' I asked Peter. Clare had gone to make the old man's lunch. The old man himself glared at us across his living room. A television in the corner battled out some inane German panel game.

'Sure. No one knows this fellow exists. Clare's past is well hidden away.'

'Wasn't she vetted?'

'What for? She doesn't have a job with us. She just ran a few messages for me. If we vetted everyone who did that . . .' His voice trailed off. Peter stood and pulled a briefcase out from behind the old man's sofa.

'Tell me the rest of the story,' I said. 'You approached someone. Who?'

'Okay. An American. Someone I'd known during my time there. He put me in touch with people in the American security hierarchy who were dying to get their hands on such a story. What I was saying fell in line with some of their prejudices about the British. They believed me because they wanted to, just as people in England have not believed me simply because they didn't want to. They needed Emma, they needed to believe her. The Americans had no such hang-ups.'

Clare came in and put a plate of sausages and potatoes in front of the old man, then withdrew again without speaking.

This domesticated side of her was completely new to me. The old man began to eat noisily, competing with the TV, sucking plump little white sausages through badly fitted false teeth.

'Why are you here? Why aren't you in Washington?'

'Politics. It wouldn't be very good if I was discovered there at the moment. I'm here to do my writing, Jimmy. I've been writing my story up.'

'Where's Tim?'

'I sent him home. He'd got the sack over the phone. I told him he'd got all he was ever going to get and he should push off.'

'And why were you outside Clare's house that night . . . the night Tim followed you here?'

'I was supposed to see Palmer just after Clare had gone. The plan was for him to organise a party to raid her house just after she'd gone. All the blokes he took were his blokes, SB. They weren't going to tell anyone that he'd met me. I was supposed to be coming to England especially to meet him. Of course, that wasn't quite true . . . but that doesn't matter. Unfortunately the raid went a bit wrong. Palmer's lot got there a bit early, and there was an embarrassing moment or two while Palmer had to tell his blokes to ignore Clare and her American minders and the minders had to get out a bit sharpish.'

'Which is why they didn't clear the room Palmer was in.'

'In?'

'There was a picture left of Clare and an old fellow in front of this castle.' I pointed above myself. 'A bit slack, eh?'

'A bit slack. Then you blundered in and I never did have my secret meet with Palmer.'

'Did you just use your ordinary passport at Heathrow again?'

He smiled mischievously.

'No.' He raised his voice. 'Come on, Clare, we'll be late.'

'Where are you going?' I said.

224

The old man had finished his lunch and was doling out baleful looks again. I couldn't even wish him good luck in his own language, or ask him how his lunch had gone down, or tell him to cheer up. He just sat on the far side of the room, picking his teeth under his hartshorn candelabrum and staring glazedly at a fat Hausfrau getting excited on his TV. She was going to win something but I couldn't figure out what. It occurred to me that the old man might think me a bringer of bad news. I smiled at him. He pushed his plate to one side, and absorbed himself in the TV, ignoring me.

'American Embassy,' said Peter. 'I'm all ready to go.'

'Let me give you a lift into town, Jimmy. Let me do that at least.'

'No. No . . . I'll walk.'

'It'll only take a minute.'

'Well, borrow a coat, then. You're soaking.'

'I'm okay.'

'Borrow a raincoat . . . here, here's an old one of mine.' He reached into a hallway cupboard and pulled out an old brown raincoat. 'Take it . . . take it.'

I took the coat.

'How will I get it back to you?'

'Don't worry. It's valueless.'

I took the coat and went downstairs. Peter followed. Clare was already down there. She had a green VW, a small one. It was parked in the street below the flat. Peter had shown me it from the flat. He had taken me on to the little iron railinged balcony of the flat and we had looked down at the car's shining wet roof. I peered through television aerials and empty washing lines, searching for any sign of surveillance, outsiders. People paying too much attention to whatever's under their car bonnets. People taking too long to look over a shop window. There was only one shop on the street and it was a dreary newsagent-type place, a place to be found in any city suburb of any country in the western world. I tried my best to see something wrong but I couldn't, and I realised Peter had brought me out here just to reassure me. He was safe. I was safe. Things were under control now. We were in Austria, Peter was on the side of the goodies. Everything was right in the world.

'Let me give you a lift into town, Jimmy. Let me do that at least.'

'No. No . . . I'll walk.'

'It'll only take a minute.'

I had no idea where I was but I said no again. I wanted to walk. I wanted to think. I said I'd find a bus or a taxi somewhere along the way.

I said this in the street. We were standing below Clare's father's flat. Faint sunlight painted the street pastel colours. The rain had left off for just a while. I had Peter's coat folded, lining side out, over my arm. Peter stood next to the boot of the little VW, without his beard and without the extra twenty pounds; he looked good. He smiled a lot and talked a lot and I can hardly remember the half of what he was saying. I know I said hardly anything. Was he frightened? I asked. I remember asking him that, at least.

'There's no point in being frightened, Jimmy.' He slapped the VW lightly. 'Yes, of course I am. But there's no point in being actively frightened. I'll just let myself be frightened enough to keep me healthy.'

Same old Peter.

'Someone could have followed me here,' I said. 'That man of Palmer's who followed Ewence to Heathrow must've reported it back. Someone in Palmer's office could easily have passed the information on . . . no matter how innocently.'

Peter just shook his head and smiled. 'There's nothing to worry about. This is the last lap for me. I've got her.'

The little VW was crammed in between other parked cars. I looked up and down the street. I couldn't see anyone out of the ordinary. But isn't that the point of people who are any good at it? If someone was stalking Peter surely he wouldn't know it until the last moment. He seemed so relaxed. If I'd been Peter I'd have been worried. If I'd been Peter I'd have had a tank parked outside the front door and a team of newspapermen waiting to witness any possible event.

'Why haven't the Yanks got people looking after you?' I asked.

'I'm better off buried in a place like this. Mr Anonymous. I'm perfectly all right here. Stop worrying. You worry too much.' He put his arm round my shoulders. 'You always have. I'll drive to Vienna and then we'll get a case made against Emma Black. Then I'll come home to London and everything will be as it was. It'll only take twenty-four hours in Vienna. Wait for me here, and we'll go home together. I'll take you to that joint in Soho and buy you the rest of your supper. We'll all go there together, eh, Clare?'

She'd come up on us silently. If she heard him she ignored him. Peter smiled again anyway. That was his style. I couldn't hang around Salzburg to find out how it went. If I'd waited for him I'd have stepped back ten years, I'd have become again the Jimmy Jenner Peter Moody used to explain things to, I'd have become again the Jimmy Jenner who was Peter Moody's fresh-faced sidekick.

No, thanks. When Peter put his arm round my shoulders to say goodbye again it made me feel like I'd gone back all that way. Peter would take care of things. No, thanks. New things would be made familiar and familiar new. I said nothing, just like Clare. What could we say? Peter smiled into my face and said again, 'Wait here for us. Stay in your *pension*. There's plenty to see in Salzburg.'

I said nothing still. I knew all the reasons why not to stay and I was going to take my own advice.

I said goodbye to them, then set off along the streets of suburban Salzburg with no backward glance. Peter Moody and Clare Fisher were rowing their own boat. Clare wouldn't even speak to me to say goodbye, she just trudged up and down the stairs to the old man's little apartment, carrying bags and fussing. Eyes never meeting mine. Maybe she was ashamed of all the use she'd put me to. Maybe she

227

really did have a 'thing' with Peter, and being with the two of us – Peter and me – was something she wanted to avoid. Clare seemed a long way from the stunner I remembered . . . even from the woman of a few days ago in Cyril's. Peter gave no sign that he recognised any problem among the three of us. The way things were to Peter, I was a much trusted and loved old friend who'd helped them. When things were sorted out no doubt he expected us to go back to being friends again . . . maybe at the same level even as when we'd been coppers together. Standing in that Austrian suburban street, Peter had it in mind, I think, to give me a tearful farewell. Stuff that. I just said a gruff 'I'll see you then' and limped off with his coat folded over my arm. We didn't even shake hands.

'You give me twenty-four hours, Jimmy. I'll pick you up at that dump you're staying in,' Peter called after me. I waved my hand above my head to acknowledge it without looking round.

As I walked away I knew I wasn't going back with them. I knew I'd probably never see them again. What did they need me for? I limped down the street and out of their lives once and for all. I left them still loading their bags. They were about to win their game. As far as I was concerned the game didn't exist. They were playing at the top table of deviousness. I was better off looking for missing husbands and making discreet enquiries for solicitors. I was back to Palmer and his pies and his ants again.

There were bumper-to-bumper cars in Moody's suburban street, and regular box-shaped apartment blocks around regular, box-shaped lawns. I walked down the straight street. I had it in mind that I would give Peter and Clare a cheery wave when they passed me. Then that would be it. They would pass into a backwater of my memory, just as they had done until a couple of weeks ago. I reached the end of the street. I stopped. No car yet. I half-turned. Then I heard the VW's starter motor turn. Just once. Then I heard a bang, like someone dropping a sheet of steel off a fork-lift truck, or throwing an oil drum into the street. Only louder. The bang rolled on and on, oil drum falling on oil drum, sheet of steel falling on sheet of steel. I lifted my eyes and saw an orange ball of flame rising, then I felt the warm blast of air on my face and heard glass smashing. Someone screamed, once. I sat down on the kerb. There was nothing for me to do. It would be military explosives, I knew. Czech- or Russian-made. Some anonymous Turk would have been paid a hundred American dollars by some anonymous Bulgarian to plant it. I wasn't even surprised. I felt lost and freed, all at the same time. Oily black smoke rose over the apartment blocks. There was nothing I could do for Peter and Clare. Nothing the people already running down the street couldn't do, anyway. I could already hear a fire engine in the distance, sounding its siren. Then another sounded and another. I wasn't going to be any help here.

I stood again. I had to find an *Ausland* phone box. I had to talk to Palmer, and very soon. Before the news story got going. As I walked away the first police car screeched round the corner and accelerated past me, up the long, straight, suburban street. The men inside looked pale and drawn. Determined young men going off to do whatever they were called upon to do. It made me feel so old, seeing those boys in their BMW. It made me feel so old to think that Peter was probably dead now. I set off in search of my phone box, quickening my stride as much as I could. Before I'd gone far another BMW came down the street, just as fast but without police markings. It halted next to me and a young, plain-looking fellow stepped out of the passenger side and said, 'Mr Moody. Won't you get in please? And may I take your coat?' In perfect English.

What's the good of arguing? I gave him the coat and got in.

Chapter Thirty-one

At the beginning of the third week of October, less than five days after the explosion in Salzburg, I was driving a black taxi round Parliament Square. It was after nine at night. It was cold and the rain was bucketing down. I drove round the square a couple of times, expecting a radio call. When it didn't come I parked the cab rather than let myself get dizzy. I had a parking place arranged, just along the front of the Abbey, so I had my options open ... Victoria Street or Great George Street. First exit or second from Parliament Square ... easy. It was the rest of the evening's work that was bothering me. The taxi belonged to Special Branch.

Considering the time of night the traffic was heavy, even for Parliament Square. I wasn't surprised. There was a motorcycle copper standing at the junction of Great George Street and Parliament Square, turning all taxis back into the square and causing utter confusion. He was letting other traffic through, just no taxis. Motorcycle coppers were similarly strategically stationed at the top of Storey's Gate, Buckingham Gate, all along Petty France and at the junction of Horse Guards Road and The Mall. Birdcage Walk and most of the area between it and Victoria Street were sealed off to London's taxi drivers.

I checked my taxi's dials for the hundredth time. Yes, I had enough diesel, water and electricity. No, nothing was too hot or too cold, nothing was escaping where it shouldn't, engine-wise. I made sure the window between myself and the passenger compartment was securely locked, then tried to relax. It wasn't easy. I was wearing two thick pullovers to give me some bulk and a flat cap to hide my face a little. I felt uncomfortable.

A policeman in a cape stood next to my cab's black bonnet, rain soaking into his helmet and dripping off the tails of his cape. He was guarding me from passers-by. He had no idea why. That wasn't his job. I did know why, and I didn't want it to be my job. There was no choice, though.

At nine-fourteen my radio crackled.

'It's on.'

Then a few seconds later, 'Go Birdcage.'

I acknowledged the call and switched the radio over to 'intercom'. I would now be able to talk to any passenger I should pick up without opening the glass partition. I drove to the motorcycle copper on the corner of Great George Street and said, 'My name's Scott.'

He stood back without a word and waved me through. He turned a taxi behind me away.

Palmer had a part to play in it. Of course. He had more than one part.

'We need a plan, Jimmy. We need something concrete,' he'd said. 'Some substantial piece of evidence to put her away with. Once I've got her in the nick where she can't be sprung,' he said and smiled, 'we'll have no problem. In between times we need a confession, or at least a lever to start her confessing with. Some major crime would be perfect . . . it doesn't have to be the one we're most interested in, just something that'll put the skids under her. Something that'll give me the chance to hold her and charge her without her friends at the top and their lawyers screaming.'

'What do you have in mind exactly?' I said. 'Inviting her to rob a bank?'

The answer was 'nearly'. I might have known it would

involve me ... why else discuss the pie with an ant? Once again I couldn't see the cliff before me as a mere crust from a very big pie. Palmer had been right in Spitalfields. Once again I had failed to get the overview. My mistake.

Palmer's part tonight was to keep Emma Black working in the Queen Anne house until nine o'clock. We'd planned it meticulously. Just after nine he'd break up his meeting with Emma, claiming a previous engagement. He'd take her downstairs, then offer to share a taxi ... he would have dismissed his service driver for the night. Emma's driver was under strict instructions to report sick that evening. To cover the unlikely eventuality that she would ask, the car pool was under equally strict instructions to have no cars free and no explanations available, no matter who asked. Anyway, Palmer's engagement was in Chelsea, just a couple of miles from Emma Black's house in Fulham. It was perfectly natural that they should share a taxi. A man would watch them leave the Queen Anne house. He would relay on the radio which route they took, though Palmer would suggest Birdcage Walk as offering a better chance of an empty taxi.

As Emma Black and Detective Chief Superintendent Palmer descended the steps to Birdcage Walk there was plenty of traffic on the road, but just one taxi was cruising in the traffic. It had its 'For Hire' lamp on, flag up, all its gauges were working, it had plenty of fuel and it wasn't overheating. I knew. I was driving it.

Palmer held his arm out. I stopped.

'Chelsea, Sydney Street will do. Opposite the Town Hall. Then my companion wants to go on to Fulham. She'll give you the address.'

Emma Black was already sitting in the back. Palmer was standing at the luggage door, giving the orders. I had the window down. Palmer's grey eyes looked into mine but he gave no indication that he knew me.

'Sydney Street, guv,' I repeated. I drove towards Buckingham Gate. On my left the tarmacadamed space of Wellington Barracks' parade ground was soaked in floodlight and rain. On my right the park was dark. In the back of my cab Emma Black was trying to show Palmer a piece of paper from her briefcase in the light of the parade ground flood-lights. She tapped on the glass and mouthed something. We reached Buckingham Gate. The motorcycle copper was still there, but it was perfectly normal to have one seated a hundred yards from the Queen's London home. I pushed the intercom button and talked into a mike extending from the cab's roof. I could just distantly hear my electronic voice in the passenger compartment, harsh and tinny-sounding.

'I can't hear you, madam. This is a new one with all the security devices. Push the button next to the light button if you want to talk to me.'

She pushed the button.

'The light won't come on,' she said. 'I want to show my friend something.' The loudspeaker distorted her voice slightly too, but there was nothing in her tone to say she'd recognised me.

'No. I'm afraid it's broken, madam. It needs a bulb.'

'Typical.'

There was an electrical 'clack' sound every time either of us pushed our intercom buttons. That would be the police radio connected to the intercom cutting in. It was broadcast-ing our conversations, but the 'clack' sound could equally be generated in the intercom, if you didn't know.

I drove to Chelsea. The traffic was still heavy, even though it was well after half-nine when we reached the Town Hall. I tried to spot the following cars. I couldn't, and Emma was a desk jockey, so she certainly wouldn't. All I could see keeping pace was a Jaguar. That wasn't ours. It was just keeping pace coincidentally. I let Palmer down out-side the Town Hall. He had some words with her I didn't hear, then I pushed the button to free the passenger-compartment door locks and Palmer got out and walked briskly away.

Emma Black pushed the intercom button again.

'Junction of Fulham Palace Road and the New King's Road.'

I turned the cab around and started up Sydney Street, heading north-west.

'Didn't you hear me? I said the junction of Fulham Palace Road and New King's Road.'

'I thought you were going home, Emma. You don't live there. You live in Sloane Street.'

'What the hell . . .' shouted her muffled voice from behind the glass. She stared at my back. I could see her in my rear-view mirror. She spoke again.

'Push the button, Emma.'

She pushed the intercom button.

'What are you doing in England, Moody? You're a wanted man.'

'I'm all right. Just you sit back and relax. We're going for a little drive.'

Emma tried the door.

'It has an electric lock. I have to release it. You're stuck, Emma. Why don't you relax a bit?'

'Where are you taking me?'

'Wales. I've got a house there. A little retreat. A lonely place, it's true, but it suits me. You and I are going there and we're going to have a discussion.'

We'd reached the Cromwell Road before she replied.

'You're mad, Moody. I'm not discussing anything with you. You're wanted, don't you realise that? You're a traitor.'

'Don't be stupid, Emma, I don't know anything to be a traitor about.'

'Clack,' the radio went. I thought, 'I only hope you fellows are getting all this, because I'm sweating here and it's not because it's hot.'

'Clack' again.

'Once the police find you, you'll stand no chance, Moody. Let me out. Be sensible. Take your chance and run back to wherever you came from while you can still do it. I'll give you an hour. Drop me here and drive to Heathrow now. I promise I'll give you an hour before I phone in.'

'No, Emma. I want a signed sealed confession from you. I want names and dates. I want to clear myself.'

'Clear yourself? Are you serious? Let me out.'

We went over the Hammersmith flyover. The lights shone below us. The Jaguar was gone.

'Here?' I said.

'Of course not. On the other side.'

'No. I'm afraid not. You're just not getting out without talking to me.'

The traffic moved forward again. I was still watching her in my rear-view mirror. The street lighting was reflected on the partition glass. Rain poured on to my windscreen. The wipers pushed it, slip slop, slip slop. We slowed. The water streamed down the side windows. She delved into her briefcase.

'No, Moody. I'm not doing anything for you. You're doing something for me.'

She moved on to the jockey seat behind my head and began to speak again.

'Push the button,' I said into my microphone. 'You have to push the button. It's no good sitting there and yelling. Push the button at the back.'

There was a queue of traffic coming off the flyover. We were almost stopped. She moved back on to the rear seat and pushed the button. Clack.

'Listen, Moody, you bastard. I've got a gun. I'm sure you know I'll use it. Now, if you don't pull over I'll shoot you. Here . . . turn left.'

I turned left. I could see her in my mirror, hanging on to the grab handle with one hand, a little snub-nosed revolver in the other. The side road was full of tall, substantial Victorian houses. Full of security, the way the Victorians knew how. I hoped the cars following had spotted which turning we'd taken. I hoped the cars following were there. I hadn't seen any.

Clack. 'Stop,' Emma ordered.

I stopped. We were next to the river, on Chiswick Mall. I couldn't see the river because there was a wall between us and it. I could see the blackness of the night above the river, though. It seemed to have a different quality. My mouth was dry, my heart was pounding, and it wasn't because I was going to kiss her.

She smiled. 'You've made a big mistake, Moody. You no doubt expected to get away with this. But you've made a mistake. I'm not going to be driven off to the country and killed by you and your pals. You're going to let me out now. Then I'll decide what to do with you. Open the door.'

I didn't answer. There was no point. She waited a few seconds, then moved quickly forward on to the jockey seat behind me again and raised the gun. Still no Palmer, still no witnesses. I wished they'd given me a gun too, then at least I'd have been able to shoot back. In my mirror I saw Emma's hand tense on the gun. I flinched but didn't move. Then the glass partition exploded next to my head, seeming to bulge out beside me and covering my head and shoulders in fine particles of glass. My good ear went nearly as deaf as my bad one. I tumbled out of the driver's door of the taxi and went for the wall. Gammy leg or not, I would have beaten all comers for the Chiswick Mall wall-jumping competition that night. Gammy leg or not, I must have beaten the world record for running along that bank of the Thames and hiding behind a boat. I'm no one's idea of a hero. The armoured glass behind my head had held but just, only just held. The cab's side windows weren't armoured glass and I didn't want her taking pot shots at me from them. I ran as best I could for that boat and the wonderful darkness that surrounded it. Here I am, dark, take me and hide me. There was another shot, then another. I peeped. Nothing. There was a sound of torn steel moving. She'd shot her way out of the door. I hid, then I peeped again. I saw Emma's head peering over the top of the wall. I didn't know if she'd seen me. She must have known I was down there somewhere. I leaned back on to the boat's hull and I stood perfectly still for a long time. I could hear Emma squelching about on the mud, then I heard a movement behind my boat. Maybe it was one of her friends. It wasn't one of mine. Mine should have come with sirens wailing and lights flashing. Mine should have bullhorns to shout through and guns to wave around and a girl to grab me and kiss me when it was all over.

I knelt, and moved forward slowly and quietly on my hands and knees, hugging the shape of the craft I was hiding behind. There were some more boats pulled up on the strand near me. If I could make it to those, and then make just one dash of about a hundred yards, I could make the shelter of some buildings. I knew the buildings included the Dove pub. A pub would provide electric light and boozy patrons and telephone calls and witnesses. No one could or would shoot you there . . . I think. It wasn't much, but it was the best I had by way of a plan.

'Moody!' Emma called. She was still squelching around on the strand, but now she was nearer my boat.

'Moody!' Her voice again. She'd moved. She was yet closer. 'There's nowhere to hide. Come to me. We'll make a deal.'

'Moody . . .' Closer still, her voice soft and hoarse and whisper-like. I could hear her footsteps in the mud as she moved along the side of the boat, separated from me only by its hull. Where was the other person? Was he with her? If it was Palmer he was playing his hand late. I looked towards the lights of the pub. The dash of a hundred yards might as well have been a hundred miles. I stood, started to move forward. Emma's figure appeared, standing by the hull, out-lined against the artificial lights of the Mall behind her.

Emma raised the gun towards me and took careful aim.

'Now, Moody. I want you to walk towards me.'

I couldn't hear Palmer and his boys. No 'just drop that gun' from some reassuringly large and deep-voiced Special Branch copper. No joy for Jenner. I said nothing and I didn't move.

'Come here," she said. 'Come here.'

'No,' said another voice. 'He's all right there.'

He stepped out from behind the boat and stood beside Emma. Close by her side. He held a handgun to her head. They were both outlined against the street light. Rain splashed around us. I felt like laughing. Peter Moody said, 'Walk towards the lights, Emma.'

A voice back on the wall called, 'Peter! Peter!' Along the strand another voice took it up.

I stayed in the darkness between the boats. Peter and Emma before me looked as if they were on a stage set, silhouetted by light. They moved forwards, Peter still at arm's length but still holding his gun up to her. I could see Peter's gun outlined against Emma's head. I saw her begin to hand her gun to him. She just raised it a little from her side. It didn't seem to be a threat to him. But Peter fired. Just a short, sharp report, a cracking noise, and Peter's hand leapt up a couple of inches and Emma Black's head jerked away from him and she went down like a felled ox, never saying a word nor uttering a sound.

'Peter!' the voice called again. More urgency this time. 'Peter, are you okay?'

Peter turned towards me, still holding up the gun. I couldn't see his face but I was sure he'd fired. He must have known I'd seen it all.

'How are you, Jimmy?' he said softly. 'Scared?' Then he raised his voice. 'Here. I'm over here! Get back in the car. It's okay. Everything's okay. Under control. Get back in the car. I'll be with you in a minute.'

I could hear lots of car door slamming and then there was absolute silence. Then I could pick out the sound of my taxi's diesel, chug-chugging. Overheating. I could never be a taxi driver. I worry too much. Some more cars arrived, screeching brakes and all that. It could only be Palmer and his people.

Peter and I walked slowly back towards the river wall. Palmer and his boys had turned up at last. I could see their car lights shining and hear their voices and their radios. I let Peter have a minute on me; I stood breathing hard and it felt as if my heart would pound through my shirt. I didn't want what would come next, but I knew when we got on to that road there was going to be a confrontation. I looked back and thanked the mute boat hull for sheltering me awhile, then I followed Peter. I climbed back on to the wall via some shallow steps. When I looked back I couldn't believe how far I'd jumped. I should be in the one-legged Olympics.

Back at the cab Palmer was talking to Moody, grinning together and nattering. They looked very friendly together. Peter's friends were just two men in a big car along the Mall. The car was a Jaguar. They sat in their Jaguar and they didn't move. The big car was in darkness. A few heads were sticking out of the windows of houses around us.

Palmer called, 'Go inside and stay inside, ladies and gentlemen. This is the police. There will be no danger if you go inside and stay inside.'

But they didn't go inside and stay inside. They never do. People are too nosy. I'm too nosy. It's what causes all our problems, nosiness.

'Who's in the car?' I said loudly, to whoever would listen. 'More bloody murderers?'

'I've got to go,' said Peter Moody.

'There are a couple of other things first, Peter,' said Palmer. His voice was warm and friendly. 'Just a couple of details before you go.'

They were both so relaxed. So confident. Peter leaned against Palmer's car and smiled and said, 'Okay. Fire away.'

'I'll bloody fire away, mate,' I said. 'You shot her. You killed her in cold blood and I watched you do it. I want him arrested, Palmer. I want him arrested for the murder of Emma Black.'

Moody shook his head. 'She was about to fire. I had to shoot.'

'No, she wasn't. She was giving you her gun.'

He shook his head again. 'She was about to fire it, Jimmy. You don't know. You haven't got the judgement for these things. She was about to fire. I had to shoot.'

'I want him arrested, Palmer.'

Palmer shook his head. 'He's told me the story. He says he asked her to hand over her gun and she lifted it muzzle first with her finger on the trigger. Is that what you saw?'

'She was giving it to him. He murdered her. I saw it.'

'*Muzzle first,*' said Moody. 'Self-defence. Why don't you bloody well listen, Jimmy. Why don't you think about what you saw before you shoot your mouth off?'

'I *know* what I saw!' I yelled.

'You obviously don't!' Peter yelled back.

Palmer held up his hand. 'Peter, let's sit in the car and have this chat. It's too public here.'

Peter sat in the back of Palmer's Rover. I climbed in beside him. Palmer sat in the front with his driver.

'I'd better take your gun, Peter,' said Palmer. 'Evidence, all that, with Mrs Black back there.'

'Okay.' He handed it over. 'She was going to fire, though. Cut and dried. I had no choice. No matter what this little prat says.'

'I don't suppose you had,' Palmer said and smiled. 'I'll certainly never be able to prove that you did have a choice, if I know you.'

'You two have got this sorted out between you,' I said. 'Very cosy. It makes me sick. Let me out of here.' I tried the door, but the child lock was on.

'Calm down, Jenner.' Palmer handed the gun to his driver, who locked it in the dash. 'I wanted to talk to Moody here about something else.'

'Else?'

'Yes.' Palmer's voice changed, became formal. 'Peter Moody, I'm arresting you for the murder of Detective Sergeant Graham Timpkins. You're not obliged to say anything unless you wish to do so. . . .' And so it went on. I just sat next to Peter in the back of the Rover, both of us stinking of

240

mud, wondering what the hell had brought us so far. Wondering what the hell Palmer had on him. There were detectives standing around our car, and I noticed they all appeared to be armed and that Palmer's car was hemmed in by two other Rovers. I saw that this moment was the point Palmer wanted to get to this evening, not the business with Emma Black. That was incidental to him. He wanted Moody for killing his sergeant. I turned and saw a detective go over to the driver's window of the big car which had been waiting for Moody. Then the car sped away. I didn't see the number. I didn't even want to.

'He was here!' I shouted. 'That's all! Not much, is it? All the bloody time and you knew it.'

'I didn't *know* exactly where. I wasn't even sure he was here.'

'Well, just how did you arrange for him to turn up tonight? Maybe I can't see clearly. Maybe I'm not as clever as you but I didn't know you could just phone him, Palmer.'

'No. You're not that clever. You won't give yourself the chance, you won't listen.'

Moody had gone away in a convoy of police cars. Palmer took my arm and led me away from the group, towards the river wall. Before us was the darkness of the river and the night, behind us the lights and the beep beep of the radios and the sounds of men's voices.

'How did you know Moody killed this Timpkins?'

He shrugged.

I said, 'And if you knew, why all this farce? Why not just go round to wherever he was and nick him?'

'I didn't know where he was. But I thought he wouldn't be able to resist the temptation if he heard about this operation to close on Emma Black.'

'Couldn't resist coming along and shooting her? And how did he hear . . . I thought it was all very secret?'

Palmer smiled sheepishly. 'I eased off a little bit on the security aspect.'

'Taking a chance on my bloody life, mate! You knew he wanted her. You set me up because you thought Moody might intervene? How did he stop you getting here at the same time as me?'

'He arranged a little accident in the traffic. I thought he would, it's what I'd do. The traffic was heavy.'

'You *knew* he'd do something like that and yet you still let me go ahead? You could've got me killed! You *did* get Emma Black killed.'

He shook his head and stepped back from me. His face was sad. It was always sad. 'I'm sorry, Jimmy. Really sorry.'

'Don't give me sorry. You must have proof positive about Timpkins. What have you got?'

'Two main things. First, forensic. Timpkins's blood group on Moody's brown mackintosh he lent you. Very positively identified to him. We've got some hairs, too. Moody will have a hell of a time explaining that away. Second is circumstantial. The fact that on the night Timpkins was killed Moody phoned me. I told him Timpkins reckoned he'd found something and was coming to see you about it. There were few enough people knew where Timpkins would be and we can all account for ourselves. Except Moody. That's quite a bit.'

'But all Timpkins had found out was that Peter hadn't left the country. If you told Peter that *you* must have known Peter was in the country too. Why were you safe?'

'I didn't know. Moody was phoning *me*. From France, he was claiming. He phoned to say he thought we might have picked you up in Dover and could I look out for you. I said you had been picked up and interviewed by both Timpkins and Emma, but we'd released you again so not to worry. I told him that Timpkins had phoned my office to say he was coming to see you again. I didn't even know why Timpkins was coming. Moody obviously did. He waited for him and killed him.'

'But *why?*'

'Because clear evidence that he had never left the country

would have put Moody back in danger. Moody obviously understood from his conversation with me that none of us except Timpkins had worked out he was still here. It was important that none of us did. He didn't only need time to cobble up a case against Emma Black. Your friend Peter was trying to clean up his own trail. Peter Moody needed to move around England freely. He knew that if I believed he wasn't in France sooner or later I'd conclude that he wasn't just writing an account of Emma's doings. You don't need to be in England to do that. There would only be one reason to be in England.'

'So he killed a man rather than have his presence here discovered?'

Palmer nodded.

'And why were you meeting him in Essex?'

'It was a trap. By then I'd narrowed down the possible suspects for Timpkins's death. I told Peter we had to meet most urgently, that I had some stuff that was red hot on Emma.'

'And did you?'

'As it happens, Jimmy Jenner, yes, I did have something on her. I told your friend that I would carry out a raid on Clare's house as a pretext for being there and that he should get himself brought back to England and meet me when the raid was over. There was never any intention to get Clare, of course. We wanted Moody, badly . . . as you discovered when my boys mistook you for him.'

'And was it you who tipped off the Austrians that he was in Salzburg?'

' 'Fraid so, Jimmy. My attitude was that if I couldn't have him, someone would. I knew the Austrians had some warrants for him from a long time ago. I simply told them he was there.'

'And Moody and Emma Black? You think the stuff he was accusing her of was true? After all that he'd done?'

'Yes.'

'And her accusations towards him, too?'

'Yes. I'm sure of that now. It wasn't an "either-or". Dirty business, isn't it, Jimmy?'

'It's bloody dirty what you did to me. It's bloody dirty what you did to Emma Black too. I don't believe all these vague accusations against her. She didn't admit bugger all to me. Even under pressure. I don't believe she'd done anything. You listen to the tapes of her conversation with me tonight. See if you can find anything incriminating in it . . . because I didn't, listening to her. If you didn't have an official mask to shelter behind, mate, I'd say you were just as guilty of murder as Moody. Just as premeditated, only carried out by a third party – Moody. What were you after, her job?'

'I'm hurt you'd think that of me,' he said, sounding it, too.

'Ah, cut it out. You should be on the stage.'

'We needed to clear it up. I just did the best I could. We've got a nice clean sheet of paper to start with now, Jimmy.'

'Some clear-up. What you've got to clear up is dead on those mudflats, mate, and it's your fault. I was nearly dead there too.'

'Jimmy . . . Jimmy. We wouldn't expose you to any risk, old son.'

'Don't "old son" me, cock.' I pointed back towards the taxi. 'Look at your bloody armoured glass! I thought you said it wouldn't even dent.'

A boat passed upriver, shedding coloured flashing lights on Palmer's face and sending disco music through the autumn rain to us.

'You're okay, aren't you? What do you want?' He looked down at the strand. 'How did you know the river wasn't in?'

'Same way as you knew that glass would work. Same way as you knew Moody and his pals would step in and stop me being shot up by that bloody woman once you'd abandoned me,' I said. 'I was guessing. Give me my stick.'

We walked back to the taxi. He fetched my stick.

'You want a lift back to the Yard?'

'No. I'm going home.'

'Jimmy. Jimmy . . . there are statements to be taken. Facts to establish.'

'Facts? What facts? You must be having me on. I'm going home. I'm probably going down the road for a pint, first . . . if you want to know. You just sit around here and think up some more lies, eh?'

He stood back and smiled. 'They won't let you in a pub, Jimmy. You're too smelly. I'll get you a drink later. I promise faithfully.'

Needless to say he didn't.

Chapter Thirty-two

The next day was one of those reprieves you get in autumn. The wind stilled, no rain fell, even the sun put in something of an appearance. I strolled along the Old Brompton Road. It was full of pretty girls and smiles and big red buses, picture postcard London. I had money in my pocket and I was on my way to pick up some work. My type of work. I'd been used and deceived by Moody, Palmer, Emma Black, even Clare in her way had used me. I had to go back to playing in my own league. Tim Ewence was a local newspaperman (although an unemployed one now), I was a little private detective, both mooching around London. We were better off that way. Delusions of grandeur on my part never did me any good. No one's delusions of grandeur are any good. Moody's had got Clare and her father blown into the next world . . . and for what? So that he could be the big manipulator for a few more weeks.

I turned up a side road. Still-green fallen leaves were on the pavement. It was a road full of big, solid-looking red brick houses, Victorian ones again. Large women in fur coats walked small dogs. A man in a cashmere coat read a foreign newspaper at the kerbside. He smiled pleasantly at me as I passed. Has no one built big houses since the Victorians? The houses had leftovers of Georgian style in them, white-painted columns outside their front doors, big windows that were missing only the glazing bars to make them

246

Georgian windows. This had never been a cheap place to live. Even in the 1850s it had had delusions of grandeur. Now, in 1985, you needed to be an oil-rich Arab or renting a room in a hotel to live in the area.

I was looking for Esmerelda Potts. My telephone answering machine was blocked up solid with messages from her. I'd misjudged her. It seemed old Mrs Potts was genuine. She really hadn't been another incarnation of the various ploys Palmer and his people were using to get me off the Moody business. She was the real McCoy. She had lost her old man in England while he'd been here celebrating the victory over the Germans. Poor Esmerelda Potts. She was genuinely waiting patiently in a Kensington hotel, making her own pathetic enquiries and waiting for Jenner to get in touch. Jenner the missing detective. Jenner the jet-setter . . . there are those delusions of grandeur. I'd let Esmerelda down. I felt ashamed to have abandoned an old lady so.

I went into one of the houses. Of course it wasn't a house any more. It was Esmerelda Potts's hotel. I went into the basement bar, a confection of polished chrome and mirrors, and ordered a whisky. There was only one other punter in the bar, and she occupied a seat next to the barman. She was a miniature blond bombshell, wearing a shiny sequined cocktail dress, an expensive-looking white fur stole over her shoulders and displaying, through the tightly fitting and low-cut front of the dress, a not-inconsiderable pair of breasts . . . the kind you could use as a card table or a small sofa once you got fed up with them, the kind babies believe heaven is made of. Some men, of course, would never get fed up with them. But then some men never stop being babies. The blond bombshell was dressed to the part, to the taste of a drunken rich businessman, the sort of fellow who goes looking for a girl at midnight and asks her if she accepts American Express cards. She was all wrong for a London hotel at lunchtime. The blonde was wearing lurid red lipstick and whispering into the barman's ear. He looked as if he was about to catch fire and took about twenty minutes to bring me my drink. When he did it was American whisky, not scotch, and I had to send him back for another.

By half-one the bar had filled up. I was in a corner trying to read a copy of the *Sporting Life* by a very dim light. All around me people were scoffing peanuts and alcohol. I don't know how they can drink so much at lunchtime and then spend all afternoon counting money or selling skirts or whatever the hell they do. I'd been in the bar for half an hour past my appointment time with Mrs Potts and she still hadn't showed up. What kept me there was my feeling of guilt for having stood her up so much. Also what kept me there was the fact that I didn't have another job on. I was surprised at quarter to two when Judy came into the bar. She smiled, sat beside me and put her keys on the table.

'Hi.'

'Hi. How did you know where I was?'

'Palmer told me. What's up?'

'I'm supposed to be seeing a client, a woman called Esmerelda Potts. She's an old lady who's lost her husband. She hasn't shown up yet. I can't complain. I let her down a few times during this Moody business.'

'Never mind.' Judy leaned forward and kissed me gently. 'I've come. I've brought my keys.'

'I can see. Your flat's full of girls. Let's go to mine.'

'Not for that.' She made a mock scowl.

'Okay. What's it in aid of?'

'It's a sign, Jimmy. I've brought them as a sign. I'm giving up the dump in Acton. I want to come home.'

'No solicitors?'

'None of that.'

'Great.'

'Ten out of ten. The right response. Going to buy me a drink?'

'I can't, Judy. I really owe this old girl one. Put your stuff in order and I'll be round later to help you move it.'

'There's not much.'

'Okay . . . but leave me alone for an hour or two, Judy,

so's I can deal with this old dear.'

I looked up. The blond bombshell was standing on the other side of my table. She smiled and nodded appreciatively.

'You're Jimmy Jenner, aren't you?'

That voice.

'Who are you?'

She smiled and leaned forward to shake hands. A couple of men at the table next to me gulped their drinks. Judy scowled again, but without the 'mock' this time.

'I'm Esmerelda Potts. And we've taken a long, long time to get together. Won't you introduce me to your friend?'

But my friend was up and away, keys and all, and by the time I reached the street all I could see was the back end of a disappearing Mini. Esmerelda Potts followed me, hanging on to my arm to slow me down.

'Mr. Jenner, what is wrong with you?'

I couldn't begin to tell her.

Also available by John Milne

DEAD BIRDS - The first Jimmy Jenner mystery - £6.99

Jimmy Jenner is a retired Metropolitan policeman. Retired because of injuries caused by a terrorist bomb in Regent Street. Jimmy was always ambitious to become a detective and now he was - the Private variety. Smart but disabled - missing a foot and deaf in one ear - he lives off his wits and contacts in the East End. The odd writ here, the odd piece of divorce work there - it keeps him out of trouble. Until he is asked to do some minding - of Alison Duncan, the wife of a boxing manager. She's beautiful, of course, but unfortunately soon after, she is dead. Jimmy takes his failures personally and trying to right the wrong, he is plunged into a world of international crime, too-clever detectives and too-rich criminals. So now Jimmy is the Sam Spade character he had always aspired to be, but he all too soon finds out that the stakes are getting higher all the time as he mingles among the London and Costa del Sol lowlifes.

ALIVE & KICKING - The fourth & latest Jenner novel - £8.99

Bermondsey gangster, Tommy Slaughter and his driver were ambushed on Croom's Hill, Greenwich in 1968. They died in a hail of bullets, reputedly on the orders of Soho denizen and Maltese pimp, Mickey DeWitt. The gunshots echo even down to today.

"The noir side of London is back with a vengeance and a boot up the backside" - *Time Out*

"The real thing. Unreservedly excellent." - *Literary Review*

"John Milne is one of the truest crime writers we have. Raymond Chandler would have applauded his voice: bruised, tender, sharp, blunt and oh so sad. This novel is his best yet. Ex detective Jenner is his own man but in that bloody mindedness the sprit of Philip Marlowe is alive and kicking." - *Nicholas Shakespeare.*

Coming in the Autumn, the third Jenner novel, Daddy's Girl.

Available from our website: http://www.noexit.co.uk or direct from the publishers. Please add 10% P&P, cheques payable to No Exit Press, Mastercard, Visa, Switch accepted.

No Exit, (MM), 18 Coleswood Rd, Harpenden, Herts, AL5 1EQ.